ACROSS THE GREAT SPARKLING WATER

BY ZOE SAADIA

ACROSS THE GREAT SPARKLING WATER

The Peacemaker, Book 2

ZOE SAADIA

For more information about this book, the author and her work, please visit
www.zoesaadia.com

ISBN: 1535196114
ISBN-13: 978-1535196116

AUTHOR'S NOTE

"Across the Great Sparkling Water" is historical fiction and some of the characters and adventures in this book are imaginary, while some are historical and well documented in the accounts concerning this time period and place.

The history of that region is presented as accurately and as reliably as possible, to the best of the author's ability, and although no work of this scope can be free of error, an earnest effort was made to reflect the history and the traditional way of life of the peoples residing in those areas.

I would also like to apologize before the descendants of the mentioned nations for giving various traits and behaviors to the well known historical characters (such as the Great Peacemaker, whose name I changed out of respect even though it was translated into English, Hionhwatha, Tadodaho, and others), sometimes putting them into fictional situations for the sake of the story. The main events of this series are well documented and could be verified by simple research.

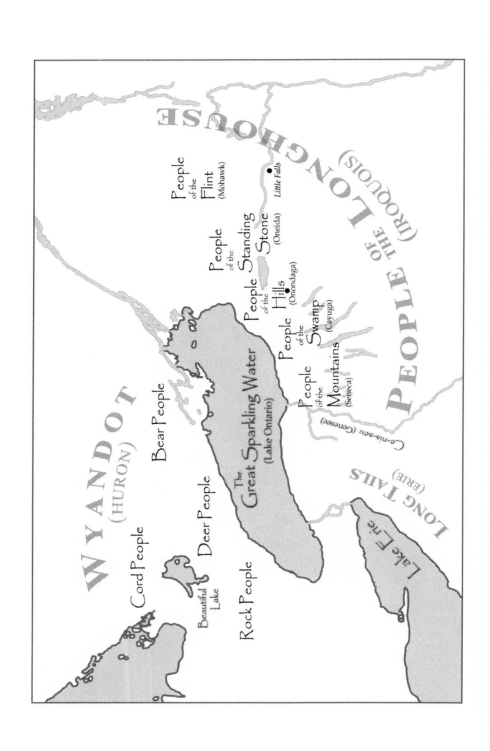

CHAPTER 1

Little Falls,
The Harvest Moon (mid-autumn), 1141 AD

Onheda shielded her eyes and watched the sun, which was blazing unmercifully in the afternoon sky. The heat was still unbearable, the humidity more so. It clung to her skin in a sticky veil of sweat, permeating her lungs with every breath.

Picking her basket up, she balanced it over her shoulder with an effort. May the Left-Handed Evil Twin take this place and make it rot, she thought, forcing her way between the swaying stacks of maize. The ground crumbled under her feet, dry after the long summer moons. She hadn't been around to plant those crops, but now here she was – forced to harvest it, curse their eyes into the realm of the Evil Twin's minions.

"Is that the best the Onondaga women can do?" called out a familiar voice behind her back.

She didn't have to turn around to recognize the speaker. As always, Anitas – tall, merry, outspoken, not missing a chance to make jokes at the expense of everyone, the foreigners being the best target, of course. Onheda pursed her lips and proceeded to ignore the remark.

"Oh, don't die on us just yet." Laughing loudly, Anitas caught up with her, treading around the stacks of the harvested corn. "Your people must have been truly lazy, you know? Our women work until the Father Sun is about to kiss the top of the trees. No wonder our people always win."

Your people are nothing but bloodthirsty beasts, thought Onheda.

And they could not tell maize from a squash, either. All they can do is to raid our lands and wave their flint clubs with such persistence one may think they have nothing better to do.

"No wonder your men are always away, raiding someone else's lands," she answered sweetly. "If you, women, spent more time at home, they might have found it more alluring to stay. But you would rather work the fields, keep your legs crossed, and let them look elsewhere."

Anitas' broad face lost its color. "You filthy rat," she hissed. "How dare you?"

The man who was supposed to become Anitas' husband had moved to live with a girl from another town. Onheda knew all about it, although the affair was hushed. There were no secrets inside the Turtle Clan's longhouses. In that aspect her life was no different among the People of the Flint than among her own Onondaga people.

While Anitas seemed as though debating with herself on what to do with her heavy basket before seizing a chance to punch the stinking foreigner in the eye, Onheda watched her opponent with sheer enjoyment, making sure her gaze conveyed her derision, willing her palms to stop trembling. *Just do it already,* she thought. *Attack me, so I can punch you hard. It'll be such a pleasure to tear your pretty hair out.*

"Come, girls, move on!" A familiar voice broke upon them. Kwayenda, a member of the Turtle Clan's Council, and the head of Onheda's longhouse, eyed them sternly, with an open disapproval; always there to make sure the work had been done properly, especially with so many young girls around. "Off with you both. There is still much work to be done."

"I'm not done with you, you stinking rat!" hissed Anitas, burning Onheda with her gaze before storming off, swaying under her loaded basket.

"What were you two arguing about?" asked the older woman.

Onheda shrugged with her free shoulder, bestowing upon her new opponent a dark glance.

The woman shook her head. "Find me after the evening meal," she said in a voice that brooked no argument. "I wish to talk to you."

"I didn't do anything wrong," muttered Onheda. "I didn't start this argument."

The elder woman sighed. "I wasn't referring to that, either. I have another matter to discuss with you. Don't forget. After the evening meal."

Uneasily, Onheda resumed her walk. What now? she asked herself. What could they possibly want from her now? She was doing her duties and not complaining. Whether in the fields or around the longhouse, she did whatever she had been told to do, never failing to accomplish her tasks. After her first unsuccessful attempt to run away, she was a model of good behavior, wasn't she?

She shivered. What had she been thinking back then, trying to escape, assuming she'd be able to find her way to Onondaga Lake and the lands of her people, crossing vast territories torn by ferocious warfare? She could have starved to death, or been killed, or captured once again.

Or, she thought stubbornly, she could have made it. There was no reason to assume she would not have been successful. She was young and strong, and she could survive in the woods. And by now she would have been back home, harvesting the second crop, living in the pretty town that sprawled not far away from Onondaga Lake, speaking a normal people's tongue and not this strange dialect the Flint People called a language. She could understand them with just a little effort, but their way to pronounce words was unpleasantly twisted. And they were the people who had killed her husband and many of her cousins and friends.

She ground her teeth. She was forced to live among the murderers of her family, among the sworn enemies of her people. Moreover, she was expected to become one of them, like the countless women who had done it before her and countless women who would have to do it after her. This was the custom. Some people were killed, others – adopted. She should have been grateful. It could have been worse. She could have been killed; or forced by some bloodthirsty warrior and then killed. But, instead, she was brought to their attackers' town, and then honored by being chosen by the Mothers of the Turtle Clan to replace a missing member, a woman who had died a few summers ago, in the winter sickness that carried away so many people. And she was expected to feel grateful about that. The rest of those captured in that raid were not so lucky. No clan had claimed them, and so they were killed. Quickly and painlessly, as there were no warriors in that particular party.

The warriors, Onheda knew, would have been honored to the highest degree; they would die neither quickly, nor painlessly. She had witnessed many such ceremonies, excited and horrified at the same time, strangely aroused by the warriors' courage and stamina. And it's not that everyone was brave up to their very end, of course. There were those who would lose their courage at the beginning of the ceremony and would beg for their lives, dying as painfully but also amidst the deepest contempt of their captors.

Oh yes, not every warrior of the Flint People was brave, she thought, grinning with satisfaction. Far from it! And her people had had the pleasure of raiding many of the enemy's settlements, too. The ceaseless warfare was a way of life, as long as she could remember herself. It seemed as if it had started from the beginning of times, but there were some who claimed it had not always been like this. They said the war should have been stopped. They said it would do no good to continue raiding each other's villages. They said the towns would perish one by one and not necessarily as a direct result of such warfare. They said all the involved nations were killing themselves.

There was such a man among her people, she remembered. Hionhwatha, a prominent leader of Onondaga Town, the largest town of her lands. Three summers ago, he had called a meeting, trying to bring together as many leaders as he could, from all over their towns and villages, to sit and smoke and talk.

His oratory skills gained him a fair audience, and some leaders did listen.

It was an unheard of affair that everyone talked about, remembered Onheda, who had not been such a young girl back then, having seen close to eighteen summers. Her man had traveled there, too, accompanying the leaders of their settlement. Many young warriors like him went, mostly out of curiosity, although her husband said there was something about Hionhwatha and what he had said.

He had turned more thoughtful upon his return, telling her all about the strange ideas of putting a stop to the feuds among Onondaga People, uniting them under some sort of a mutual management. It sounded ridiculous, but she loved to hear her man talking. He had a beautiful way with words, so she argued only mildly, to work him up into telling more.

His friends were dubious too, even those who had traveled with him. They went there out of curiosity more than anything else. It relieved the boredom of hunting and raiding the enemy's lands. It gave them something to laugh about.

However, the results of the meeting were not good. Those who opposed Hionhwatha interrupted the peaceful gathering, not above using violence, and even witchcraft, some said. The meeting disintegrated into a hopeless affair of flying insults and threats, and some people were killed before the present left for their homes, their hearts full of anger. They even heard that one of Hionhwatha's daughters had died, murdered some said, while the meeting was still on. A wild rumor, but a persisting one.

Onheda shrugged. The stubborn leader did not give up, trying to bring his ideas to life by calling more meetings. Then somehow, his other family members died, and crazed with grief, he had left his town, to disappear into the mists of Onondaga Lake. Some said he was living there now, alone, an outcast, a deranged, violent man with whom no reasonable person would come into a contact. She remembered the rumors. They said he was now feeding on human flesh.

Well, some people were strange, and unlucky, was Onheda's

private conclusion. The Right-Handed Twin had clearly given up on the struggling leader, but what could one do about it? And anyway, there was no wrong in their way of life. As long as one didn't let herself be surprised and captured, or killed. And she had been foolish enough to get captured, may they all rot for all eternity.

Atiron panted his way up the hill, struggling under the weight of a deer carcass. Sweat rolled into his eyes, and he could barely see his way.

Not that he had a cause to complain, he reasoned. If one could wander outside the safety of the town's fence in order to clear one's head and return burdened by fresh meat every time he did this, life could have been made into a bearable affair. Actually, life could have been more pleasant, if one could just walk out every time one needed to clear one's head, instead of being expected to keep oneself either within the boundaries of the fence or surrounded by others, even when needing time alone.

However, this morning's council meeting turned out to be such a depressing affair he could not resist the temptation, slipping through the opening in the double row of poles, taking a trail leading toward the river, a few hundred paces down the hill.

Of course, he didn't stroll leisurely. He had taken all the precautions, moving silently and carefully, his senses alerted. Outside the safety of the town's fence one could never be too careful, not with the enemy lurking, all these groups of foreign warriors on their way to raid this or that settlement, or even heading for Little Falls itself. People did not venture out unless in large, well-armed groups, yet, from time to time, one just had to have a gulp of fresh air and some privacy.

The Harvest Ceremony was nearing, usually one more happy

celebration, but this time the amounts of the harvested corn were pitiful, creating a problem. Reasons and explanations kept mounting, as they did now in the beginning of every fall, plenty of reasonable excuses, but their mutual nature was difficult to overlook. It towered menacingly, indicating the farmers' state of mind and even the lack of manpower. Women in the fields were busy keeping their watch, ready to sound alarm at the sight of approaching enemy, so the rest could make it safely behind the town's fence. However, for every justified warning, there were quite a few false ones and those pointed at the disoriented state of the people's minds. Nervousness and lack of confidence had been mounting for decades, reaching for all aspects of life, growing with every summer, steadily, if imperceptibly.

If only someone could put his finger on a particular event, to recollect how it had all began, thought Atiron, struggling up the hill, listening to his heart that was thundering in his ears. Then the solution might also present itself. However, who could explain how they had come to this? Although, since the dreadful winter three summers ago, when so many people had died from disease, and after the ill-fated raid of the late War Chief on the following spring, the situation had definitely worsened. The town had never recovered fully, although tremendous efforts were made to get back to normal life. More raids were sent, more captured enemies adopted, still the ranks of the clans were thinning, undermanned. There were simply not enough warriors to send out and not enough food to equip them with.

Sighing, Atiron remembered the War Chief, the closest of his friends. What a man he had been, imposing, intelligent, fierce, a good leader and a great companion, blessed with a beautiful wife and a pair of boisterous twins, a miracle in itself. Grinning against his will, he remembered the boys who had looked absolutely alike and yet different, easy to tell apart, because while one, Tekeni, was vital and handsome, having inherited the temper and the strength of his father, the other, Oni, was quiet and thin, closemouthed, a thoughtful sort of a child, much like his mother.

The boys were always together, and while it might have looked as though the smaller boy was following his impressive brother, the closer inspection showed that the opposite was true. The quiet, thoughtful twin was the one coming up with all sorts of ideas, ideas which the other boy, the boisterous one, was only too happy to implement. They balanced each other perfectly, and the whole town watched them, amused and expectant, remembering the prophecy concerning these boys. Like the Celestial Twins, they were destined to do important things, to better their peoples' lives, to change it dramatically in some unknown, unexplained way. They would lead their warriors to great victories when their time came, whispered the elders of the town.

A prophecy that was cut short by that terrible winter three summers ago. The War Chief's wife and the quieter twin died, leaving the great leader deranged with grief. Deaf to the words of the condolence ceremony and the consoling whispering of his friends and the devastated neighbors, the man spent the rest of the winter alone, talking about the raid he would organize with the coming of spring. A raid into the mists of the Great Sparkling Water, no more and no less; a reckless, unnecessary adventure, but there was no reasoning with his old friend, although Atiron did try. However, all he got was a cold grin that never reached the leader's clouded, distant eyes, and the short, cutting words, suggesting that he should bring his objections before the Town Council if he felt this projected raid was so ill-advised. Where had his friend gone?

He remembered getting to his feet, angered, hurt, offended, to encounter the anxious yet expectant gaze of none other than Tekeni, the surviving twin, huddled in the far corner, listening avidly. According to the decision of the War Chief, the boy was to come along, but by that time, Atiron had given up.

He shook his head, his sadness welling. The man had convinced the Town Council, and the Mothers of the Clans had given their blessing and a considerable amount of food supplies, and so the party of two dozen warriors sailed, never to return.

None of them. Not even Atiron's own son, who had insisted on going along, a promising young warrior, his only son. They had all died on the other side of the Great Lake, and the grief stricken town accepted it, trying to get on with their lives for two more hopeless summers of less raids and deteriorating conditions in general.

Sighing, he shifted his burden, searching for a place to hide his catch before entering the town and proceeding along the twisted alleys, washed by the late afternoon sun, spreading the aroma of evening meals being heated upon the glittering fires that doted the walls of the longhouses.

"Father!" As he neared, Kahontsi, his youngest daughter, burst from under the facade of their building, slowing down reluctantly. The smile she bestowed upon him shone. Tall and pliant, her movements as graceful as those of a young doe, her face a perfect oval, her eyes changing their color from bright to a dark brown according to the light, Kahontsi was held to be the most beautiful girl, according to the judgment of the entire town.

Atiron could not fight his smile. "*She:kon*, Daughter. Back home already?"

She shook her head and her braids jumped, sparkling with drops of water, still damp from the wash up that would seal the day in the fields.

"No, not really." Kahontsi's eyes glimmered as brightly as her wet hair. She knew of her father's affection. He could never resist her charm. "Mother is resting. Ehnita had to be taken home this morning. She didn't feel well, and anyway, she is getting too heavy to be of use. I don't think she'll be back in the fields before her baby is out. She is also resting now. I was just visiting her." It all came out in a gush, with no pause for breath. The girl was obviously anxious to be on her way.

"Wait, don't run away. I might need your help. I'm going in to talk to your mother." He grinned at her open disappointment. "Well, you don't have to, of course. Who wants freshly broiled meat for one's evening meal?"

Her eyes widened. "You are not saying…"

However, Atiron was already inside, crossing the storage space of the outer room, heading for the long passageway.

"You just wait and see," he called out, satisfied with her reaction.

"*She:kon.*" His wife's smile glimmered tiredly, as she perched on the edge of the lower bunk, brushing her hair. "What a day! We are almost done with the last of the maize. Might be able to finish harvesting it by tomorrow. Ehnita scared us, though. She became dizzy and almost fainted on us. Had to sit her in the shadow until she felt better, then two girls took her home. I'll talk to our Clan's Council today. I believe she should not be coming to the fields anymore."

"Will they agree?" asked Atiron doubtfully. "She has one more moon or so to go."

"They had better!" Her hand tore at the tangled hair impatiently. "There are other tasks a pregnant girl can do, without working to death harvesting maize."

"Look, I need your help, but if you are too tired I'll take Kahontsi. I bumped into her just outside."

The woman's eyes widened as she listened to his story, flooding with surprise and joy, yet spiced with a fair amount of reproach.

"You should know better than to wander outside unprotected," she muttered grimly.

Her nimble fingers finished braiding her wet hair, tying it behind her back with a thin leather strap. From under the bank, where the kitchen utensils were stored, she took a pot and a flint knife, and tossed them into a big leather bag, talking as she worked, "I had better come with you. You say it's just outside the fence? We can cut it there, so it won't be necessary to drag the whole carcass with us. I hope you hide it well. Wouldn't want any of the other greedy mouths claiming it for themselves. We will invite people for our meal, but it is still our catch."

Atiron grinned. Yes, this was his wife, the epitome of efficiency itself. By the ancient tradition, when a man hunted in his spare time, and not as a part of an officially organize hunting party, his catch would be hidden within a fair proximity of the town, while the successful hunter would rush back home to summon his wife, or a daughter, or any other female relative, to accompany him to the hidden treasure, as the meat carried into the town by a woman would become her personal property, not to be shared with the entire community.

Kahontsi was still outside, shifting her weight from one foot to another. At the sight of her mother, the girl's pretty face flooded with relief. "So you don't need me, I suppose?" Broadly, she smiled at Atiron, mischievous and pleading, knowing well which of the two could not resist her charm.

"Be back in time to help me with the meal!" called out her mother sternly, watching the girl's well-shaped shins disappearing down the alley. "This one is a handful. Running around, going wherever she pleases. Careless. Indifferent to her duties. Anxious to finish whatever she does and be off. I wish I knew where she is wandering and in what company. In the fields, it's just the same. We have so much trouble with the young girls. They have to be placed far apart from each other, otherwise they are gathering in groups, laughing and chatting and do nothing productive. We weren't like that when we were young!"

Atiron shook his head. "It's the war."

"There was war in our time, too!"

"But not like now. Things are worse now. Everything is falling apart. Look at the town's mood. It comes to expression in the young peoples' behavior. They feel the end is nearing and are trying to take the best out of life. I'm afraid to think what it'll look like in another few decades, in what world Ehnita's child will be living."

"Here you are again, plunging into that fatal mood of yours," complained his wife. "Full of dark prophecies."

It was an old argument, and they made the rest of their way in silence.

Kahontsi rushed toward the southern entrance, elated. Smiling at the afternoon sun as it caressed her shoulders and arms, she breathed the aroma of cooking meals, thinking about their dinner. A broiled meat, of all things! Many would come to share their meal tonight.

Several fires were gleaming near the longhouses, and the women were busy with pottery bowls, stirring a porridge of mashed corn that was prepared from the morning, and now needed to be warmed and spiced with berries and dried meat. Nothing to rival a fresh stew, of course.

Narrowing her eyes, she saw Anitas strolling beside the poles of the inner fence, pacing back and forth, impatient.

"Good that it didn't take you a whole moon to appear," called out the tall girl, rushing forward, speaking as she ran.

"I'm sorry. It's Father. He burst upon me, looking for someone to come with him and get this delicious, pretty little deer he just hunted out there. Luckily, Mother volunteered." Kahontsi waved happily. "Would you believe that? He was wandering out there – don't ask me why he would do something like this – and he ran into that deer. Just like that! And then, whoop, one good shot and we are having a fresh meat for our evening meal." Her braids jumped as she tossed her head and laughed. "I don't suppose you'll be coming visiting tonight."

Anitas' eyes widened. "Wild bears could not have stopped me. In the name of the Right-Handed Twin, how long has it been since I've eaten a fresh meat! When did the last hunting party leave? Five dawns ago? Weren't they supposed to come back already?"

"Not a chance. Give them another five, if at all." Kahontsi's face darkened, and both girls proceeded in silence for a while. In these war times, the hunting expeditions were as dangerous a business as a raiding party.

"Look at her!" exclaimed Anitas, pointing at the slender figure of the Onondaga girl, as she stormed out of the second Turtle Clan's longhouse. Stumbling into the cooking facilities spread beside the building's wall, the foreigner cursed softly and rushed on, paying no attention to the watching eyes.

"What about her?"

"The most annoying, stupid piece of rotten meat I ever met. Never smiles, never speaks to anyone unless it's something nasty. They should never have brought her here, if you ask me. They should have killed her with the rest of her filthy people. Or adopt into another clan, as far away from mine as possible. Stupid fowl!"

Kahontsi shrugged. "I guess it's not that easy to get used to a new place. Think about it. You and I could do no better, maybe. I'm not sure I would be all smiles if forced to live in one of her former settlements."

"Oh, how nice of you." Anitas raised her eyebrow and sneered, "Why don't you go over there and befriend her, if so?"

"I may, when I have time."

Anitas laugh. "But you never have time, do you? That's the catch. And I have to see her ugly face every day, all day long. Today, in the field, I wanted to punch her, I swear. She has such a dirty mouth."

They reached the end of the fence and glanced at the ceremonial grounds and the children running around it, throwing sticks at improvised targets. No adult appeared to be walking by. Relieved, they sneaked out and made their way along the outer side of the inner palisade, crossing tobacco plots.

"Did you bring everything?" inquired Kahontsi eagerly.

Anitas waved a small pouch, in which warriors and hunters carried their sacred objects. Dropping to her knees, she brought out a tiny pottery jar, which Kahontsi took reverently, peeking in, eyeing the glowing coal. In the meanwhile, her friend brought out a pack of corn husks wrapped around the smaller, brownish ground leaves. Next came a pipe – an old, cracked, unpainted affair. The amount of tobacco was hardly impressive, enough to fill only half of a pipe, but the girls went to work on it diligently, excited but cumbersome, lacking the experience.

"This time I had to take it from my brother's cache," murmured Anitas. "Father was beginning to wonder why his stockpiles were melting away."

They laughed.

It took them even longer to light the old pipe. They puffed and blew and panted, fiddling with the coal, until the thin line of smoke appeared. By that time, Anitas relaxed and leaned against the warm poles, taking a deep breath, calm and confident, in perfect control.

Kahontsi's experience was not as advanced. She inhaled nervously, unsure of herself. Their hide-and-smoke escapades began not so very long ago, but Anitas had done it previously, from time to time.

"No games tonight?" Making a face, Kahontsi passed the pipe back to her friend.

"No, I don't think so." Anitas' lips twisted. "Not enough people to make up the teams. Everyone worthwhile is out there, either raiding some filthy enemy, or hunting, or doing the Left-Handed Twin knows what. There is no more life in this town. In the end only women will be left, to play with each other. Yuck! Let us hope some of the warriors or the hunters bother to come back in time for the celebration."

"Father is upset about it, you know? I don't know why, but I think something is wrong. He wouldn't talk about it, but I know him, and what is bothering him these days is the Second Harvest ceremony."

"What is wrong with that? No! They can't do this to us. No ceremonies, no celebration, no ball games, no nothing!"

"Who are 'they'?" grinned Kahontsi.

"I don't know! I don't know and I don't care. Whoever they are."

"Don't get all warmed up about it. The ceremony will be held, maybe in a smaller form but it will. No one would think of canceling the celebration. The Great Spirits need to be thanked. We can't make them angrier than they are now. Besides, maybe the warriors and the hunters will come back in time, and then wait and see what a great celebration this one will turn out to be."

Anitas pulled a face. "Somehow I don't think they will come back in time. Everything is bleak and boring. The Great Spirits are angry with us, or indifferent."

Kahontsi eyed the pipe, now lifeless and temporarily forgotten. "It'll be well." Trying to make it work again, she talked between the puffs, "Trust me. Besides… what do you think… the warriors and the hunters know very well when the ceremony should be held…" The pipe came to life suddenly and, unprepared, she inhaled too deeply and began coughing and choking. Tears flooded her eyes, but determined to finish her line of thought, she struggled to continue, "They are waiting for this ceremony just like us…" She swallowed and coughed again, her face burning.

Anitas giggled. "Too bad I didn't think to bring water. For a beginner like you." She winked and took the pipe, resuming her smoking, at peace with the world once again. "Maybe you are right. These boys are not supposed to miss the ceremony. It's not one of the most important celebrations, but still. They would be insane to miss it."

Kahontsi shook her head vigorously to the offered pipe, taking a deep breath of an evening breeze, smelling the aroma coming from the woods just across the ditch and down the hill.

"I'm going to participate in, at least, two ceremonial dances. Grandmother promised to prepare two more turtle shells for me, to make it up to eight pieces. Last year I was dancing with six."

She remembered the rustling sound the turtle shells made, when tied to the leg with a wide leather strap, preventing the rattle from bruising the soft skin of the thigh. A skilful dancer would make their rattling merge perfectly with the trill of the flute and the monotonous beating of the water drums. It was a challenge to control the heavy shells. The girls had to practice a lot to be accepted into the circle of the true ceremonial dancers.

Anitas shrugged. "All those girls are running around with a rash on their thighs."

"No, they don't. You just have to make sure the leather straps are wide enough to protect your skin. And, of course, you do not forget to rub enough of the bear fat, a little before and plenty after."

"And you think it helps?"

"Oh yes, it does. Last year, my legs were just fine."

"You had only six shells. Now it's going to be eight. A serious weight."

Kahontsi grinned. "Stop whining and come with me to do this. You are dying from boredom, anyway."

Anitas pulled a face. "I bet the warriors are having better time than us. The fields are such a bore!"

"Those who survive, maybe," murmured Kahontsi, her sense of well being deteriorating rapidly.

Two summers earlier, her only brother had been killed in a raid. He died far away from his family, somewhere across the Great Sparkling Water, along with the War Chief and the rest of the warriors who went with him. Even that handsome boy, the War Chief's surviving twin son went on that ill-omened expedition. Not to return, any of them. Oh, how the people of Little Falls were devastated, how reluctant to reconcile themselves to the bitter reality.

Yet, none suffered as she did, she knew, no one! Her brother was the best boy ever, her invincible hero, strong and funny and always there, solving her childish problems, knowing everything. He had a great future, everyone had said that. And somehow, somehow, she knew he did not approve of the way the war was going. He and Father had talked about it often, deep into the nights.

She had seen close to fifteen summers back then, never recovering from the shock of his death. She never talked about him anymore. Neither did Father. But on the rare occasions, when she allowed the bittersweet memories of him to enter her mind, she knew for certain that if he had managed to survive, he would have found the way to make things better. Some way that was unfamiliar to her, or even to Father.

Her mood spiraling downward in a way she could not control, she sprang to her feet.

"What happened to you?" asked Anitas, startled. "Do you feel bad? Because of the smoking?"

Kahontsi shook her head violently. "I have to help Mother. I'll see you there."

As she rushed away, she could imagine Anitas gaping at the place she was sitting just a heartbeat earlier, thinking that her friend had gone completely mad. She didn't care. All she wanted was to be left alone now, truly alone, at least for a little while.

Onheda stared at the small fire, watching the shadows bouncing off the walls, creating strange patterns.

"Sit down, girl," said the heavyset women, indicating the low bank opposite to her.

Sitting down obediently, Onheda did not take her eyes off the fire. *Come on*, she thought. *Just get on with it already.* She could hear the clamor coming from the longhouse next to this one, its dwellers gorging on the fresh meat, happy and unconcerned. Some simple-in-the-head council member, she knew, had gone outside and hunted a deer. As though there was no danger in doing so; as if no raiding parties were likely to wander about. Would serve him well to get captured or shot, she thought, raising her eyes and meeting the gaze of the older woman.

"So tell me, how do you feel now that almost two moons have passed since you joined our longhouse?"

Oh please, you are not expecting me to pour my heart out, are you? She cleared her throat and tried to keep such thoughts off her face.

"I feel well," she said, clutching her palms tight.

"Are you happy here? Is there anything that bothers you?"

Onheda shook her head, her uneasiness mounting, the scrutinizing gaze of her interrogator making her stomach tighten.

"What happened today between you and Anitas?"

"Nothing."

"It didn't look like nothing to me."

She shifted uneasily, perching on the very edge of the bank, where blankets and pelts did not cover the hard, wooden surface. It felt uncomfortably harsh against her legs.

"We were just arguing about things, that's all," she said finally, wishing to be outside, away from the suffocating dimness and the threatening pictures the dancing shadows were painting upon the wall.

The stocky woman sighed. "I know it's not easy to get used to a new home. I know it takes time. We are making every effort to accommodate you, to make you feel at home, but with no cooperation from you, we cannot make a good progress, can we?" She paused, and the silence that ensued was heavy, pregnant with meaning.

Onheda dropped her gaze, suddenly finding it difficult to breathe. This compartment truly did not have enough air. They ought to have kept the smoke hole in the roof opened. Glancing at the ceiling, she saw the opening gaping into the night sky, not covered at all.

"I… I'm doing my best," she said, surprised to hear her voice ringing steadily.

"It doesn't seem that way."

The fire flickered as a gust of wind swept through the corridor, making the shadows on the walls jump.

"Look at me, girl!"

The older woman's voice rang sternly, full of authority, not friendly anymore. The flinty gaze held hers. Onheda bit her lips and tried to look calm, and not like the cornered animal she felt.

"I know what you are going through, girl. You are not reconciled to your new life, not yet. You are fighting it. But it's time you made up your mind. Our clan does not need resentful members. We are patient, and we don't change our minds easily. But we can't wait forever for you to adjust. You will have to make up your mind soon. Do you understand me, Onheda? You were offered a chance of a new life. But the question is, what are you going to do with this offer?"

Out there, in the clear evening air, someone was beating on a drum, slowly and mournfully.

Onheda swallowed. "I... I do everything I'm asked. I give no trouble."

The penetrating gaze held hers. "Is this your model of a good behavior? To do as you are told? Have you been as good of a girl in your previous life?"

She licked her lips. "I don't know."

"Is that how you plan to go through your life? Doing as you are told and giving no trouble? You have many moons to go yet, many summers, many hunting seasons. Your life is still in its very beginning, girl, even if it did not go the way you had planned. Are you prepared to give up on everything? To do as you are told until you get old?" The glittering eyes were now like a pair of dark, glowing coals. "Or do you plan to change your life once again? Are you cherishing ideas of running away to your former people? Would you help them attack us, having a chance to assist? Are you still our enemy, Onheda?"

Shivering, she stared at the woman, unable to answer, unable to shift her gaze. It was a nightmare. The annoying hag was reading her thoughts.

"Like I told you, I understand what you are going through." The stocky woman got up, a look filled with a certain amount of pity creeping in her eyes. "But it is time you made up your mind."

She turned and began rumbling through the clothes piled upon the bank. Onheda clenched her hands to stop them from trembling.

"It's time you took yourself a husband," said the older woman without turning. "There is a man of the Bear Clan. His longhouse is just across the ceremonial ground. A good man; good hunter, good warrior. He should make a fitting husband for you."

"I don't want to take a husband," whispered Onheda.

"Why-ever not?" The older woman was still busy arranging the bank. "You are free, and you are of a right age. Why wouldn't you want to take a husband?"

She clenched her palms tight, feeling herself back on the banks of Onondaga Lake, on that horrible day of the early summer, with her cousin killed, her friends dying, and herself tied and hurt, and for the first time realizing that she could do nothing, nothing at all, to fight back and take control of her life – a feeling unfamiliar up to that warm summer day.

She took a deep breath. "I don't want to take a husband," she repeated, voice firm. "Not yet. I will let you know when I'm ready."

Her adversary turned around, losing some of her composure; the sight that pleased Onheda, in spite of her plight.

"You know that the last word in this matter belongs to the Clan Council?"

"The clan's member is also privy to such a decision." Her anger welled, banishing the last of the fear.

"The clan's member, yes."

"I am a clan member!" She stared at the older woman, almost welcoming the developing confrontation. *I know my rights.* Her thoughts raced through her mind, frantically, fervently. *I will not be intimidated.*

The eyes in front of her took a different shade. "No, you are not." The voice of her tormenter was soft, almost compassionate. "Not yet."

Onheda felt her heart coming to a halt. It missed a beat, then began racing wildly, unevenly.

"But I am," she said breathlessly, the sensation of helplessness returning. "I was adopted... I... I would not be here otherwise."

"You didn't go through the adoption ceremony, yet. You

didn't receive your new name. You are not officially a member of the Turtle Clan. You are allowed to live in this longhouse, you are allowed to work our fields, but you are not a member of our clan, yet. Nothing is decided."

The emphasis put on the word *live* was unmistakable. It bounced off the wooden walls. *Live, live, live. Do you want to live? Are you ready to die?* There had to be a way out of this nightmare.

"You will be adopted should you show a proper attitude. Not by doing as you are told; or pretending to do so." The woman reached for Onheda's shoulder, pretending not to notice her wincing, recoiling from the touch. "You have to make up your mind, girl. You have to understand that your past does not exist anymore. You have to reconcile yourself to this reality. This clan is your only family now. This town is your only home. This is the only life you can have. Either this or nothing at all."

The face in front of her was so blurry she could not make out its expression. She fought the welling tears.

"I'm certain the council will be willing to give you a few more dawns. Maybe half a moon. Maybe a whole moon, even. You will have to show this clan it will be poorer without you. Work as hard as you have worked so far, but do it cheerfully. Make friends. Take a husband. Either this or there will be no adoption ceremony. Do you understand me? Your time is limited now."

Oh, Mighty Spirits! She stared at the fire stubbornly, remembering the other small flame, the one she would light in this pre-dawn time when everyone was asleep and she would sneak out to make her secret offering to the Great Spirit, the Right-Handed Twin himself. She had done so several times, with no one to notice, no one to know. And if no one had noticed so far...

She almost shut her eyes, as another thought hit, swelling inside her head. She had not been formally adopted, not yet. The woman said so, thinking to intimidate her further, but actually, doing her a great favor. She was free to go. She could have done this every night, every time she had sneaked out. The Right-Handed Twin was showing her the way, but she had been too blind, too cowardly to see it.

CHAPTER 2

The river sped ahead, flowing strongly, wider than any waterway he had seen so far. Two Rivers narrowed his eyes.

"Impressive," he said, having difficulty seeing through the grayish pre-dawn mist. "So that's *the* river?"

"Yes, that's our Great River." His young companion nodded impassively, with no sparkle brightening the dark eyes, no expression crossing the closed up face. It remained sealed, cold, indifferent.

Used to the sudden spells of gloom in his companion's moods, Two Rivers still raised his eyebrows, surprised. Wasn't the youth happy to see his homelands?

"Well, we had better make ourselves comfortable somewhere in there," he said, glancing at the trees adorning the low bunk. "Before your country folk run into us, entertaining the idea of dumping my juicy parts into their stews before we have prepared our explanations."

"My country folk will not run into us here," said Tekeni, coming back to life all of a sudden. "Onondaga, The People of the Hills, will be the ones feasting on your juicy parts. Or maybe the People of the Standing Stone. Our river begins somewhere between their lands."

"What? When you said 'your river' I thought you meant your lands, too. Weren't you bragging that your Flint People were the most powerful on this side of the Great Lake?"

"They are powerful, but not that powerful." A grin stretched the generous lips, lifting the scars that were crossing them now. "Unless too many things changed through the last two summers."

The defiant sparkle was on, bringing back the boy Two Rivers remembered. Regardless of the circumstances of his people, the youth himself had changed into something unrecognizable. Whether because of the scars adorning the handsome face now, painting a strange pattern upon it, or the way it had thinned to look older, losing its youthful look, the change was there, deep and subtle. The boy had grown to be a man.

"And they will be as happy to dispense with my body parts as with yours, so there is no need to feel threatened by me just yet," the youth was saying, his grin challenging. "In a few more dawns? Maybe. If we make good progress."

"With the flow of this current and the moon getting thinner and thinner, I may be safe for longer than that," said Two Rivers, studying his companion with his eyebrows lifted high.

You cheeky skunk, he thought. *You are growing too sure of yourself.*

Careful to conceal their tracks, they carried their canoe along into the safety of the woods, then made a quick meal by mixing the remnants of the sweetened powder Tekeni's girl had been shrewd enough to toss into their bag. In these foreign woods it was not wise to try and spread the traps in order to enjoy some fresh meat, but after a whole moon spent in the uninhabited lands on the northeastern side of the Great Lake, they could not complain of being underfed.

Stretching and stifling a sigh of relief, Two Rivers stared at the brightening sky, remembering the past moon, the first moon of the Shedding Leaves season, and the wonderful days spent at leisure, resting and talking and hunting, preparing their plans.

The youth needed time to recover, and he himself welcomed the delay, enjoying the tranquility of the woods with no people. Five days of sail separated them from his homeland's bay, five days into the wilderness of the abandoned parts of the great water basin. A safety at long last. A wonderful opportunity to relax and to think. His plans needed to be formulated, or maybe just aired aloud. He had never dared to face his ideas fully, to put them into words with no gnawing doubts or misgivings.

Not until now. The luxury of it made his head reel, and so he had taken his time in the wonderful loneliness the uninhabited woods provided.

The youth did not argue, needing this time to recover his former strength. His cuts were deep, not healing as fast as expected, and his cracked ribs needed the benefits of full rest. Not to mention his spirit, which needed to recuperate as well. His moods changing interminably, the youth seemed to be constantly torn between spells of rage and depression, one moment hopeful, busy making plans to get his girl back, the other growling, full of anger at everyone, from the men who had made their flight necessary, the men who had tried to kill him in humiliating, painful ways, to human beings in general.

"I wish Yeentso were still alive," he would murmur from time to time, eyes glimmering eerily, telling without words what he would have done to the man now if he could. Not a pretty sight.

"Yes, the filthy lowlife got an easy death," Two Rivers would agree, shrugging. "But he is dead, and this is the main thing. Stop living in your past."

"I'm not living in my past. I'm thinking about my future," the youth would maintain stubbornly, face sealed. "I'm making plans to come back and take Seketa away from them. It is my future."

"Oh yes, it is. But it's not your near future, so stop wasting your time thinking about it. When the time comes, you'll get her."

The gaze shot at Two Rivers was as dark as a stormy cloud. "We should have taken her along!"

"Where? Here?" Glancing at the clearing they had been staying at, a pretty pastoral place, Two Rivers lifted his eyebrows. "Yes, I'm sure she would be happy to live in the woods, skinning rabbits from our traps."

"She might have liked it. She would have taken care of our needs."

"*All* of our needs?" With a murderous glance being his

answer, Two Rivers laughed. "Forget it, wolf cub. Forget your girl for some time. She'll wait like she promised. She seems to be a serious young woman, not a lightheaded little thing. So if she chose you, then it's that. She won't be looking at other men."

"She may be forced to take a man. The Mothers of her Clan are mean hags, every one of them. They may be angry with her for being involved with us." The youth sat up abruptly, hugging his knees, his lips pressed tight, the healing cuts glaring. "What if they know about her helping us? What if someone saw her when she brought us things?"

"No one saw her, and she is capable of taking care of herself, this pretty Seketa of yours. If you didn't notice, she was a good girl, a respectable member of our society, before you drew her into the wild whirlwind that is called your life. So she will be back, working the fields, grinding maize, dancing through ceremonies. Maybe breathing with relief, eh?" Meeting another dark gaze, Two Rivers brought his arms up in a defensive gesture. "All right, all right. But all the same, she is not the person to be intimidated easily, and she is better off in the town for now. When we cross the Great Lake, you will be happy you didn't bring her along. The adventures that await us are not for a woman, upright or wild. You had no right to risk her life and her well being in this way."

A grunt was his answer.

"So what will we do when we cross the Great Lake?" asked the youth after a while.

"We'll go to your Little Falls."

"And?"

"And we'll see if they are prepared to listen."

"Why would they?"

Disregarding the defiant, openly challenging glance, Two Rivers shifted closer to the fire, making himself comfortable.

"The situation must be as bad in your lands as it is in mine. So any of your people's settlements can be a good start. But in Little Falls, we might have a better chance due to your old connections. Even though you were no more than just a mischievous boy back then, they must still remember your father, if he was as great a war leader as you claim."

"He *was* a great War Chief, you can trust me on that!" called the youth hotly, forgetting his previous cause of gloom. "He was a great leader, and no one will forget him in a hurry, no one! He led his warriors for many summers, men from Little Falls and from the surrounding villages. He was always victorious, and they always listened to him."

"He must have been a good orator," commented Two Rivers thoughtfully, glad that such an opponent would not be standing in his way. A warrior of this vast influence might have proven a real obstacle.

"Oh, yes, he was. They always listened to him. He could talk passionately but reasonably, so even those who disagreed found nothing to say."

"Where there those who disagreed with him? On what subjects?"

"I don't know. Some raids were less advisable than the others, I suppose." Frowning, the youth narrowed his eyes, as though trying to remember. "His closest friend, Atiron, also from our clan, was always arguing with him. In a friendly manner usually, but sometimes they would grow angry with each other." Reaching for a small branch, the youth threw it into the fire, watching it thoughtfully, concentrated. "Their conversations would last well into the nights, in our compartment, or outside by the fire. They worried about our town and our people. And about our enemies, who grew stronger and fiercer with each passing moon. My brother used to sneak closer and listen. He didn't think it was boring, what they were talking about."

"This man, your father's friend, was he a leader too?"

"Well, he was a member of the Town Council and very esteemed and respected." The youth grinned. "He liked to disagree with my father. He enjoyed listening to his passionate speeches, defending his views and our way of life. My brother said so. He said the man was doing it on purpose. But they were great friends, so Father did not get angry for real, not usually."

"I do hope this man is still there in Little Falls," muttered Two Rivers, his mind racing. He forced his thoughts to slow down, studying the youth, pleased to see the large eyes clearing of shadows. "Your brother might still be there, you know."

But the handsome face closed again, abruptly at that. "He is not."

"How would you..." The rest of the question died away, answered by the empty, sealed eyes staring at the fire, refusing to look up.

How did the other cub manage to die? he wondered. Was he also a part of that raid that the oh-so-highly-praised War Chief decided to drag his underage sons on? What a stupid decision it was, and across the Great Sparkling Water, too. Into the very heart of the enemy lands.

"He died three summers ago, of a winter disease," said the youth quietly, his voice hardly audible, ringing eerily in the thickening dusk.

Two Rivers sighed. "I'm sorry to hear that."

The silence hung, uncomfortably heavy, unsettling.

"Anyone else of your family still alive?"

It took yet longer for Tekeni to respond, and Two Rivers thought he would not hear the answer at all.

"No, no one."

He threw more branches into the fire, then got to his feet, intending to check the traps. Their evening meal needed to be attended to, he thought, welcoming the opportunity to busy himself, to escape the heavy silence. Life could be too cruel, sometimes.

He glanced at the youth, his heart going out to him. So young and yet so disillusioned already, having been forced to face more than some men would see in a lifetime. His own life seemed to be sheltered and uneventful when compared to this boy.

"So what will you do if my people agreed to listen?" asked

Tekeni after a while, getting to his feet to fetch the rabbit Two Rivers brought back. Businesslike, he took out his knife and began cutting its back legs off. "Besides a lot of talking."

"Well, besides a lot of talking…" Shooting a direful glance at his younger companion, Two Rivers stirred the glowing embers, to make it ready for the cooking. "We'll be busy organizing your people and their neighbors, and later on, my people too, in a way that will enable them to work together, without the need to war on each other."

"How would you do that?"

"Through councils, of course."

"Town Councils?"

"No. The Town Councils cannot control the whole nation, can they? There are too many of them." Receiving the legless rabbit, Two Rivers sliced its stomach, emptying its contents into the hole he'd dug in the ground. "There will be the need to form a council of a nation, where chosen people would be responsible for dealing with troubles between the towns and villages. Just the way the Clans or the Town Councils are working, but on a larger scale."

The youth was peering at him, his eyes full of curiosity and again free of shadows. "And the trouble between the nations?"

"What do you think?" Two Rivers hid his grin, pleased with his companion's quick thinking.

"Councils too, on an even larger scale."

"Yes, but not many of them. Only one general council, comprised from a group of representatives from each nation." Slicing the fresh, dripping meat into neat pieces, he frowned, sensing his companion's doubts filling the silence. "It will work, because it works on a smaller scale. Our people are living this way, they are familiar with this sort of arrangement, so all they need is a cause to stop warring and get organized."

"And there will be no wars and no warriors?"

"Oh, that I can't promise you. It depends on the amount of nations that would be willing to listen. Not all of them will be able to open their minds, to overcome their prejudices."

"I'm not sure one single nation, or person, will do that," muttered the youth, picking a bowl Two Rivers carved earlier through the day out of a solid piece of wood. "I'll bring water."

"Yes, do that." Grinning, Two Rivers busied himself with impaling the meat on the sharpened sticks.

The cheeky bastard was learning, he thought. And he was gaining confidence. Which was a good thing. He'd make a good partner.

CHAPTER 3

The light breeze rustled in the trees adorning the ceremonial ground next to the double palisade fence. Pleasant and calming, it put the men into a lazy mood. Squatting more comfortably, Atiron grinned, sucking on the pipe when his turn came.

The members of the Town Council had come to deliberate quite a few pressing issues, but now they fell silent, enjoying the coolness of the early afternoon. The Shedding Leaves season was at its most enjoyable stage, before the days turned cold and the wind started blowing for real.

"Well," the Head of the Council inhaled deeply, holding the smoke in, deliberating. "The second harvest, indeed, came as non-abundant as predicted. The first of the *Three Sisters* did not favor Little Falls this season."

"Too many enemy attacks undermined our women's spirits," murmured a thickset man, one of the two Bear Clan's representatives. "They had to leave the fields more often than not. No wonder the crops were not tended properly."

"The enemy grew too bold!" exclaimed the Wolf Clan's man. "The People of the Standing Stone and the Onondagas grew too bold. They should be punished for their brazenness."

Some heads nodded in agreement, while others just shrugged.

"To ensure our well being through the upcoming winter, we will have to send out as many hunting parties as we can organize," said Atiron, taking the pipe in his turn. "The men will have to leave their clubs in favor of their bows and their fishing spears. We have close to two moons to do as much hunting and fishing as we can." He let the smoke linger in his throat, enjoying the sensation. "The women will finish their winter preparation sooner than usual, due to the small amounts of corn to grind, and so they will be free to gather more of the forest fruit, and plenty of firewood." Passing the pipe on, he sighed. "Our duty is to ensure the well being of this town, so the Frozen Moons will not prove as terrible as three winters before."

They fell silent, remembering the terrible winter when the illness spread like a lethal storm, killing people in its wake, unmerciful, oblivious of the identity and the age of its victims. All due to the lack of food and firewood, Atiron knew. Not to the displeased spirits as many chose to believe.

"And what about the raiding parties?" asked the man of the Wolf Clan. "Do you suggest we send no warriors to the enemy lands before the coming of the Awakening Season?"

Atiron stood his peer's heavy gaze. "Yes, I suggest we postpone our retaliation until the well being of this town is ensured."

"This town can stand the hardships. Our people are not afraid." The gaze of Ohonte, his fellow Turtle Clan man, the representative of the neighboring longhouse, held no enmity, only an open concern. "We should let our warriors raid the Onondaga lands. We should send not one, but two, maybe three raiding parties. And another one into the lands of our immediate neighbors, the People of the Standing Stone. Our enemies have grown too bold, and they will grow bolder if we do nothing but defend our town. They will deem us weak, afraid."

More vigorous nodding. Atiron paid them no attention. It was an old argument, repeated all over again at every meeting of the council. But this time, with the crops being so pitiful, he knew he had to press his point, unpopular as it was.

"Yes, they might deem us weakened, but this should not be our main concern. We are not weak, and we are not afraid. And we do not need to prove it to anyone. We know what we are, and the well being of our people, our old and our young and our womenfolk, is more important than the opinions of our enemies concerning the valor of our men. We need to make sure this town will not starve. This should be our main concern."

"We can do both," said another Bear Clan's man. "The way we have always done. Last autumn, we sent two raiding parties and a few hunting ones."

"The harvest was more abundant on the summer before," said the Head of the Council mildly. "We could have done with less meat dried and stored."

"Then we can send more hunting parties than the warriors' ones."

"The harvest is too pitiful. Even if we sent every man capable of hunting, we may still have not enough food stored for the winter."

He knew he should cease arguing, because the proposed solution of more hunting parties than the raiding ones was acceptable, a good compromise. Still, he could not keep silent. It should have been done two moons ago, when the first harvest of the sweet green corn was small and the signs of the main harvest were alarming. Back then, they should have stopped equipping warriors. If only he had been listened to!

"We should have started storing meat two moons ago," he repeated. "Now it may be too late. Unless we put in a serious effort."

"With all due respect, brother," said the Wolf Clan man. "The decision of sending raiding parties belongs to the War Chief and the people of the War Council, ratified by the Mothers of the Clans. We are not the ones to decide as to the advisability of this or that raid. We only advise, which we will do, should we reach an agreement between ourselves." The man's eyes flashed. "You are in the minority, brother. In the glaring minority. Why would you go on arguing?"

"Because I care for this town and its people, and not only for the prestige of its name," flared Atiron, enraged. The man was challenging his authority too openly. "The well being of this town is my main concern, and this is what I was elected to do."

"Like all of us," said the Head of the Council, placating. "Now please, both of you. Put your anger away, and concentrate on the possible solutions to our problems."

They went on discussing the size of the hunting and raiding parties, but Atiron stopped listening, knowing that it was hopeless. Their ears were deaf to reason, as they always had been. The terrible winter three summers ago had taught them nothing. Nothing had changed, and this winter, more people would die of disease and malnutrition.

He stifled a sigh. Miraculously, his family came out of that terrible winter unharmed, he, his wife, and his three grown children, while many dwellers of their longhouse perished, suffering terribly, coughing and burning until their senses would leave them. No amount of prayers, brews, and tobacco smoke offerings helped. His closest friend, the former War Chief's heavily pregnant wife had been among the dying, her and one of the twins. So needlessly, so untimely. But now Atiron's older daughter was pregnant, too. Would she, or her baby, survive the upcoming winter?

So much had changed. The War Chief and the other twin had died in the raid that the man, mad with grief, rushed to ensue with the coming spring, and so had Atiron's son, his only son. The stony fist was back, pressing his insides in its crushing grip. He clenched his teeth tight and concentrated on the words of his peers, knowing better than to let the wave take him.

"How long has it been since the girl disappeared?" one of the men was asking.

"Two dawns, I think. Maybe three." Ohonte, the other Turtle Clan's longhouse representative, grimaced as though he had eaten an unripe fruit. "The Mothers of our longhouse kept the trouble between themselves and the other longhouses of our clan. But now that they want us to send a party, to look for the girl, they deigned to let us know."

Atiron narrowed his eyes, mildly interested. "Who disappeared?"

"The Onondaga girl." Ohonte made a face. "A wild, unruly thing. Since her adoption, she gave nothing but trouble. Kwayenda was complaining about her. She kept nagging and nagging that the girl was not doing well, but the other women said she was being overly suspicious. Well, apparently she wasn't."

"Maybe the girl just got lost in the woods," said Atiron, shrugging. He did not remember the object of this conversation, never interested in his Clan's Council and their problems with young girls. Those were always a problem, whether local or adopted. He thought about his youngest daughter.

"Kwayenda says the girl disappeared at night, and quite a few useful things with her. Blankets, some dried food."

The others laughed. "Now we know whom we should blame for our lack of supplies to withstand the winter."

"Oh, how the Clan Councils are always eager to throw their problems on us!" exclaimed the second representative of the Wolf Clan, half amused half put out. "They tell us to mind our own business most of the time, then they come crying for help the moment someone gives them trouble."

"They do that," agreed one of the men, and Atiron found himself nodding vigorously. Sometimes the Clans' Councils were nothing but nuisance.

"So the girl ran away?" He shrugged. "If she always gave trouble, then they should thank the Great Spirits and breathe with relief."

"They want us to send a party to look for her."

"Oh, please," said the Wolf Clan's man. "As though we have not been discussing our lack of men to do all that needs to be done. Between hunting parties and raiding parties, we have no men to spare in order to track down stupid girls who did not want to belong to any of the clans, anyway."

"And who might be either dead by now or safely among her own people." The Head of the Town Council grinned. "Well, not among her people yet, but probably well into the lands of the Standing Stone People. Which means it would be up to the War Chief and his council to decide. Good for us."

But Ohonte shifted uncomfortably. "The Mothers of the Turtle Clan will not be happy."

"What do they need the girl for?" asked Atiron, knowing the answer.

The others shrugged, shifting their gazes. They all knew that the enraged Turtle Clan women wanted to make an example out of the stupid girl.

He sighed. "Will you put this to the vote?" he asked, addressing the Head of the Council.

"We have to," insisted Ohonte, not about to give up.

But of course. This man's longhouse was the one to complain. If he didn't press the matter, the Clan Mothers might get angry, replacing him with another man. The headstrong women were always ready to do that, the moment they sensed the representative did not care enough for the well being of the longhouse he represented. Atiron shook his head.

"We will not discuss this matter until I have talked to the War Chief," he heard the Head of the Council saying. "The Mothers of the Turtle Clan's second longhouse cannot put their private matters before the well being of this whole settlement. But," he raised his hand before Ohonte's protest could be sounded, "it depends on what the War Chief suggests. I may reconvene you in order to vote on the proposed solution."

"I will vote against this," said Atiron, unable to hold his tongue. "It is as futile as it is inhuman. The Onondaga girl was nothing but a captured woman. To hunt her down and make an example out of her would be a needless cruelty. We do not war on women and children."

"We certainly do not." The Wolf Clan man nodded, in agreement with Atiron for a change. "To do that would be a needless waste of our resources."

"How can you?" cried out Ohonte, turning to Atiron. "It may not be your longhouse, but it is your clan that is now poorer by one member."

"By one *unwilling* member." He allowed his eyebrows to climb high. "They will not put this girl back to work the fields, will they? They will put her to death and make an example out of her, for the other adoptees to fear. I oppose their revengeful strike, and it is nothing to do with either my clan members or anyone else's."

"So all the adopted people of our, or any other, town may just leave if they wish it so?"

"I didn't say that. People get captured all the time. Sometimes they get killed, sometimes they get adopted. It is the way of life, a sensible thing to do." He pursed his lips, not happy with being pushed into this particular corner. Hadn't he annoyed them enough, while arguing about the raiding parties? "But once in a while, there are adoptees who do not fit, who cannot forget their former people or lives. And I say, those people should be set free. We are better off without them. If this young woman chose to go, then so be it. We should let her go."

They watched him, some thoughtful, some dubious, some indifferent. No one felt strongly about the newly adopted people. This issue did not matter. Not like the harvest and the raiding parties. No one but Ohonte, whose anxiety originated in his private considerations.

"How very considerate of you," the man said now, his deeply set eyes blazing. "I want to know what you would say if it were your longhouse pressing to solve the matter."

"I would tell them what I think!"

"Of course you would. When were you keeping your thoughts to yourself?"

They glared at each other, as the Head of the Council hurried to raise his hand.

"We may meet again tomorrow with dawn or when the sun reaches its zenith," he said, clearly anxious to prevent another exchange. "There are many matters that are waiting to be discussed with the War Chief and his people. When I'm done, I will summon you all back." He encircled them with his gaze, his eyes amiable, but blank. "I thank you for giving this town more of yourself, brothers."

They were getting to their feet, well pleased, as though having solved the problem of the pitiful harvest and the meager amounts of meat or fish and wild berries that had been stored so far. While, of course, they had solved nothing, thought Atiron bitterly, retracing his steps, contemplating sneaking out of the town again.

CHAPTER 4

The moon was not strong enough to illuminate the path trailing along the river, but Onheda went on, determined to make good progress. It had been too long since she had left Little Falls, sneaking away in the dead of night, stuffing her bag with food and all sorts of useful things for the long journey. She was not a young girl of no experience, and she would not be caught, starved and afraid. Oh no! This time she would make it all the way back to her people; and she would be successful, too.

Halting for a moment, she watched the clouded sky, the wind tearing at it, powerless to scatter the heavy clouds but managing to make her yet colder. She hugged her elbows and hurried on.

It could have been such a wonderful night, but for her hunger and her exhaustion, and the persistent dizziness that kept making the trees around her blurry and the damp odor from the river nauseatingly strong. She was feeling like this for the second night in a row, and it was not a good thing, she knew. Not good at all.

Oh, but for one single night of rest, she thought. A night of no struggle and no walking and no cold. It had been ten dawns since she had left, or maybe more. She had lost her count, but judging by the state of the thinning night deity, it must have still been Hunting Moon.

The trail turned upward, and she wanted to curse, fighting the urge to sit down and rest, to curl around herself and hide from the cold. Yet that would be disastrous. She would not be able to get up again, just like the previous night, and so she would spend more time drifting between sleep and reality, open to all sorts of dangers, from sniffing coyotes to the wandering enemy. And who knew if she would be able to get up at all when the next night would come. She had had a difficult time doing this on the last evening.

The river gushed just below the cliff. She could hear its fierceness, the current violent and strong, raging in the darkness. Maybe it was the time to offer the Great Spirits, the Right-Handed Twin himself, more than just a mere prayer. She might have run out of food, but she still had the pieces of flint she had been careful to bring along.

Putting her bag down and fighting the urge to lie alongside it, she shifted around for a while, gathering grass and dry sticks in order to make a small fire. How far were her people, Onondaga Lake and her town? Would she manage to reach them at all? It didn't look that way now. But then, anything was preferable to the life in Little Falls, curse them all into the realm of the Evil Left-Handed Twin, every one of them!

Her fingers busy with pieces of flint, she remembered making many such offerings through the time spent with the enemy. She would sneak out every other night, in this pre-dawn time when everyone would be truly asleep, making her way down the hill and up the high river bank, where the roaring of the falls would drown out every other sound. Always shivering with fear and being very careful, making sure her fire was small and with just a little smoke coming up. Just a sliver of it, really. The Right-Handed Twin was as happy with small offerings as with the large official ones. She had been sure of that.

With the last of her strength, she rubbed the pieces of flint against one another, clenching her teeth and shutting her eyes with an effort. Oh, but she *needed* to succeed. This time, she truly needed it! Back in Little Falls it was important, but not that important, and she didn't want to draw attention should anyone happen to wander around. Neither an enemy, nor a friend. As though she had had any friends in the accursed town, as though she wanted to be friends with the disgustingly haughty, violent, annoying Flint People lot. Oh no, she had no friends, and she had preferred it this way. There was some pretension on her part in order to put the Clan Mothers off guard. She was civil, and she smiled when required, and she never picked an argument with Anitas anymore. Had this pretended niceness fooled Kwayenda? Maybe. Maybe not. The formidable woman was impossible to read. But since Onheda had agreed to marry the man of the Bear Clan, the one Kwayenda had indicated, the powerful woman seemed to be satisfied.

As if something like that would matter! She sneered to herself, fingers busy with sharp pieces. As if the fact that she agreed to admit a local man onto her bunk at the end of the Hunting Moon mattered. As if it would reconcile her to her fate. Well, she was not reconciled, and by now, they had learned all about it.

Oh, but it had been such a difficult journey! To progress along the Great River was not as simple as she expected and she had lost her way constantly when forced to detour through the woods, backtracking her step and spending too much time, precious food, and energy on doing this. If only she could have sailed. But to steal a canoe was out of the question, a difficult task, certain to bring many pursuers eager to retrieve the valued property. And anyway, she would have to make her way against the current, paddling all alone and at nights. Not a promising prospect. So she had set out on foot, but now, ten days into her journey, she wasn't sure it had been a good decision after all.

A gust of wind swept the clouds away, bringing her back from her reverie. The small flame, achieved with such difficulty, had flickered and died.

She cursed softly. Her offering to the Right-Handed Twin was not going to succeed, not tonight, and she had no strength left to either gather more grass and sticks, or to rub the flint again; she had no strength left to get up, for that matter. But for a little of the warmth the flame would offer. She curled around herself, shivering uncontrollably. There was a blanket in the bag, but she had no strength to reach for that, either.

Resigned, she closed her eyes. Just for a little while, until she gathered enough power to get up. The roaring of the distant rapids was calming, making the cold recede, the dizziness now pleasant, cradling her into a blissful sleep.

The sun was blazing unmercifully, blinding her, but bringing no warmth. She shut her eyes tight, trying to dive back into the tranquility of the darkness with no cold and no violent trembling, but the hand kept shaking her shoulder, annoyingly insistent, like a hungry mosquito.

"Open your eyes, girl. Don't go back to sleep."

"Leave me alone," whispered Onheda, the effort of saying the words making the trembling worse.

"Get up, come, get up," repeated the commanding voice, and as she obeyed reluctantly, she saw it belonged to a wrinkled face with a pair of squinting, worried eyes. "Come on. Get up. Put forth an effort. We have some way to go, and I can't carry you. You are too big for that."

Squinting in her turn, still finding it difficult to see against the glow of the rising sun, Onheda tried to understand what the woman wanted. *To go where? To carry whom?*

"Come on, girl." The pull on her arm was annoying, not letting go. "Do it now!"

Straightening up, she swayed and almost fell back but for the supporting hand that clutched her arm, hurting it with its desperate grip. She wanted to know where they were going and why, but with all her energy bent on the effort to stay upright, it was not possible to formulate the words.

"Yes, that's better," muttered the woman, whose head seemed to be bobbling now somewhere around Onheda's shoulder. "Be a good girl and make an effort. I can't take all your weight, so try your best to go on until we reach home." A wrinkled hand brushed against her forehead, sliding down her cheek. "You are burning up, but try your best, will you?"

Onheda just nodded, concentrated on her steps. One after

another. It was like walking in the swaying mist, with nothing stable, not even the earth and the sky. It forced her to pick her every step.

Sometimes she would lose it and fall, grateful for the respite, but every time she would close her eyes, the annoying woman was back, urging her to get up, pulling on her arm, threatening to leave her there for coyotes and wolves to feast on, but never making her threats real. Why was the old hag so insistent? If only she would leave her alone! She didn't care who would feed on her, not if the prize would be the opportunity to lie down and be allowed to close her eyes.

However, the nagging witch was like a mosquito, impossible to shake off. Maybe in her regular state, Onheda might have had an upper hand, but as it was, she could summon no strength to argue, and so they went on, toward the rising sun as it seemed.

How that journey ended she did not remember, but at some point, she was awakened and forced to drink the most bitter-tasting brew she had ever tasted. Coughing, she tried to spit it out, but the old woman was uncompromising, once again winning the day by making Onheda keep the disgusting beverage down. Yet, it made the sleep come, the real, deep, blissful sleep, and she pulled the blanket closer and curled around herself, happy at long last.

The next time she opened her eyes the light was not as cruel, seeping softly through the low opening in the hut's wall. Glancing around carefully, she made sure she had been alone before disclosing her state of awareness. It was obvious now that she had been in a house, someone's house. Treated well, apparently. So far.

Sitting up with an effort, she looked around, taking in the pieces of bark and the woven branches of the wall, with more light flowing in through the splits. Such a strange dwelling!

Her wet, sweat-soaked clothes were gone, and she pulled the blanket higher, afraid. Who had taken off her clothes? The old witch? She tried to remember the woman, but nothing came to her mind, except the glimpses of the round, wrinkled face in the light of the cruel sun and the arm pulling her on, making her suffer.

Shivering, she tried to get up. If she was to escape her captor, it had to be done now. Whatever the woman intended to do with her, it would be no good. Judging by her accent, she belonged to the Standing Stone People, that much Onheda remembered. The immediate neighbors of the Flint People she, Onheda, had just managed to escape, and her own Onondaga people, a blissful land only a few days away from here.

The Flint People turned out to be all right, although an arrogant, oppressive lot with no sense and no finesse. But who knew what kind of people these neighbors of theirs were. There were stories, persistent stories, about twisting snakes for hair and all sorts of eating habits, with some of the enemy reported to feast on human flesh. One could never be too careful when dealing with the fierce foe, and she was in no position to deal with a sick squirrel even. Her only hope was to put as much distance between her and this strange hut's dweller now.

Panting, she got to her feet, the attempt taking the remnants of her strength away. A few heartbeats later still saw her in an upright position, and it pleased her. She would be able to do it, even if the cramped space between the mats and the piles of pots and bowls kept swaying, making her nauseous. She needed to regain her strength, but there was no time for that.

Clutching the blanket close to her body, she made her way toward the entrance, only to stumble and grab the woven twigs adorning the doorway, making the whole construction shake. The bowls piling nearby went rolling in a deafening cacophony.

"What are you doing, girl?" The woman was upon her, so small she barely reached Onheda's shoulder, but fierce, intimidating, her hands clutching a basket of berries, her grizzled hair flying behind her back.

"I…" She wished the world would stop swaying, afraid to leave the support of the tottering pole, but not trusting it now, either. "I needed… I wanted, wanted to see…" For the life of her, she could not find any possible explanation for her stumbling all over the house, wrecking the place as she went.

"Get back to bed, you silly girl." With her free hand, the woman took hold of Onheda's arm again, propelling her back toward the mat. "You are not strong enough to wander about, not yet. Be patient, you foolish thing. If you need something just call, and if I don't hear, then wait, with no fuss." The old eyes studied her patient kindly, flickering with amusement. "I'm yet to hear how you got to that riverbank, starving and half dead with exhaustion. I know there is more to that story than just you being lost. You are not a local girl."

Dropping her gaze, Onheda examined the prettily embroidered hide that served her as a blanket. It had beautiful patterns made out of white and purple shells.

"Let me bring you more medicine. You are shaking again."

Turning around, the woman waddled off, back into the world of the soft sun, leaving Onheda wondering. Her hostess seemed kind enough, and if she didn't mean to kill and eat her weakened guest right away, then maybe she truly didn't have any plans to detain her, Onheda, for more than necessary. The moment her strength would return, the old woman would be no match for her, that much was obvious, powerless to hold a strong girl like her against her will. Carefully, she leaned against the wall, not trusting the woven construction too much.

"Here, drink your medicine, and then we'll fix you something to eat." The woman was back, carrying a bowl in her hands. "I don't have any meat as of now. No warriors or hunters passed here through the last moon, which is a wonder." Her hostess shrugged, sighing. "But a decent bowl of sweetened porridge will do you nothing but good."

"Warriors?" Onheda's heart skipped a beat. "Why would the warriors raid this place?" Grimacing, she sipped the brew, determined not to throw it all up. It did her good on the previous occasion, she remembered.

"Don't sip it, girl. Just drink it in one gulp," said the woman, kneeling to pick up the scattered utensils. "It's a medicine, not a maize beverage for your pleasure." The plates and bowls back in the pile beside the doorway, the woman got to her feet, regarding Onheda with another glance full of amusement. "You are a wild thing, I can see that. I'll bring you your porridge, and you will tell me your story." The old eyes narrowed. "And you will not lie to me. I will see if you lied, so don't even try."

The drink was as bitter as she remembered, probably worse. Holding the nausea back, Onheda returned her rescuer's gaze.

"Why would I lie to you? I'm not from anywhere around, you can tell that easily. Anyone could tell that."

"Yes, I can tell. Your accent is this of the Onondaga People. But why would you wander our woods, equipped as though for a long journey?" Offering Onheda a bowl of water, the woman grinned. "I went through your bag. It has a blanket and a dress, and another pair of moccasins, and a flint to make fire. And it, evidently, held some food before. To where were you journeying, pretty girl? What was your destination?"

Onheda felt like choking on her drink. "I was going back home," she muttered, studying the earthen floor.

"Back home?"

She nodded, and thought about this promised porridge, knowing that it would be terribly impolite to just ask. As though reading her thoughts, the woman grinned and went out again, to return with the steamy bowl, its aroma filling the hut, making Onheda's mouth drool.

"So where were you returning from?"

"Little Falls," mumbled Onheda through the spoonfuls of the most wonderful-tasting porridge she had ever eaten. It was scorching hot, but she could not muster enough self-control to let it cool. The smell alone drove her to the verge of destruction, and the fresh berries mixed with the ground corn made her want to gulp it all at once. "Flint People. Large town. By their Great River."

"I know where Little Falls is!" cried out the woman, startled. "It's at least four days of sail, more by foot. No wonder you came here half dead." She regarded Onheda soberly, with not a hint of her previous amusement. "You ran away from those people."

As those were phrased as a statement, Onheda felt free to pay the words no attention, sorry to see the bottom of the bowl showing.

"How many moons have you spent there?"

"Two moons."

"Captured? Adopted?"

She felt the familiar tightening in her stomach. "No. Well, I was adopted, but not formally, not yet." She swallowed. "They wanted to see if I fit in, before making the adoption ceremony for me."

"But you didn't fit." Another statement.

"No, I did not." She scraped the bottom of the bowl with the spoon, liking the sound it made, wood rubbing against wood, softened by the greasy remnants of the mashed corn.

"So you ran away?"

"Yes, I had to leave. I could not stay. I hate those people. They are the enemies of my people. The adoption ceremony would not change that."

The woman nodded, getting to her feet and taking the bowl away, to Onheda's profound disappointment. There was still some substance to scratch off the sides of the bowl.

"How long had you been wandering the woods?"

She hugged her knees, suddenly dead tired. "Ten dawns, maybe more." Eyes firmly upon the floor once again, she sighed. "I knew I had to follow the river, but sometimes it was not possible, and then I would lose my way." She hesitated. "It happened twice."

"I see." Once again turning to go, the woman shook her head. "You are a brave girl to attempt something like that," she muttered.

And stupid too, I know that much, thought Onheda, enraged. But she was almost adopted. Almost! She had broken no law by running away. Yes, there was a custom, an old, solid tradition, which said that the adopted people would forget their past, would start anew with their new adoptive clan and new nation, would forfeit their past loyalties. It was the law, and yet… She was not adopted formally, was she? Kwayenda had said so, threatening her quite openly while pressing her into taking the man of the Bear Clan in.

"So where is the town of your former people?" asked the woman, coming back with her bowl half full again.

Onheda's stomach responded with churning, but her heart fell at those words.

"Onondaga people are not my former people. I was not adopted, not formally. The People of the Flint are not my people."

However, her heart kept sinking at the realization that the dwellers of her town might think she had broken the law as well. There were plenty of adoptees all over her lands, from all sorts of nations. What if they all decided to leave the way she had? The whole way of life would be disrupted dreadfully, if it happened.

The woman's smile was light, non-committal. "Well, where is the town of your childhood and your youth, then?"

"The town of *my* people." She pressed her lips tight. No, she did not go through the adoption process. No law had been broken and no tradition disregarded. "It is some days of walk toward the Onondaga Lake." Now it was her turn to be non-committal. Why would she tell things about her town to this strange woman, the enemy of her people?

Emptying another bowl, she studied the broad, wrinkled face of her hostess, taking in the slightly foreign-looking features, the wideness of the woman's hips.

"You belong to the People of the Standing Stone, don't you?" she asked, unable to keep her curiosity at bay. "Why do you live here alone?"

The woman's laughter was free of anger. "I'm many things, girl. But yes, I belong to the People of the Standing Stone. I have called them my people for more summers than you have seen in your entire life, much more than that. Yet, I was not born in these lands or among these people." Smile widening, the woman shook her head. "I live alone now because since the death of my husband I needed the solitude of the woods and *my* people's way of living. I thought it would pass, but it did not. So now I live here, regarding this clearing as my own, feeding the warriors when they pass my way." The woman's grin widened. "This location is important, although I didn't know it when choosing this place to be my home. Here lays the path leading from the west to the east, and the other way around. Many warriors are passing here, large and small parties, on their way to their various destinations."

The cold wave was back, washing over Onheda, making her blood drain from her face. "Then you should move to another place," she said, stumbling over her words, her appetite gone. "You don't, you don't have to... It's dangerous!"

"Oh, girl, what danger can an old woman like me be in, eh?" The gaze regarding her was motherly, full of condescending amusement. "I have nothing to offer, nothing but a friendly face and warm food. And believe me, the warriors cherish this above anything else, every last one of them. If I had many valuable things they would still not touch any. What I offer is of a greater value to them." Her gaze wandering, turning dreamy, the woman stared at the space, forgetting her guest as it seemed. "They are nothing but tired, hungry youths and men, those formidable warriors. Their aggression is just a show. They are craving moments of peace no less than anyone else. They just don't know what to do about it, and they are afraid to speak their minds. Or their most inner thoughts and feelings. If only..." Shrugging, the woman got up, picking the bowl once again.

"But how can you do this?" cried out Onheda. "How can you feed the enemy warriors? They are enemies. They may have been on the way to raid your former settlement, or any other of the Standing Stone People's towns. How can you feed them and be friendly with them?"

The woman did not turn to look back, but there was an obvious smile in her voice.

"When you are as old as I am, you'll see things differently, pretty girl. Quite differently." A shrug. "Now rest and gather your strength. When you are better, you will stay for some days to help me out with my field, to gather, grind, and store my corn. Then you will be free to go wherever you want. Or stay for that matter."

For a moment, they fell silent, listening to the roaring of the river not far away.

"It's good you came here on foot," muttered the woman, heading out again. "Those rapids are dangerous. Many canoes have crashed there, some to their deaths."

CHAPTER 5

The rapids roared ahead, invisible in the pre-dawn mist. Two Rivers stifled a curse. Five days of sailing along with the current of the mighty river did not see them making good progress. The necessity to keep their watch and the diminishing moon slowed them down so badly, they had hardly left the lands of the Onondaga People, only now entering their smaller, neighboring nation.

A long, pretty lake should let them know that they had been about half way, maintained Tekeni, but no pretty lakes happened on their path so far. Only the endless rapids, some smaller, possible to negotiate, some powerful enough to force them into paddling toward the nearest bank, dragging their belongings and their canoe upon their backs, sweat covered and exhausted despite the chilliness of the nights.

"Are those *the* rapids?" shouted Two Rivers, trying to overcome the growing noise.

Perching on the prow of their boat, peering into the grayish mist, Tekeni just shrugged.

"I don't know," he called, turning his head. "I think it might be the Raging Waters, but I can't be sure. We came from the other side back then."

During the last five dawns, since crossing the Great Lake and finding the wide, powerful river, the young man had made tremendous efforts to remember every detail of his two-summers-old journey, the only time he had traveled these lands. His memory admirable, he managed to recognize a multitude of landmarks, finding the main river despite the tortuous way many smaller streams and tributaries mixed with each other until creating this powerful flow.

And he was helpful with more than a mere guidance, more than a pleasant companionship. Because upon the day of the crossing, rowing since sunrise, relieved to see the land with the beginning of dusk, Two Rivers remembered how his heart missed a beat as he peered at the nearing bank, seeing a silhouette of a man standing upon it. Oh, how could that be? He remembered the sudden surge of panic cascading down his spine. Now, here, of all places? Discovered just like that, helpless in their canoe, able neither to fight nor to hide. What were the chances of that happening? Did the Great Spirits despair of him, abandoning him, taking their benevolence away?

The man upon the bank did not move, and so they kept rowing, nearing the land. What else was there to do? He could hear the youth moving behind his back, picking up his bow.

"Don't," he said quietly, hardly moving his lips.

The man upon the bank stood motionless, not grabbing his own weapons, clearly a hunter, his bow and quiver of arrows hanging behind his back. As they neared, Two Rivers could see the colorful patterns upon the man's leggings, his shirtless torso, and the way his hair was arranged, partly shaved, partly tied high, proclaiming some sort of a status, along with the richness of the clothing.

"How do the Onondaga People greet each other?" he whispered, without turning his head or taking his gaze off the nearing figure.

"*Sge:no.*" The word rustled, whispered in a steady voice.

Good. He rose to his feet, trusting Tekeni to steady their vessel against the mild current.

"*Sge:no*, brother" he called out, pleased to hear his own voice firm, hoping that his face related the same. "What are you doing here?"

The man frowned, hesitated. "We are hunting for our living," he said finally.

He tried to understand the answer. Hunting, the man said something about the hunting. Good.

"And where are your companions?" He hoped he was not taking it too far, speaking in such a patronizing manner.

Keep him off balance, whispered his inner voice, *don't let him ask questions; keep pressing.* Still, the arrogant questioning could do only up to the certain point.

The man's frown deepened. "What?"

Before he could lose more of his confidence, he heard Tekeni's voice behind his back, talking quietly, sincerely. Fighting the temptation to turn his head, he studied the hunter instead, keeping to his pretense of the important visitor from a distant land.

The puzzlement upon the local's face grew as he brought his eyes back, to meet Two Rivers' gaze.

"My companions are back there, in the woods," he said. Another heartbeat of hesitation. A nervous licking of lips. "Who are you?"

Grateful for the youth's prompt translation, whispered hurriedly behind his back, Two Rivers let his gaze thaw a little. "It is I who came from the west and am going eastward and I am called Two Currents Flowing Together in this world."

It came out well. The man seemed as though about to take a step back. With the translator at hand, he could make his speech as flowery as he wanted to. It was a blessing.

"You will now return to the place from whence you came. And I want you to tell your leaders that the Good Tidings of Peace has come. They shall hear from me soon."

The man's face lost its color. "Who are you?" he whispered, eyes wide.

"The Messenger of the Good Tidings of Peace." *Was he taking it too far now? Definitely.* He moderated his words. "What is the name of your settlement? How far away is it?"

"Two days' walk." Suddenly, the man's face came to life. "There is strife in our village and our lands. It's good you came." Eyes traveling, obviously taking in his clothes and his companion, widening at the unusual coloring of their canoe – it was, indeed, startlingly bright, almost white, really - the man nodded, then turned around, disappearing into the deepening darkness.

Two Rivers stared after him, surprised. He had taken it too far, that much was obvious.

"The Messenger of the Divine Spirits?" Tekeni stifled a giggle. "Not bad."

"Oh please!" He ran his hands through his hair, feeling it sticky with sweat, unpleasant to touch. "He will be too unsettled to call for his friends and have us shot with their arrows. And by the time he decides to check any of it, we'll be gone."

"Will we sail along the shore?" Practical as always, the youth took the paddle and hesitated, studying Two Rivers, his eyebrows lifted high.

"Yes, and let us hope we will not run into any more of these people, not before nightfall." He watched the shore, listening to the calm splashing of the paddle. "What were the chances of this man being exactly at this point in exactly the right moment? Unless there are many more of these Onondaga People, more than I assumed."

"They are quite a large nation." Thoughtfully, Tekeni shrugged. "But not that large. We have more people than they have, bigger settlements, and our woods are larger." He frowned, watching the shore in his turn. "I thought it could have worked well if this man had invited us to come to his camp, to his town even. He seemed friendly enough, open to your words."

"Yes, I know. I should have talked more simply. I got carried away." He narrowed his eyes, seeing the small inlet behind the bend. "Get closer, I want to see this shore." Liking the way the youth steered the canoe, bringing it smoothly toward the low bank, he smiled. "I should thank you. Your translation came in time, and you did it well. You could have panicked, but you did not. You are a worthwhile partner."

And now, listening to the distant roaring of the rapids, pondering as to the advisability of steering back toward the shore, he felt the calming effect of having this youth along. Oh no, he would not have gotten so far all by himself.

"I think we can make it," called out Tekeni, standing on the prow, looking strange in the brightening air. "It's getting wider, and there are quite a few courses we can take."

Careful not to tip the boat, Two Rivers straightened up, studying the river which, indeed, became wider, as though pushing the towering cliffs away by the sheer power of the angrily raging water, with the sleek stones protruding everywhere. He eyed the white foam spitting around a large rock in the middle of the stream.

"We avoid this one," he said, bringing his paddle up. "Sit back there and do what I say. We steer to our right, keep to that course all the time."

For some time it went according to the plan as they passed the first rapids, tossed but passably so, their canoe steady. It wasn't that bad, he decided, eyeing the protruding rock in the middle of the river, the water raging around it, spitting in anger.

"Keep on paddling," he shouted without looking back, inspecting another step made out of rocks, small whirlpools forming all around it. "Keep clear of those."

The canoe tossed wildly now, soaking them in sprays of cold water; still they managed to reach another quieter pool. Blinking, he tried to clear his vision, blessing the sun for appearing at long last. Enemy warriors or not, they needed the light to come out of this enterprise. Those rapids were bad enough, worse than anything they had encountered so far.

Racing with the strengthening current, he did his best to slow their progress down, then saw the new set of rocks springing out of the brightening mist, the water jumping around, seeping through the small openings, not nearly deep enough.

"Steer to the left," he yelled, paddling madly, knowing that upon hitting this obstacle they would be either stuck or overturned.

The current caught them the moment they were out of the shore course, not giving them an opportunity to breathe with relief. Dragged toward the large rock they had tried to avoid in the first place, he listened to the screeching of their boat as its sides rubbed against the underwater stones, concentrated on pushing the nearest obstacles away.

From the corner of his eye, he saw Tekeni doing the same, taking care of the other side. Yet soon, they were tossed into the side cataract formed between two protruding stones. Apparently, there were more of the cascades than they could have seen from their previous course. Hurled into the narrow passage, they could do nothing but clutch their paddles and hope for the best.

A futile hope as it turned out. A load screech intermingled with the roaring of the water as the boat came to a sudden halt, throwing them forward, gasping and groping for something to cling to. The hollering current rushed beneath the prow of their canoe now, stuck at the straight angle, looking like the worst possibility of them all.

Clinging to his paddle, Two Rivers tried to shove the half stuck boat which kept turning slowly, unhurriedly, pushed by the current but not with enough force.

"We need to empty it," he shouted, turning to Tekeni. "Swim ashore and be ready to catch the bags."

The youth did not pause even to nod, but scrambled up toward the lifted back of the boat, sliding into the water, making an obvious effort not to get caught in the current. Still, soon he appeared in front of their canoe, bounced and tossed rather than swimming, struggling not to be pulled into the chute.

Worried, Two Rivers tried to reach him with his paddle, then felt the boat beginning to turn as the current pounced at the suddenly lightened vessel. Before he could think of something to do, it slid forward, straight into the roaring water, turning upside down as it went.

The thundering roar disappeared all at once, replaced with the darkness and the deafening silence. Hurled violently, flipped and hit by all sorts of hard surfaces, he pushed himself up, swallowing water and air all at once, trying not to succumb to the surge of wild panic. No light reached his eyes, until he realized that he'd surfaced under the overturned canoe, probably stuck between one more set of rocks.

Another dive into the swirling water, to be bounced like a straw doll, rewarded him with the view of the distant bank to his left and the quieter pool just ahead. Clutching to his paddle, reluctant to let it go, he steered himself forward, then felt the abrupt pull as it stuck in the underground stones, with his right arm twisting, as though about to be torn from his body. Gasping at the piercing pain, he was tossed forward once again, without the paddle this time, his struggle to stay afloat made difficult with his arm not reacting properly.

The water was calmer now, but it didn't matter because he was underneath again, not feeling any hard surface this time, trying to push with his legs, the panic too powerful to think sensibly. As the light neared, he gulped more air and more water, struggling to stay afloat, not caring for his direction, the hissing foam making it impossible to clear his vision, or to breathe, for that matter. But for the lost paddle!

Going down again, he kicked wildly, then felt a palm clutching his hurt arm, pulling him strongly, making him gasp with pain and swallow more water. It was like a bad dream, all the water and the roaring of the furious rapids behind his back, and the wild, mindless pain. Dizzy and desperate to keep his face above the surface, he let his rescuer pull him on, clenching his teeth and keeping his other hand from clutching to the laboring silhouette's limbs. It was the worst thing to do; he had enough presence of mind to remember that.

Dragged up the slippery rock, he coughed and coughed, finding no strength to even look up, the pain in his right arm blinding, his throat hurting, eyes blurry. At some point he knew he had been alone under the warming sun, shivering with cold. It made him worried, but only for a heartbeat; he had been too busy breathing the sweet morning air, discovering that if he laid still, his arm hurt less, even if it wasn't so with the rest of his battered, bruised body.

"Feeling better?" Tekeni's face swam into his view along with the fierce glow of the high morning sun. *Was it mid-morning already?*

He tried to nod without moving.

"Good. I wasn't sure I would know what to do if you didn't cough out that water all by yourself."

"The boat," groaned Two Rivers, wishing the grazed, bruised face would stop swaying. It made his nausea so much worse.

"It's here. Came into that pool, following us, like the good boat it is." The youth grinned. "Even if it did throw you out to make its journey down the waterfall easier."

"The damn thing did just that." He tried to make his mind work. "We need to bring it to the shore. This pool has currents, too."

"Yes, of course. I dragged it out first thing." A frown. "But our other things sank. Almost everything."

Two Rivers sat up, grimacing with pain. "What was left?"

"The bag itself. It got stuck on the rocks, so I managed to fish it out."

"Oh, then the weapons are safe?"

The youth nodded readily. "Yes, and the birds' trap, too. But the food and the other things are gone."

"We'll manage." He looked up, measuring the sun. "It's mid-morning."

"Yes, the sun is not far away from its highest."

"I didn't think I was wandering other realms for so long." Blinking, he watched the youth, taking in the bruises that made the scars stand out eerily. "How badly were you hurt?"

"Not badly. It was a smooth slide." The handsome face crinkled with laughter. "Smoother than yours."

"You saved my life. I will not forget."

But his companion's face closed with the typical suddenness. "You owe me nothing. You saved my life before." He shrugged. "Also, you might have made it without me, too. Even with the broken arm. You were near the shore when I caught you."

He remembered the feeling well, the sensation of the most primitive dread gripping his stomach again, making him wish to fill his lungs with more of the fresh air.

"No," he said hoarsely. "You saved my life, and I owe it to you now." Careful to shrug with his left shoulder only, he winced at the pain all the same. "Also, my arm is not broken. Just twisted badly. It happened to me before. So first thing, I need you to pull it in a certain way, to make it right again." He breathed deeply, preparing to withstand the torture. The youth wouldn't manage on the first try. "I'll tell you what to do. And then…"

He tried not to think about their further survival. With no food and no opportunity to hunt or place their traps, they were in serious trouble. The euphoria was over, that first surge of relief and the thrill of being alive. Indeed, they did not drown, and didn't even break their limbs, but they were still in the enemy lands, and now with less basic means to survive.

CHAPTER 6

Crouching behind the cluster of trees, Tekeni watched the strange, mushroom-like constructions, one large, about a man's height, the other smaller, with smoke coming out of it. A storage room? A place for cooking?

Frowning, he tried to make sense of what he saw, having watched this place for some time. The larger cabin looked like a dwelling, but why would someone live in such a manner he couldn't tell. He had happened to see an occasional hut while traveling with his father, but those also looked like longhouses, only smaller, made out of customary sheets of bark. Yet, a house made out of twisted branches he couldn't recall even envisioning.

The old woman came out again, heading for the smaller hut, a straw basket in her hands. Squinting, she looked around, frowning, the suspicion written clearly across her broad, foreign-looking face. Tekeni held his breath, diving deeper behind the cover of the trees. Was the old witch sensing him?

The sensible thing was to come out and try to talk to her. They needed help, and the lonely place, with its obviously lonely dweller, provided a perfect opportunity. Too good to be true, even. He could not believe his good fortune, when first smelling the aroma of the cooked food coming from this clearing.

Still, something held him back, made him wish to know more before disclosing their presence; and their plight. Two Rivers was in bad shape, his arm still useless, causing the man much pain. He had made Tekeni try to twist it in a way that might have put the dislocated bones back in place, claiming that he knew what he was doing, that it had happened to him before.

But it didn't work. As much as Tekeni tried to follow the instructions, he didn't manage to pull sharply enough, or in the correct way, causing the poor man more pain and bringing no relief.

In the end, the formidable man was barely conscious, and all Tekeni could do was to drag him to the relative safety of the woods, along with their canoe and their now meager belongings, making him as comfortable as he could, while venturing into sniffing around in the hope of finding some food and no enemy lurking.

Fighting off his exhaustion and the temptation to just close his eyes, he followed the woman with his gaze when she disappeared behind the opposite cluster of trees, muttering angrily. Was she living there all alone? It appeared to be so, still he wasn't sure. If the woman was not disturbed by the foreign presence she might have sensed, then she was looking for someone who wasn't around but supposed to be.

He shifted his aching limbs, all scratched and bluish from his fall into the rapids. What a devious place, he thought, remembering the tales his father's warriors were telling about this pass on that eventful journey two summers ago. He should have recognized the spot, he thought angrily. Once again, he'd proved useless.

A branch cracked, and his heart missed a beat as he froze, all ears. No more sounds came, but now he sensed the foreign presence himself. Someone was there in the trees, watching him, maybe. Human or animal? It made no difference.

His hand slipped toward his knife, fingers fastening around the hilt, its touch reassuring.

One heartbeat, then another.

No more cracking interrupted the silence, not a leaf rustled, but he knew he was not alone, now he knew it for certain.

More of the agonized waiting, then came the soft rustling from his left. A footstep. His instincts deciding for him, he sprang to his feet, hurling himself into the trees with the same movement, his body just a tool now, lethal and ready to kill.

A silhouette darted aside, but he changed his direction too, crashing through the bushes, feet hardly touching the ground. His hands claws, he grabbed something, a fistful of hair, pulling powerfully, making his prey lose its balance. Not letting the slender body fall, he caught it by the shoulder, pulling it up and crushing it against the tree instead, his knife pressing into the delicate throat, his senses in panic.

The girl didn't cry out, but stared at him with enormously large, glazed, terrified eyes. Blinking, he stared back, his sanity returning. Another heartbeat and he began backing away, still slowly, not trusting his own judgment, ready to fight, peering at her as though she were an *uki*, her terrified eyes making him shiver.

It lasted for another heartbeat only, because without his assaulting support, the girl slipped down the trunk, to curl upon the wet ground, just a heap of sobbing and trembling limbs. He shook his head, trying to slam his mind back into working.

"I'm sorry," he muttered. "I thought… I thought you were a warrior." Helpless, he watched her, not daring to come closer. "I didn't mean to hurt you."

Her trembling was bad now, an open shaking. He knelt beside her.

"Please, stop crying. I didn't mean to scare you like that."

"I wasn't… wasn't scared," she mumbled, stammering. "I just…" Raising her head, she peered at him, her pupils too wide, face thin and haggard, lacking in color. "You must be insane! To attack people like that."

"You were spying on me," he said, startled. "I didn't know you were just a girl."

"I'm not just a girl," she said, voice growing firmer, although her lips were still trembling. "I live here. I live here for now, and you were the one to spy on this place."

"You live here? In this strange thing?" He motioned in the general direction of the clearing with the huts.

The girl regarded him with a glance that made him feel stupid.

"Yes, I just told you that." She frowned. "I live here for now, until Jikonsahseh gathers her crops. I'm helping her." Her eyes narrowed, grew defiant. "And you can't raid this place. No one does this. So stop entertaining those silly thoughts and go away."

"No one raids this place?" he repeated, puzzled. "Why not?"

The girl pressed her lips and got to her feet, her legs shaking but holding on. "You are truly dense, aren't you? Or maybe desperate. Go and find a better spot to fight, to get captives and goods. Use your head next time when you are looking for a suitable place." Another challenging glance measured him with an open contempt. "And what are you doing here anyway, running around these woods all alone, like the stupid foreigner Flint that you are?"

He got to his feet in his turn. "It's not of your concern. Go back to your old woman and her crops. Leave the decent people in peace."

She glared at him, her chest rising and falling, eyes ablaze. A pretty thing, he reflected, admitting that almost against his will. With her face returning to normal coloring and her eyes to acceptable size, she did look attractive, her lips full and slightly opened, her cheekbones pleasantly high.

"Don't tell me what to do! I've had enough of your filthy people giving me orders for days on end. Go back to stupid Little Falls, or whatever other filthy town you belong to, and leave these *decent* woods alone."

He stared at her, aghast. "How did you know about me and Little Falls?" he muttered, trying to calm the wild pounding of his heart. "Who are you? What do you know about me?"

"I don't know anything about you, and I don't want to know a thing!" She tossed her head high, making her beautifully thick braids jump. "But I can tell where you are from. You have their dreadful accent."

"Like you can talk any better," he cried out, enraged. "You belong to these lands, to the People of the Standing Stone, or maybe the Onondaga People. Cowards and dirty liars, every one of them." He took his eyes off the glaring line his knife had left on the smoothness of her neck. *It was her fault, wasn't it?*

She gasped. "Your people are the worst beasts that have ever roamed the Turtle Island, the creation of the Sky Woman. They are dreadful beasts with no feelings and no decency."

"Oh, yes, like I said, liars, every one of you." Pleased, he watched her burning cheeks, seeing her lips pressing into such a thin line they became almost invisible. "And cowards, too. That's without me mentioning no decency and all the rest." She looked as though she would explode like a thunderbolt. "Anyway, I'm going to talk to your old woman. I hope she has more sense than you do."

"She won't help you," she cried out after him. "I'll talk to her, and she won't give you a single trampled on berry from her food supplies!"

━━━━━□─◻◆◻─□━━━━━

Two Rivers stretched his legs, then shifted, trying to find a better position. His arm, now fastened in a sling, hurt as much as before, although the support it received helped. His shoulder was swollen badly, mainly from Tekeni's morning ministrations in order to put it back in place. Unsuccessful attempts that made it go numb with pain. Still, he thought, it was back in place now, and the moment the swelling went away he would be able to use it again. He hoped so most sincerely.

"So you are coming from the lands of the Crooked Tongues," said the old woman, her face kind in the light of the small fire.

He nodded, hiding his grin. Tekeni had told him all about this nickname, referring to the peoples from his side of the Great Lake, *all peoples.*

"Yes, I'm coming from the other side of the Great Sparkling Water," he confirmed, talking slowly, simplifying, trying to be understood. Until he learned their tongue, he would have to get used to this sort of speech, he realized, sighing inwardly. He, who was held to be a great orator.

"I see." The woman nodded, studying him, the unspoken question in the eyes. While washing his wounds and taking care of his damaged shoulder, then organizing their meal, she had asked no questions, ordering Tekeni and the pretty young woman about, making them assist, but now, relaxed in the rapidly descending darkness, she was obviously ready to abide her curiosity. "What is the purpose of your journey?"

He remembered the man on the banks of the Great Lake. "I'm bringing the message of peace," he said, holding her gaze. "The time has come."

She frowned, and he heard Tekeni talking quietly, like back then on the bank, translating but speaking at length, saying more. He could hear the combination of words 'good tidings of peace' and some more sentences. He hoped his young companion didn't make it sound as flowery. This woman was no simple hunter.

The glint in their hostess's eyes made him understand that the youth had taken it too far.

"The Messenger of the Good Tiding of Peace, eh?" Her eyes flickered challengingly. "A presumptuous mission. And a difficult one."

He wished he could speak with no need to translate. "It's time people stopped warring on each other. It does no good; neither to my people nor to yours. It's time they talk."

"Oh, it is definitely the time to talk." The woman grinned lightly, her eyes sobering. "I wouldn't disagree with this argument of yours. But will they be ready to listen? You would need to talk to many deaf ears, convince many closed minds. The hunger for blood is clouding their judgment, the hatred and the thirst for revenge is weighing upon their spirits like a mighty mountain, impossible to move."

He glanced at Tekeni, frustrated.

"She says you don't have much chance to convince all the bloodthirsty people. She thinks it's impossible to achieve."

"Please, try to translate word for word," he said quietly, smiling at the youth with his eyes, making sure his words did not sound like a reprimand. Turning his gaze back to the woman, he caught a glimpse of the girl, who squatted on the other side of the fire, staring at him, fascinated. "I didn't think my mission would be an easy one. But I will do it all the same. It is time to do that." He hated repeating himself, sounding so clumsy, like a child learning to talk. "You are feeding the warriors, you said. Any warriors? Or only the warriors of your people?"

"Any warriors," said the woman firmly. "They are all the same to me."

Ridiculously pleased to understand her with no aid, he nodded. "That's the beginning. I see no difference, either."

"Because you came from across the Great Sparkling Water and can't tell one nation from another? Or because you truly see no difference between anyone, even your Crooked Tongued people?"

Fighting off his impatience, he waited for Tekeni's explanation.

"I saw no difference between my people, too. This brave young man can testify to that matter."

They all looked at the youth now, even the girl whose frown did not sit well with the delicate features of her exquisitely shaped face.

He listened to Tekeni's halting explanation, glad to enjoy the moment of respite. He was so tired, so ill-prepared for this conversation. Yet, he would not be better prepared until he learned their tongue, any of their tongues. If he wanted to be listened to, the faltering speeches in barely comprehensible language of the Crooked Tongues may not be enough. Any more of the stammering moments while talking to the warriors' leaders, and he might pay with his life, achieving nothing.

"Quite a tale," said the woman, when the youth had finished, talking for a relatively short span of time. His companion obviously did not mean to tell more than necessary.

Two Rivers hid his grin. The boy was growing fast, and he was turning into an excellent partner, quick, enterprising, courageous, sure of himself. Who would have thought he would blossom into any of this, looking at the wild, cornered cub he had noticed just a moon and a half earlier?

The woman's eyes were resting on him again, regarding him with a kinder gaze. "I shall help you all I can."

"Thank you," he said, warmed. "I owe you more than a simple gratitude."

Her grin widened. "I was living here all alone for quite a few spans of seasons. Waiting for nothing, expecting nothing. Feeding warriors who were passing by, giving them a resemblance of home. And it didn't matter what nation they belonged to – People of the Mountain, People of the Flint, People of the Hills, it made no difference. They were exactly the same, apart from their accents. Just groups of young or middle-aged people, misled, taught to hate other people who were just like them." The woman sighed. "I didn't try to tell them that. I just made this clearing into a place where there was no war. And they appreciated that, I can tell you. They respected my rules. No one ever argued, or tried to do something violent while staying on my clearing." A silence prevailed as the calm, even voice trailed off, the woman's eyes clouding, staring into the fire, wandering other places. "Somewhere deep down, I probably wished that it would have been this way all over the land. Why should it not? If they could be so peaceful, so respectful of one another here, why not anywhere else?" The smile was back, glimmering out of the old squinted eyes, the wise, slightly amused, know-it-all smile. "Did I expect you to appear one day? Maybe. Sometimes I would dream of strange things, of a man crossing the Great Sparkling Water in a white canoe made out of stone, of a man uprooting a tall tree in one powerful pull in order to bury our weapons in the bottomless cavity it created. I don't remember all the dreams, because I tried to pay them no attention. They made no sense, and their vividness was disturbing. And yet..." The thin lips quivered, stretching into a playful grin. "You did not chance to own a white stone canoe, did you?"

"Well, it is bright, yes, but it's made out of bark, no stone," he said, grinning back, mesmerized, feeling at home all of a sudden. It was easier now to follow the woman's words, spoken slowly, softly, caressingly. "Stone bad... difficult to sail," he tried to speak in the way they spoke. He would need to learn their tongue, anyway. "Problem to float."

"Heavy to carry when on foot, too," said Tekeni, his grin obvious, one of his typical unguarded grins, rare to flash out these days. "Our backs would be broken by now."

They all laughed, all but the girl, who curled there, on the other side of the fire, hugging her knees, scowling, clearly not liking any of it.

"So what are your immediate plans?" the woman enquired, sobering once again.

"We have not formulated our plans yet. Not to the fullest degree." He glanced at Tekeni, giving him the courtesy he deserved. "But your information can give us a clearer direction."

"Oh, you can start anywhere. In every place you are likely to encounter fierce resistance." Her chuckle dying away, the woman frowned. "The Onondaga People are in a state of turmoil now, with their prominent leaders and towns fighting for dominance. It will not be long before they start fighting each other in the way they are fighting the other peoples. But this time town against town."

The girl's gasp startled them, exploding in the darkness. Two Rivers watched her covering her mouth with her palms, embarrassed.

The woman paid her no attention. "You might wish to start with other peoples. The People of the Standing Stone may be more open to unusual ideas, presented in a passable way. Backed by anyone, just anyone, even the smallest, most meaningless village, you might have a better chance."

Not waiting for a questioning glance, Tekeni translated, knowing by now what speeches his companion could not understand.

"What about the People of the Flint?"

"Oh, the People of the Flint are another challenge. I wouldn't go there all alone. The temptation to make you and your young companion run the gauntlet upon the carpet of glowing embers may be too great to resist. The taste of your flesh may add to their stews, now that the harvest was rumored to be bad in their lands."

This was unsettling news. So even the locals feared the fierce, warlike Flint up to the point of advising to go anywhere but there. Involuntarily, he glanced at Tekeni once again, seeing the frown and the pursed lips.

"My young companion is in no danger of being cooked in the Flint People's pots," he said lightly, anxious to conceal his uneasiness and at the same time to reveal the youth's origins, to save them any more awkward moments. "In Little Falls they might be relieved to see him back and alive."

Another gasp from the girl, but this time quieter, suppressed more easily. They paid her no more attention than before.

"Have you grown up in Little Falls?" asked the woman, a little too curtly.

"Yes, I have." Tekeni's voice was strained, ringing strangely in the tranquility of the night.

"How old were you when you were captured?"

"I saw fifteen summers."

"And how many summers have you seen by now?"

"Close to eighteen."

Two Rivers had found it easier to follow the curt interrogation, watching them, forgotten for a few blissful moments. The girl's eyes were upon him, staring. Returning her gaze, he saw that she was a truly pretty thing. Too thin, obviously underfed, her face had this exquisite quality that no hardship could ruin, this wonderful structure of the bones few women could boast. Delicate and strong at the same time, enhanced by large, luminous eyes, and generous lips, now slightly opened, in the most tempting of ways, although he was sure she was not entertaining any ideas this particular evening.

"So you will be remembered in Little Falls." The interrogation was simmering down as it seemed. He took his eyes off the girl, who blushed, before dropping her own gaze.

"I don't know," said Tekeni gruffly, looking more of his old aggressively cornered self. "Maybe I will be, maybe I won't."

"We are yet to find this out," said Two Rivers, trying to help the youth out. "And like you said, any place is a good start."

"Any place but the towns of the Flint People," muttered the woman, not pacified. "A certain way to end your mission before it begins."

Oh, Mighty Spirits, he thought, his tiredness welling, his headache getting worse, a dull pain turning into sharp hammering of many axes inside his skull. The damn accident. He shifted his arm, feeling it swollen and numb, worse than before, disturbingly so.

"We are yet to determine our first destination," he said tiredly, wishing to be left alone and in peace. "We are yet to formulate our plans better."

The woman sighed. "Well, I can tell you of places you had better stay away from unless accompanied by more than a barely armed young man. There is great strife in the Onondaga lands. A few summers ago, a man tried to do something about it. He was a prominent leader of a large town, and so he called the meeting of leaders from many settlements, in an attempt to unite them, as it seemed." Shaking her head, the woman stared into the fire. "He talked well, so they say. The people listened. But his opposition was strong, led by one man, a man who was not above using violence. It broke the meeting, and then the next one. Threats and violence came, riots, quarrels and uproars followed, a murder even. The enterprising leader's family died. Violently, some say." The woman shook her head. "The man either left of his own free will or, maybe, he was banished. No one knows. Since then the Onondaga People are quiet, groaning under the rule of the bloodthirsty Tadodaho, the one who had fouled the meetings. Some say he is a powerful sorcerer.

Another place you should avoid going to if you value your life and want to do more than just die bravely."

"It happened in Onondaga Town, near Onondaga Lake." The girl's voice tore the silence that ensued. "Two summers ago."

They all turned to stare.

"What do you know about that?" asked the woman sharply.

The girl swallowed. "My town was not far away, and…" She hesitated, obviously uncomfortable in the center of their attention. "Many warriors went to the first meeting. My man was among them."

"Did you go with him?" asked Two Rivers, his tiredness forgotten.

The girl shook her head and said nothing, returning his gaze, a challenge in her eyes, the challenge of a cornered animal. He moderated his eagerness.

"What did he tell you about it when he came back?" Startled by an unsettling thought, he narrowed his eyes. "He did come back, didn't he?"

"Yes, he did. Why wouldn't he?" Again her eyes sparkled. "He talked about this meeting. He told me all about it."

"What did he tell you?"

"He said that that leader, Hionhwatha, talked about the fate and the destiny of the Onondaga People. He wanted to unite us, to make us strong." A furious glance was bestowed upon Tekeni this time. "United, we would be invincible. He wanted to achieve that." She shrugged. "But the other leader of the same Onondaga Town, this Tadodaho, he envied Hionhwatha his power and his strength, even his family, they say. He made other people, bad people, listen to him, and they came and broke up the first meeting with threats and violence. There was much fighting, and the leaders of the other towns went away, some scared, some angered. My man said that Hionhwatha talked well. He said he wanted to follow him."

The girl fell silent, staring at the fire, biting her lips.

"And then what happened?"

"And then there were two more meetings, and more violence, there and in Onondaga Town. More people died." She nodded, as though agreeing with her own thoughts. "Hionhwatha's family, too. He had a wife and three daughters, so they say. They all died as a result of sorcery and despicable deeds. None of them saw the end of the winter."

"Three summers ago there was a very bad winter," said Tekeni to no one in particular. "They may have died of sickness and nothing else."

"They did not!" cried out the girl, her fury spilling. "I know what I'm talking about. I lived nearby, and my man was involved. You don't know any of it. Your disgusting Little Falls is situated on the other side of the world!"

"Which is a mercy," growled the youth. "Any place nearer and we would die of the stench coming out of your filthy towns."

She gasped, and for the moment, just stared, fighting for breath, her eyes seeming to be capable of lighting fire. If gazes could hurt, his young companion would now be thrown upon the ground, dead.

"How dare you," she hissed in the end. "You and your people are the most despicable, lowly creatures that have ever roamed the earth. They are the creations of the Evil Twin himself and—"

"Look who is talking about being evil! The stinking lowlife bunch of people who cannot even hold a meeting without killing each other."

The old woman's laughter shook the air. "And among those very people you intend to go about, offering peace and brotherhood?"

With his translator busy trying to stare the furious girl down, Two Rivers grinned, understanding the general gist of the argument and the following comment too well.

"I never said my mission would be an easy one." He looked at the youth. "Come on, wolf cub. Stop making our hosts angry." His glance back upon the two women, he sobered. "So this man, Hionhwatha, did he die, too?"

The girl paid him no attention, too busy with the glaring contest, but the old woman shook her head.

"No, he did not. He lives to this day, alone, in the woods. Not very far away from here, in fact. In some sort of a hut." She sighed. "Another place you would be better off to avoid visiting. They say he has turned evil, living alone, feeding on human flesh."

"He was not banished," muttered the girl through her clasped lips. "He went out of his mind at the death of his family and just wandered off."

This time Tekeni translated promptly, his gaze still burning, but his voice calm.

"Actually, it seems like a necessary place to visit," said Two Rivers quietly, now more than ever wishing to be left alone, to think it all over.

"This man will not listen. He has lost his mind."

"If that is the case, I will leave him to his own devices." Forcing his thoughts to slow down, he glanced at their hostess, taking in the aged, tired features. "I thank you for the wonderful evening, for your kind treatment and your invaluable help. I will repay you your kindness."

The woman's smile flashed out, wide and free of shadows. "There is no need to repay anything. I'm glad to be of help, to you more than anyone." She began to get up. "I'll bring mats and blankets for you two. And I will urge you to stay here for more than a few dawns, until your wounds are healed. If you are to roam the woods in search of a madman, you would need to be at your best."

CHAPTER 7

Grinding maize was the task Onheda hated with all her heart. A boring, thankless work that was forcing her to crouch at the same spot for shameless amounts of time, toiling hard, but not moving, not doing anything to interrupt the dull activity; sleepy, restless, *bored*.

Yet, this time she didn't mind. The round bowl clutched firmly between her knees, she let her hands do their work, with her mind free to roam, along with her eyes. The swish of the knife was calming, interrupting the silence, as it sliced against the hard wood, monotonous and soft, not disturbing the peacefulness of the clearing, washed in the soft afternoon light, swept by the pleasantly warm breeze.

Stealing another glance at the awkwardly squatting figure, Onheda pursed her lips. Because of the damaged shoulder, the foreigner was forced to hold the large piece of wood he was working on with his knees, the way she held her bowl, crouching with difficulty, obviously doing his best to disregard the pain.

He should have been resting, she knew. Jikonsahseh had told him to do so, to go and sleep inside the hut, to gather his strength. But of course, the stubborn man did not listen, and while his annoying young companion took the bow and the misshaped quiver of arrows, both looking pitiful after their dive in the river, and went to hunt something for their evening meal, the foreigner wandered about, restless and frowning, carving things out of wood, fighting the pain and the exhaustion with the stubbornness typical to men. Why would one listen to sensible advice?

She studied him carefully, unwilling to be caught doing this. Although pale and haggard, his shoulders bent awkwardly, disheveled hair tied carelessly behind his back, he did look impressive, an air of strange confidence surrounding him, making him look calm and aloof, but not in an arrogant way. Alien, outlandish, a true foreigner.

She happened to meet an occasional person from across the Great Sparkling Water. In her settlement there had been this captive girl with sad brown eyes and an outrageous accent, and there were a few more women in Onondaga Town, always easy to tell apart because of the way they spoke, as though having difficulty moving their tongues. All the peoples across the Great Lake were called Crooked Tongues, and this man had spoken as badly.

She watched his bared back, the way his muscles moved with every swish of his knife, the way his head was tilted, immersed in his task, presenting her with a glimpse of his eagle-like profile. She wondered what his eyes held. Was he concentrated on the club he was carving, or was he thinking about other things? Those presumptuous, strange sounding 'tidings of peace' whose messenger he claimed to appear, according to the words of the scar-faced, violent youth from Little Falls.

She ground her teeth, her anger rising anew. How dared the damn Flint say bad things about her people, he who had come from the accursed Little Falls itself, of all places! Why, why did she have to run into a person from that same stinking, disgusting town? As though she'd not had enough of them all, the annoying People of the Flint, may the Evil Left-Handed Twin take them all into his realm under the earth, with this youth being the first, such a violent, sure of himself representative of his nation. She remembered his face and the way his scars ran down his high cheekbones and across them, making a strange pattern, setting it apart, handsome and peculiar at the same time.

Glowering, she doubled her efforts, pounding the dried seeds of maize, making them crumble. How dared he call her people liars and thieves, with his country folk being the worst of the enemy? And how dared he talk about his outlandish companion and his mission, about those 'good tidings of peace', as though this man were the messenger of the divine spirits. What gall! But, of course, a typical attitude of the arrogant Flints.

She glanced at the crouching man again, trying to see the signs. Some proof, something that would tell her one way or another. Was he truly the messenger of the Great Spirits; or was he just a foreigner, no more sane than the crazed with grief Hionhwatha. To come to their lands and try to talk to anyone was the height of stupidity. He would not be listened to, he could not, not even by the Flint People, them less than anyone, despite his annoying companion's self-assurance.

"This pottery must be very strong. I don't know how this bowl of yours is holding on against all the pounding."

His voice made her jump, the foreign words catching her unprepared, deep, calm, amused. Did he say something about the bowl and the grinding?

"What?" She cleared her throat, desperate to sound calm and aloof, the way he had. "What do you mean?"

"The maize, you are beating at it, not grinding. You better look at your bowl, instead of staring at me."

Now that he talked in short, simple sentences it was easier to understand, although he didn't change his position, didn't turn to look at her. Which was a mercy. Her face felt as though a hot water had been poured upon them, or maybe burning coals.

"I'm not... I was not staring at you." Licking her lips, she dropped her gaze, seeing the dry seeds mashed rather than ground. *How did he know?*

He didn't raise his head, his knife chopping at the wood at rhythmic intervals. "Of course, you were. I can feel the holes in my back, where you were staring." A few more slashes, then he studied the shaft, satisfied, running his fingers alongside it. "So what's your story, Onondaga girl?"

The smugness of his tone made her angry. "I don't have to tell you anything. My story is no concern of yours."

That made him turn his head at last, moving with his whole body, obviously sparing his damaged shoulder the effort. The large eyes measured her, reflecting no resentment but only a genuine curiosity, curiosity mixed with a flicker of an amused admiration, this pure admiration of a man seeing an attractive woman, not afraid of a challenge.

"No, you don't have to tell me anything." The spark in the dark eyes intensified. "Although, I'm sure it would make an interesting story."

"And how about you?" Desperate to put him in his place, unsettled with the way his gaze made her stomach flutter, she pursed her lips. "What would make a man leave his people and go to his worst enemies in order to tell them something? Is that how desperate you are? Why don't you talk to your own people? Why choose to betray them, instead?"

It had the desired effect. Satisfied, she watched his smile disappear, replaced by a frown.

"You have to talk simple. I don't understand what you say."

"See? You can't even talk properly or understand." She glared at him, her agitation mounting, rising like a river after the Frozen Season, impossible to control. "Why did you come? Why leave the Crooked Tongues? Why cross the Great Sparkling Water?"

"Oh, that." He shrugged, his face closing, turning into a mask. "That is a long story. I have my reasons."

"I heard them all last night," she pressed on, satisfied with her victory. He was not smug or playful anymore. "Good tidings of peace? You explained nothing. You just made a pretty speech through this scar-faced, bloodthirsty interpreter of yours." She made an effort to control her voice, hearing it rising, taking a shrill tone. "Maybe you should start preaching to him first, talk to him about behaving peacefully, so he won't attack people every time he sees a person. He attacked me, you know? Almost slashed my throat." Raising her chin, she pointed at the thin line that still hurt whenever she touched it.

"Who? Who tried to kill you?"

"Your companion, your follower, your interpreter! The youth, who is translating your words, claiming that you are the messenger of the Great Spirits themselves." She peered at him, trying to see the signs of him being angry, or maybe thrown out of balance. She hoped for the latter. "Are you? Are you the messenger of the Right-Handed Twin?"

"No, I'm not," he said quietly, his gaze not wavering, holding hers, as deep as the moonless night, and as undecipherable. "But what I say is worth listening to. It may scare you now; may make you fight it. I understand that. You are scared. But you will listen in the end. And your people will listen, too."

She fought the intensity of his gaze, wishing to look anywhere but into the dark orbs and the strange glow they radiated. Clenching her teeth, she struggled not to drop her gaze. He would think she was truly afraid. How dared he?

"I'm not scared. I'm not! I left Little Falls, and I made my way here. A cowardly person would not do this. You don't know me. You can't say such things about me."

"I didn't say you were a coward," he said hurriedly, shaking his head as though awakening from a dream. "I said you are afraid, afraid of a change. A brave person can be afraid of such things without losing one's dignity." His eyes narrowed, concentrating. "But a wise person may stop and listen. Do you think yourself to be a wise person?"

"I don't know," she said stubbornly, not liking the urge to hear him talking, to listen to this calm, even voice of his. It was, again, more difficult to understand his words, as he clearly forgot to talk simply. Yet, she wished she could understand every one of them now.

"I think you are. A simple-minded girl would not run away from her captors. She would adjust; she would grow used to her new surroundings, to her new circumstances. It takes a person of courage and broader thinking to undertake this kind of a journey." He shrugged. "Jikonsahseh seems to be fond of you, and she is a very wise woman. Maybe she sees in you something, something that you don't see in yourself."

Mesmerized, she tried to follow the foreign words, desperate to understand. He did not squint, although the midday sun shone directly into his face, enhancing the sharpness of his cheekbones and the strong line of his jaw.

"You feel strongly, and you've been through much, one can see that. But your anger does you no good. It poisons your mind. Originated in frustration, or maybe a grief, it poisons you inside and does not let you start living your life. It is directed into objects that do not deserve it. My companion, for example. Why do you hate him so? Would you be so angry with him had he been a member of your nation, had he been a warrior from your lands?" Raising his hand to stop her protest, he nodded. "Yes, you told me he had his knife at your throat. Well, knowing this young man, he was probably surprised, not knowing who you were before acting. He would never have harmed you on purpose. He didn't cut your throat, after all." His face twisted as he brought his other hand up. "Before you start yelling at me, tell me this. Had he been a man from your lands, would you be so unforgiving of this meaningless mistake? No, you would not be. You don't hate him; you hate his people and his town. You just don't want to admit it."

Oh, why couldn't he speak in normal people's tongue? She tried to put the fragments of what she understood together, staring into his eyes, unable to take her own gaze away. They were so large, so dark, bottomless, radiating power, calming but unsettling too, as though there were a fire behind these orbs, a blazing, peculiar fire. And his voice! Whatever he said, she wanted him to keep talking. If only she could understand better. She forced the strange sensation away.

"I don't understand half of what you said," she said, pressing her lips. "And I don't want to understand any of it. You should have stayed to orate before your people. You should have never come. You are not welcome here."

The gaze peering at her grew cold all at once. She watched his jaw tightening, her heart beating fast.

"Well, I hope your people are wiser, more tolerant than you

are," he said curtly, turning away, back to his knife and his half finished club, his shoulders stiff but not due to the damaged arm anymore. She knew what his eyes held, even though his back was turned to her now.

"And I hope you have more patience than this," she said, unable to hold her tongue. Just who did he think he was, to finish their conversation so abruptly, turning his back on her, as though she was not worthy of the time he spent on talking to her. "You don't want people to listen to you. You want to be obeyed. You just told me what I should do or feel, and when I don't agree with you, you are turning away, disappointed, telling me that I'm not wise." His knife did not move, and it made her stomach flutter with anticipation. "You talk with the arrogance of a person who knows better than anyone. No wonder you had to come here. I'm sure your people did not want to listen. And neither will my people. And nor will their enemies. They will not listen to you. The people of your disgusting companion more than anyone."

He didn't turn back, but neither did his knife resume its work. "My people did not listen, yes," he said coldly. "But this is not why I left." Turning back at last, he regarded her with his eyes still cold, but attentive, more thoughtful than before. "Yes, I may have told you how to feel, and yes, it might have been said wrongly. But I'm right about your hatred. It is not directed on the right objects." His gaze flickered, lost their aloofness. "So tell me more about your people. Why do you think they will not listen?"

"There are too many reasons. Jikonsahseh is a very wise woman, indeed, but she is not an ordinary person. She is strange. Like you. My people are not like that."

"She belongs to the People of the Standing Stone," he said thoughtfully. "Are they like her?"

"No, of course not. I just told you. She is strange."

His grin flashed, surprisingly playful. "I didn't make the mistake of thinking anything else. But tell me what are *you* doing here with her?"

She fought the sudden spasm of fear, remembering the woods and the hunger, and the helpless acceptance of the impending death. "I'm here to help her with the harvest. The moment the maize is ground and stored, and her squash and beans are picked, I will go home."

"Where to?"

"To my people, of course. Why do you ask such obvious questions?" She glared at him, her anger back, making her chest tighten.

"Because it seems strange to me that you are helping her harvest her crops and not those of your people."

"She saved my life."

He frowned. "Oh, I didn't know that. In what way?"

"I don't have to answer you!"

"No, of course you don't. You keep telling me that over and over." His smile was back, an amused, superior smile. "And yet, here you are, telling me how to go about my mission. Or how not to go about it."

"You asked me!" she cried out, wishing to sink her nails into the sharp smoothness of his face, to scratch off the smug expression.

"Yes, I did that. You are right," he said, growing serious again. "Tell me about that man, Hionhwatha. Tell me what he was trying to do?"

Pacified a little by his admitting the truth, she shrugged. She didn't have to answer his questions, but she could have, if she wanted to.

"I didn't meet this man, but my man met him twice. He was impressed. He went to both of the meetings, and he told me all about them."

She paused, collecting her thoughts, wishing to present her account in the best of ways, so he would see that she was anything but a silly girl. He would not understand all of her words, but she was determined to talk like the best of orators.

"Hionhwatha was a prominent leader, the head of the Onondaga War Council. They said he was a great warrior. There was no one who could best him, in a combat or a preparation for battle. When he and the War Council's members would come to the sacred ground declaring that the time for the War Dance had come, there was never a lack of volunteers, never. Every warrior wished to follow Hionhwatha. They knew they could not lose as long as he led them."

His painful frown made her pause, her sense of superiority growing. The messenger of the Great Spirits had had a hard time following her words, clearly desperate not to skip a single one of them, but missing out on more than he understood.

"Then came the summer of the bad harvest. The *Three Sisters* grew poorly, yielding little food for the people. The dances and the prayers did not help. Both harvests were bad, and so the people prepared to withstand a harsh winter. Men tried to hunt and fish as much as they could, and women – to gather wild berries and roots. But the enemies didn't let the people prepare properly. Many raids came from the east and from the west. Our towns suffered. Yet, the people of Onondaga Town and the surroundings, our town included, did not despair. Before the Frozen Moons came, Hionhwatha led many raids, many attacks, and our enemies were made sorry. This is when my man met Hionhwatha first." She smiled at the memory. "He was honored to be allowed to join the famous leader, along with many others. Our Town Council wanted the men to go hunting, but the brave warriors would not hear any of that. They wanted to punish the enemy."

Forgetting her audience, she sighed. It was such a difficult winter, but their warriors were victorious. Her husband came back just before the first snow storm hit, bringing a pair of beautifully embroidered moccasins for her, and a necklace. They were invincible, making People of the Flint suffer, burning down two villages and making the life of one town a misery for some time. It was well worth the hunger of the following Frozen Moons, she decided, now sorry only that this town was not Little Falls. Their warriors didn't venture that far.

"They raid where? Whose lands?" The voice of the foreigner

brought her back from her reverie. Fully absorbed, he stared at her, beads of sweat adorning his forehead, the knife and the half finished club forgotten in his hands.

She blinked, concentrating. "The People of the Flint."

"Little Falls?" The twinkle was back, sparkling out of the dark eyes.

"No. Little Falls was too far away."

"How far?" he asked abruptly, the spark gone.

"Four, five dawns of sail. It was already Shedding Leaves season. They had not enough time."

He nodded thoughtfully. "And then what happened? There was little food, you said? Bad harvest?"

"Yes, it was. But it didn't matter. They came back victorious, bringing many spoils and some captives. They made us proud!"

She glared at him, expecting him to argue, to say something about the futility of the war parties, maybe. There were people who claimed that the men should have gone hunting instead of warring. It was truly a very uncomfortable winter. However, he just nodded, watching her, clearly expecting her to get back to her story.

She frowned. "Well, it was not an easy winter, and by the springtime, Hionhwatha called the meeting of the leaders. He must have been planning it for some time, talking to people. He could not have organized it all in a mere half a moon." She paused again. "Also, in the dead of the winter, his wife died, and the eldest of his daughters. His grief was terrible, people said, but he still went to the gathering he had summoned."

"His family died? His whole family?"

He was so obviously desperate, having such a difficult time following her words. She felt something close to compassion.

"No, not his entire family. Only his wife and his oldest daughter."

He nodded. "Go on."

Not liking his tone, she shot him a furious glance, but he seemed too absorbed to notice.

"Well, like Jikonsahseh told you on the previous night, the

meeting went well, until Tadodaho and his men came."

"Who is Tadodaho?"

"He was one of the other warriors' leaders, but now he is the War Chief of the whole region. No one dares to go against his wishes. Not after what happened to Hionhwatha."

"A War Chief," he muttered, pressing his lips. "Of the Hills People?"

"Of many settlements, yes. Not all of them, of course. We are a large nation. Many towns and many villages." She took a deep breath, suddenly sick with longing for home. "We are many and powerful, and there is no strife among my people."

But his eyes narrowed, turned challenging again. "That is not why I heard."

"What did you hear?" This time she truly had a hard time restraining herself from jumping to her feet. "What could you, Crooked Tongue, have heard about my people? What stupid rumors could have reached your distant lands?" The thought hit her, and she had a yet harder time pretending to be calm and thoughtful. "It was your companion who said that, wasn't he? Well, then know that he lied to you, the despicable liar that he is. All his people are like that, and he is probably lying to you all the time. Maybe all he wants is to lure you to his dirty Little Falls, to give his people the honor of slaying you."

But his grin deepened, turning openly amused. "I heard that from one respectable hunter, only five, six dawns ago, while traveling through your lands. He said there was strife, strife in his lands and even in his settlement. There was no reason for him to lie to me. He had told me the truth."

Now it was her turn to struggle with his rapidly flowing, foreign speech. Why couldn't the Crooked Tongues speak more clearly?

"This hunter, maybe he did lie to you. Maybe he had his reasons," she insisted. "Why did he agree to talk to you in the first place? My people do not speak to Crooked Tongues."

"Well, obviously they do. I talked to this hunter, and I talked to you." He laughed into her eyes, unbearably complacent once again. "Out of two Onondaga People I have met so far, all of them talked to me, quite readily at that. Although the hunter was nicer, a polite, well-mannered person." As she was too busy glaring at him, speechless, he raised his good arm in a defensive gesture. "Wait. Before you get too angry, please, finish the story of Hionhwatha. It is important, important for your people no less than for me."

She still glared at him.

"Please?" His smile was wide, confident in his ability to win her affection back.

She ground her teeth. "I will finish his story, but I will not tell you one more word," she breathed in the end.

He nodded readily, more amused than ever. What filthy skunk!

"Well, like I said, the first meeting broke because of Tadodaho and his men. There was much violence, my man said. They started to fight each other, but Hionhwatha stopped them and made them all go home."

"What was the meeting about? What did Hionhwatha say to them before Tadodaho's people arrived?"

She frowned at his constant interruption. "He wanted to unite people, to make them fight together against the enemy, and not against each other."

"Oh, a soundly good idea." He nodded, satisfied.

"Well, it has nothing to do with your ideas. He wanted to fight the enemy more efficiently. He wanted to strike them hard."

He sighed. "Yes, I understand that. Still, he arrived at half an idea and this may be enough for the beginning. I truly need to find him and talk to him."

"You can't. He is not himself anymore. He lost his spirit when his family died, after the second meeting at the Awakening Season."

He frowned. "They died in the winter, of starvation?"

"No," she said firmly. "His beloved wife and his oldest daughter died in the winter, not of starvation but of sickness originated in sorcery. Tadodaho is a dangerous sorcerer, too."

"Then what happened to the rest of his family?"

"They died, too. First his second daughter, then his last one. The young girl was killed in the melee that followed when the meeting broke so violently he could not prevent their fighting this time. She fell down the cliff. No one pushed her, she just tripped, but everyone knew who made it happen. There was a terrifying looking bird circling in the sky just before she fell to her death. My man was there. He saw it all."

His gaze was upon her, suddenly soft, sincere, penetrating. "And what happened to your man?"

She felt it like a cold wave, sliding down her chest, all the way to her stomach, to freeze her insides. He had been dead for a whole span of seasons, and she had been through much since then. Still, it was happening every time anew, every time she remembered, this dreadful wave, washing her, wiping the life out of her body.

"He came back from the meeting, and he told me all about it," she muttered, studying the small stones jutting against her knees.

"Is he still alive?"

She shook her head.

"How did he die?"

If only she knew! Her throat was too constricted to form words. She clenched her teeth to stop them from clattering, then heard him getting to his feet, slowly, clumsily. His shoulder must have still given him a lot of pain.

"*Wipe away the tears.*" Somehow the customary words of the condolence ceremony sounded better when spoken in this strange accent of his, barely understandable, but familiar nevertheless. "*Cleanse your throat so you may speak and hear.*"

She glanced up as he knelt beside her, his face blurry but more visible at such close proximity, the sharp features softened, radiating compassion.

"I know," she whispered, shivering. "I heard these words when we readied his spirit for the Sky Journey."

But the sensation was different, not like back then, in the condolence ceremony, at the sacred ground, with his body lying on a platform tied to a tree and the people crowding, talking, not letting her concentrate and think about her loss. Oh, how she had wished they would go away back then! But this time, she needed this man to stay and say more, she realized, her heart thumping.

"Restore the heart to its right place, and remove the clouds blocking the sun in the sky."

He went on, as though certain of her wish to hear that. His hands were upon her shoulders, touching lightly, not threatening. They gave her courage to meet his gaze.

"Wipe away the fallen tears so you might look around peacefully."

Those were the words she didn't know, and she peered at him, puzzled. Was this the way of his people to console? His gaze did not waver.

"Open your ears so you may hear readily. Remove the obstruction from your throat, the grief that is choking you. Ease the burden off your mind by speaking to your friends."

Spellbound, she stared at him, seeing his eyes, luminous and large, the smile in them obvious, a kind, good-hearted smile.

"Is this how your people console the mourners?" she whispered, not trusting her voice to talk aloud.

"No," he said, taking his hands off her and moving away, to try and make himself comfortable against the shaky wall of the hut. "I made them up just now." There was a grin in his voice again, a light, comfortable grin.

"Why?"

She watched his face twisting, as he was obviously having a difficult time settling, the sling holding his arm in place hindering his movement.

"I hope the stupid arm gets better by the next dawn," he muttered. "The worst of timings."

"It will. Jikonsahseh has all sorts of medicine." The thought hit her and she sprang to her feet, her heart beating fast. "I'll go and ask her to find something to put on your shoulder. Maybe some leaves. Something that will take away the swelling. I remember there was such a thing."

He frowned. "Medicine, you mean?"

"Yes, medicine."

Turning around, she smiled, oddly elated. Jikonsahseh's little garden behind the cooking hut contained similar looking plants. She remembered noticing it while first wandering the clearing, the moment her body stopped burning. Was it only five, six dawns ago? It seemed like a lifetime had passed, as though she had lived in this hut for summers, waiting for this stranger to appear.

"What is your name, Onondaga girl?" he called, back to his good natured, complacent self.

"You can call me Onheda," she said without turning back, not annoyed at all this time. "No one uses my full name, anyway."

"Onheda means porcupine, isn't it?" He laughed. "How appropriate."

Before diving behind the corner of the smaller hut, she turned her head. "Oh, yes? And what is your name? Must be something involving a lot of talking. A squirrel, maybe."

"No, no talking and no squirrels, I'm afraid." She watched his eyes twinkling, lips twisting with an open amusement, their corners going down in the way that made her heart beat faster. "It's about two currents of the same river, flowing together. Don't ask me what it means." He shook his head. "But you can call me Two Rivers, like everybody else."

"Two Currents, I like Two Currents better."

"Suit yourself." His eyes turned serious, narrowing, boring at her. "Will you come with us, Onheda, a porcupine girl? When we set out to look for that strange leader of yours, that Hionhwatha, will you accompany us? It won't take us more than a few dawns or so, and we will escort you back here safely."

"Why would you want me to come with you?" she asked, her heart making strange leaps inside her chest.

"You can help us to find him more easily. You can help us

talk to him. He is your country folk. He may feel more at ease with you around, maybe translating, or at least explaining some things, helping to avoid misunderstandings."

"I don't know." Aware of her acute disappointment – *what did she think he was inviting her for?* – she frowned, anxious to be on her way, to reach the small field and to look for an appropriate plant, craving some privacy all of a sudden. She needed that, to think it over, to understand something, about her and about that strange man. "I'm not sure I can come, but I'll think about it. I will let you know."

Diving behind the low wall, she saw him nodding absently, back in his thoughts.

CHAPTER 8

Afraid to breathe, Tekeni pressed against a tree, peering at the wide glade below his feet, desperate to see better. The men upon the clearing were busy, some making fire, others cutting a carcass of a deer, occupied, purposeful. They talked quietly, but the breeze was coming the wrong way, and he could not hear what they said.

His back covered with sweat, despite the coolness of the late afternoon, he pondered if it was wise to follow the trail leading down the hill in order to come closer. If he heard them talking, he would know what nation they belonged to. Also, he would learn if they were hunters or warriors as the slain deer gave no indication. They could have been warriors, making sure of their meal. But if they felt safe to light a fire, then they may have been the Onondagas, at home in their own woods, so near Onondaga Lake.

He shivered, then shrugged. Their own progress toward the long, misty lake was satisfactory so far. Only three dawns since leaving the sanctuary of Jikonsahseh's clearing and here they were, wandering Onondaga Lake, looking for the mysterious man that was supposed to live somewhere around in these woods. A dubious mission, but he had grown to trust Two Rivers' judgment up to the point that he asked no questions. The Crooked Tongues man knew what he was doing, and so far, they'd gotten into no trouble, although it had been almost half a moon since crossing the Great Sparkling Water, heading to their deaths, according to any possible estimation.

He stifled a sigh. Half a moon, spent on his side of the Great Lake, heading toward his town, his people. He should have been excited, elated, thrilled – home at long last! – but he was not. In fact, every day that kept them still close to the shores of the giant water obstacle made him feel hopeful, made him believe that he would be able to cross it back in the not-so-far away future. Somehow.

The Green Corn Moon was over, and the Harvest Moon as well. The Hunting Moon was in its highest, the time for the women to grind the corn, preparing for the upcoming winter. How good was the main harvest back in the Crooked Tongues' lands? Did the Beaver Clan finish picking their crops in time? Were they grinding maize now, drying the squash, and the wild berries?

The dull pain was back, familiar by now, but still difficult to deal with. What was she doing in this same twilight? Grinding maize? Cutting meat or fish in order to dry it and make it ready for the winter? Serious? Sad? Happy? It had been almost two moons. One moon and twenty-two dawns, to be precise. Was she thinking him dead? Did she give up on waiting already?

He clenched his teeth until his jaw hurt. She wouldn't wait for summers upon summers. How could she? If only there were a way to send her a word, to let her know that he was still alive and well, making plans to come back and kidnap her just like he promised.

A kidnapping! Back then, upon the dark shore, amidst his pain and their bottomless desperation, the word 'kidnapping' made them laugh and feel better. He would come and spirit her away, into the lands of the savages, to cook people and comb the snakes out of his hair. He remembered the way her face shone at him, more beautiful than ever, despite the scratches and the smeared mud, despite the paleness, or maybe because of it. She was not just a pretty girl anymore but truly a goddess, the Sky Woman who had known suffering already, but who was strong enough to overcome the hardships. Not a girl, but a woman. *His woman.*

He bit his lips to swallow a groan. She had given herself to him, and they made the promise. But then the dirty lowlife

Yeentso came along, ruining it all! Oh, but for a chance to hurt the disgusting, ugly bastard, to make him suffer the way he had made them both suffer. However, the despicable man was dead, killed by Two Rivers in a single, well aimed shot, not suffering even a little bit. The dirty piece of rotten meat! He ruined it all for them, all of it.

Touching his cheek, he ran his fingers along the scars. Would she still love him, looking like this? He would peer at his reflection every time he happened around a source of water, studying his face and the patterns the scars made. It looked strange. Repulsive, probably. In a reasonable amount, scars were good, welcomed, displaying one's bravery and achievements. Like the marks the old bear had left upon his chest. A sure way to let people know that he was a brave man. But to have one's face and chest crossed by the long, twisting lines, like a war painting? No, it was anything but good, or attractive. She had fallen in love with him when his face was still clear of marks.

The aroma of roasted meat brought him back from his dark thoughts, made him concentrate. The men within the clearing gathered near the fire now, all ten of them, squatting or strolling around, clearly expectant. He envied them their prospective meal. Back on the journey, rowing against the current this time, mostly at nights again, their nourishment consisted of dried meat, berries, and mixed maize powder. Not a feast to make one drool.

He squinted against the glow of the setting sun, eyeing the weapons that heaped not far away from the fire, bows and quivers mainly, but with an occasional spear peering out, and obviously more than a few clubs. *Warriors or hunters?*

Had he been more familiar with these surroundings, he would have dared to come closer, to listen to their speech, to determine their identity and intentions. Yet, the prospect of the scouts lurking could not be disregarded. If caught, he would ruin it all for Two Rivers, and not only for himself.

One last glance at the feasting people, and he dived back into the bushes, hurrying along the invisible trail. They would be ready to sail, anyway, crossing the long Onondaga Lake like the girl maintained they should. She said it was full of strong currents, despite its deceptively calm appearance. Fully absorbed, her lips pursed, eyes narrow, she had kept watching the shore as they sailed alongside it, barely visible in the pre-dawn mist. There was a good crossing point somewhere nearby, she promised, scanning the high banks. Before the next night was over, they would be camping on the other side.

He remembered watching her covertly, admiring her against his will. She was an annoying piece of rotten meat, aggressive, arrogant, sharp-tongued, but maybe Two Rivers was right in bringing her along. These were the lands of her people, and if she was all of a sudden willing to help, then why not to use her. And yet...

Making his way through the darkening woods, he frowned. What happened to the '*how can you think to drag your girl into the enemy lands with no supplies and no clear destination*'? All of a sudden it was all right to bring this girl along, the girl Two Rivers clearly found attractive. These two were talking a lot, doing their best to understand each other with no need of his translating services. And there were all sorts of glances running between them, stealthy, covert glances when the other thought he or she was not looking. Like two silly children, when both had seen well over twenty summers and more, grown up people as they were. He scowled.

They were still there, not far away from the shore, not talking this time. And not making love, either. Tekeni snorted. He would not have been surprised to run into them, panting and sweating one above another, to have a quick pleasure. Maybe he should have stayed in the old woman's hut, to rest and eat properly, while those two made the journey to meet the strange, crazed-with-grief leader.

"What?" asked Two Rivers, raising his head, his pointed eyebrows knitting in a frown. He was crouching above their overturned canoe, his hands sticky with sap he was smearing upon the cracks in the old wood.

"Ten armed men, not far away from here. Either hunters or warriors." He didn't spare a glance for the girl, who stopped stirring her small pottery bowl and froze, all ears. "Onondaga People, most probably. We would be better off back in the water, crossing the damn lake."

"Where exactly?" In a heartbeat, Two Rivers was on his feet, the newly carved club just an extension of his hands, one moment thrown aside, the next – there and ready. With his arm back in place and the swelling gone, the man was his old self again, as agile and as dangerous as before.

"On the clearing, down that hill, to the east."

"How well-armed?"

"Bows and clubs. Also, at least one spear."

"Did you see them from a close proximity? Did you hear what they were talking about?"

"No. I couldn't hear them talking. I watched from the top of the hill." Shrugging, Tekeni strolled toward the boat, inspecting it in his turn. The sap was still wet, but it would hold. It's not like they were attempting to cross the Great Sparkling Water.

"How do you know those were Onondaga People?" This time it was the girl speaking, challenging his authority, as always. "If you didn't hear them talking, you could not tell for sure what peoples they belonged to, could you?"

"Of course, I can tell." Helping Two Rivers to cover the remnants of their small smokeless fire, he glanced at her, meeting her daring gaze. "They felt at home, confident, careless, making a large fire, roasting meat, strolling around and laughing. Who would behave like that in the lands of the enemy?" The open contempt in her eyes made him wish to strike her. "Also they were ugly, like only the Onondaga People can be."

That did it. She was on her feet, too, breathing heavily, her eyes blazing, oblivious of Two Rivers' quiet but hearty laughter.

"One needs no better entertainment than to watch you two bickering," said the older man. "Come, let us eat your porridge and be gone."

"I'm not giving him my porridge," she tossed, not taking her burning gaze off Tekeni.

"Of course you are. This food was packed for the three of us." Two Rivers took the bowl and grabbed a spoonful of the thick dough it contained. "Oh, it's really thoroughly sweet," he commented, whether trying to lighten the atmosphere, or genuinely at ease. "Jikonsahseh did not spare the maple syrup. Good."

"He can mix his own porridge," insisted the girl. "There is still enough powder in the bag."

"Like I want any of the things you stirred." Kicking a stone, Tekeni strolled toward the bag, fishing out a piece of dried meat. "She may have poisoned it," he added, addressing Two Rivers. "She is well capable of using dirty means like that."

But Two Rivers just shook his head, refusing to be pulled into their argument, which wasn't their first.

"You two sort it out between yourselves," he said, giving the half full bowl back to the girl. "But not before we are safely away from this shore." He motioned to Tekeni. "Help me with the boat. You can nibble on your meat later on."

CHAPTER 9

The cabin was small, low, its angles sharp. Made out of logs and bark sheets, like a short version of a typical longhouse, it should have been in a better shape than Jikonsahseh's hut, but it was not. An air of neglect surrounded it, a feeling of untidiness and dirt. No smell reached their nostrils, but Two Rivers felt that if he tried hard, he would catch the odor of filth and decay. Not an inviting place.

Crouching behind the cluster of thick bushes, he eyed the grass-covered ground that was clearly taken off from the forest, with the stumps of old, cut down trees peeking everywhere. It was also littered with garbage, broken tools, weapons, pieces of hides, remnants of old and not-so-old fires. Such an unappealing mess! His gaze scanned the piles of river shells, scattered everywhere, mostly white and purple, its coloring darkly alluring.

"What was he doing with those?" whispered the Onondaga girl, leaning forward, pressing against him, trying to see better.

The sensation of her nearness sent shafts of excitement down his stomach. She was wearing a long-sleeved dress, but the well-tanned material did not seem to hide the warmth of her body. He felt it burning his skin. An uncomfortable sensation. They were here for a reason, and he needed his full concentration for the encounter that awaited him.

"We'll find out," he said curtly, moving away as though trying to see better.

He would need to get her out of his sight before he met that Hionhwatha man. Her presence was distracting. Many were the times when he would lose his line of thought while talking about important matters, when she would peer at him with those huge, luminous eyes of hers, drinking in his every word – the ones she managed to understand, that is – then saying something clever, contradicting, challenging him in a provocative but somehow temptingly feminine way. She was high-tempered and sharp-minded, and very appealing to look at. Not a good combination at all, not for their present situation. Were she ugly or old, he would have actually liked her to stay and help. The crazed-with-grief former war leader was her country folk.

"He is not here," breathed Tekeni, appearing behind them soundlessly. "But he did spend the night here."

"We can see that," whispered the girl angrily.

"Good for you!" Tekeni's snort bore an equal amount of hostility.

Two Rivers rolled his eyes.

"You know what? You two, go back and guard the boat. Make yourselves comfortable, and wait for me there."

Both pairs of indignant eyes peered at him.

"I want to talk to this man in private. He might feel threatened if pounced upon by all three of us."

"He'll feel threatened anyway, and he won't understand a half of what you are saying," said the girl. As always, through the three dawns of their journey, it was her to sound the objections, with Tekeni just frowning doubtfully.

Two Rivers grinned. "He'll manage. You understand me well enough, and so will he."

"I understand you because I want to understand you, and it is still difficult, believe me on that." Her frown matched that of Tekeni now. "But he is likely to be even less responsive."

He acknowledged it with a nod. "Yes, I see your point, and yet, I want you to wait for me by the boat."

"He may be dangerous." Now it was the youth's turn to argue.

"Yes, I know. I will be careful. Now would you two, please, go away?"

Their gazes flashed at him, united in their mutual resentment for a change. Then they were gone. He sighed with relief. Now he could concentrate properly, could think about the strange man that lived in this hut, and about his sad history.

How would it feel to lose one's entire family? he thought. Whether to sickness, tragic accident, or ill wishes and sorcery, it didn't matter. Like Tekeni, falling in captivity while losing his greatly admired father, and that after seeing his mother and brother on their Sky Journeys. Like this Onondaga girl, so sharp and daring, then suddenly unable to control her tears at the memory of her lost husband, the man she had evidently loved. So many deaths, all caused by war.

Silently, he got to his feet and went toward the mess of the house, stepping over overturned pots. Yes, the wolf cub was right. The place was deserted but not for a long time.

He listened carefully. The owner of this dwelling would be back, and he had better not be caught doing the unspeakable, going into a person's home uninvited. The custom concerning hospitality was old and uncompromising. Everyone would be invited in, to feel at home and partake in the hosts' meal. Even the captured enemy was fed and offered a pipe before his ordeal would begin. The custom was the same on both sides of the Great Lake, he gathered. But never was a man, or a woman, allowed to go into the house, into the town even, uninvited. The arriving guest was expected to sit outside, smoking and waiting patiently to be invited in. And yet, the opportunity to learn more about the mysterious man, before he would have to face him, was tempting. He had brushed aside too many customs, too many reasonable ways of doing things. One more transgression would not harm his conscience.

The bark-sheet door slid aside, screeching. Now he could feel the smell. Oh yes, rotting meat, most certainly, coming from a half covered pot upon the bed of cold embers. And from all over, too, with the earthen floor dotted by pieces of food and tramped upon berries and roots, more so around the pile of hides that clearly served as a resting place.

Involuntarily, he shivered. Jikonsahseh assumed that the man had resorted to eating the flesh of humans. She had said so more than once, the accusation he had dismissed as imaginary like the other things of its kind. Tekeni's people, the savages from this side of the Great Lake, were supposed to feed on human flesh too, and to have snakes in their hair, but so far, he had not seen evidence to any of that. And not that he had expected to find any. Sometimes people were silly, suspended to stupid superstitious lies, no better than small children.

Still, the oppressive semidarkness and the stench wore on his nerves as he went over the place, careful to touch nothing. Entering this house with no invitation was bad enough in itself, without adding more to his mounting list of transgressions. He was here not to steal.

The resolution to touch nothing came to severe temptation when he stumbled upon a strange looking bow with multiple strings stretched against its curved shaft. What, in the name of the Great Spirits, purpose did it serve?

Kneeling to inspect the mysterious object, he studied the strings that seemed to be made out of fiber, twisted together and tied to the bow-like construction with leather tongs. Puzzled, he looked around, his gaze encountering a stash of beautifully woven belts of white and purple shells. Different in length and width, their patterns strange, curving and twisting but in a pleasant way, they lay there arranged neatly one next to another, presenting a glaring contradiction to the cluttered mess of the rest of the house. Whoever made those belts was evidently fond of them, keeping them safe, adding to the collection.

He fought the urge to touch, to pick up one of the wonderful strings. Now the heaps of colorful pieces outside the hut made sense. Working the fragile shells was a difficult business. For so many belts one would need plenty of material, and there would be more broken shells than not. So, the question of the Onondaga girl was answered. He grinned fleetingly, kneeling to inspect the nearest string, long and thin, more purple than white, its patterns pleasing the eye. She would enjoy wearing it, and the beautiful piece would enhance the elegance and the smoothness of her neck.

Frowning, he eyed the other decorations, their patterns disturbing, making him think of its maker's frustration, of violent urges, of grief. So that's what the strange man was doing, living all alone for more than one span of seasons. Did making the strings help to ease the pain?

The sound of the hurried footsteps brought him up in time to face the furious owner as the man burst in, blocking the light with his massive body. Wild-eyed and wide shouldered, his broad face contorted, sweat-covered and scratched, the long, unkempt hair flowing wildly behind his back, the man held his club high, its flint spike glittering darkly, reflecting some of the outside light.

"Don't," he hissed in a cracked voice, eyeing Two Rivers and the way his hand reached for his knife. "Drop it. Your pitiful knife can do nothing against my club."

Two Rivers swallowed, willing his heart to beat slower. It was pounding madly, interrupting his ability to think. There was something about this man, something unsettling, powerful, making one think of all sorts of dangers, although what was one single man with a club? He could best him, if careful. He was not a bad warrior himself.

"I didn't come here to fight you," he said, pleased to hear his voice steady, not trembling.

"What?" The man frowned, thrown out of balance for a heartbeat. "Why you talk strange?"

"I came from across the Great Sparkling Water." He tried to talk slower, frustrated. He should not have sent Tekeni away. "I want to talk."

A knife appeared out of nowhere, flashing in the air, swishing beside his ear. Afraid to take his eyes off the man, whose lips now twisted in a maliciously satisfied grin, Two Rivers glimpsed the wooden hilt fluttering at the corner of his eye, stuck in the wall, too deeply to fall out.

"Still want to talk?" The derisive grin was wider, flickering with scorn.

He watched the hate spilling out of the dark eyes, struggling to keep calm, aware that his own knife was still in his possession, clasped tightly in his sweaty palm. He should have brought his club here, instead of leaving it back by the boat.

"Yes, still want to talk."

Another knife came out in a flash. How many knives did this man have in his sash? He threw himself sideways, not mistaking the deepening glint of the narrow eyes. This time the knife was intended to kill.

A fleeting glance at another wooden handle fluttering out of the crack of the wall that had supported his back only a heartbeat ago confirmed this conclusion. He clenched his teeth. Desperate to have a better weapon than merely his own knife, he grabbed the bow-like stick with multiple strings, but it only served to make the owner of the house yet angrier.

"Don't touch it!" The man howled, leaping forward, his club high.

Darting aside, Two Rivers tried to block the blow, the curved stick too thin, breaking with a loud crack, the multitude of strings falling downwards, hanging limply, defeated.

"Oh, you are a dead man!" screamed his host, bringing his club forward without much calculation. It crashed against the pole holding the frame of the dwelling in place, making a hollow sound, missing Two Rivers' shoulder by a fraction as he threw himself sideways yet again, not planning his own moves, either. He needed to get out into the open. In the cramped space of this house, between the wild attacks of its insane owner, he had no chance.

The man attacked again, bringing his club sideways this time, intending to cut and not to crush. Had Two Rivers not noticed his assailant's intentions, the razor-sharp spike would have cut into his stomach. As it was, it brushed lightly against his side, leaving a stinging sensation and a crimson line in its wake as his body tilted once again, acting as though on its own accord.

He fought to keep his balance, then saw his chance when the man brought his arms up, his club again high in the air. Desperate, he flung himself forward, to crash into the momentarily exposed torso with all his weight, his fist shooting forward, to make contact first, knocking the air out of his rival, his shoulder coming to his aid, reinforcing the effect.

The man groaned, wavering, but not losing his fighting spirit. Older than his intruder, he still seemed to be as agile in a simple struggle of limbs as when wielding a weapon. His kick was vicious, making Two Rivers gasp at the pain in his shin.

Paying it no attention, as did his rival before, he watched the club rising, his instincts in conflict, crying to leap aside in an attempt to escape the lethal blow, urging to reach for the temptingly defenseless throat.

He did both things. As his body darted sideways, careless of a fall anymore, feeling the hard wood of the club brushing against his recently healed shoulder, his palm shot upward, straight and rigid, like a flat stone, colliding with the man's windpipe but sliding, not crushing it, having not much strength put into the blow.

Evidently, it was enough. His rival collapsed onto the floor in a heap of twisting limbs, gasping for air, while Two Rivers groped for the nearby pole, desperate to stay upright. The hut wavered, swayed, still he clutched to his slippery support, gasping for air too, but not as loudly as the man on the ground.

Another heartbeat, or maybe more, and the world was right again. Clenching his teeth against the pain pulsating in his shoulder and under his right arm, he rushed to retrieve the club. To have it well away from its owner's reach made him feel safer, not as anxious to flee outside, into the clearness of the autumn high noon. The carved weapon was impressive, a weighty, perfectly polished object covered with patterns, its spike long, piercingly sharp, lethal. He shook his head, then twisted to study the cut at his side, bloody but thin, bearably painful. Not a dangerous wound, but one that needed to be washed. Kneeling, he put his attention to the groaning man.

"Wait. Don't get up," he said, not trying to stop his victim, afraid that the touch may make his unwilling host lose his sanity again. The large eyes reflected pain and wariness, but no madness. "Do you have water somewhere around here? Water? Drink?"

The man motioned toward the dead fire, then wiped the saliva off his mouth with the back of his palm, suppressing another bout of coughing. Behind the pot with the old foul-smelling meal, there was a pottery bowl half filled with water. He fought the urge to drink it all by himself.

"Here, drink."

The wary gaze did not waver, glued to Two Rivers' face, but as the man got up with a visible effort a crooked grin twisted his lips.

"You don't have to be that tense. I won't kill you, not now," he said hoarsely, accepting the bowl.

"I know that well enough, don't I?" Incensed at the way he, indeed, tensed the moment his host seemed to be capable of getting up, Two Rivers shrugged, then forced his face into stillness. The eyes were still upon him, calm, undecipherable, as dark as the moonless night.

"So what do you want? Why did you come here?"

"I came to talk."

"No one comes here to talk. Tell me the real reason."

He stood the intensity of the dark gaze. "That's the reason. Others don't see what I see."

Something flickered in the depths of those eyes. "What do you see?"

"I see a man who needs change. I see whole peoples who need change. They don't have courage to admit it. You do have courage. You tried to change things already."

Oh, but for a chance to make a better speech! He suppressed the familiar frustration, aware of the effort it took him not to shift his gaze. The intensity behind his opponent's eyes was nerve-wracking.

"You can offer me nothing."

"How do you know before you hear?"

"What do you want?"

"I want you to help me stop the war."

The eyes peering at him widened, then narrowed. The pressed lips began to twitch.

"You what?" The hoarse laughter erupted, rolling between the walls, making the man cough. Breathing heavily, he reached for the bowl, gulped the remnants of the water, then laughed again. "You talk strange. It must be the Crooked Tongues' thing. I thought you said…" More laughter.

He waited patiently, watching the man, seeing the nervousness, the uncertainty. Oh, he wanted to hear more, he wanted to hear it all. The rudeness, the coarse toughness, the derisive laughter were just a show. Deep inside, this man was lonely and scared. He needed the change, he needed the direction.

"I need to go and wash my wound," he said, getting up with an effort. "Think about what I said. I'll come back."

The laughter died away abruptly. "Let me see."

As the man got up, Two Rivers fought the urge to grab his knife, just in case.

"It's nothing," he said. "Just a cut. But I need to wash it."

"I have more water in the pot outside," said the man, his steps ringing heavily between the overturned possessions. "I'll bring it, and the leaves of that plant they usually tie to the wounds, too. Make yourself comfortable, in the meanwhile." Turning his head, he gave Two Rivers a furious glance, his eyes sparkling darkly. "Don't touch anything. Anything! You may be a foreigner, but even the savages from across the Great Lake must have some manners. To enter someone's house uninvited? To touch things?" The large head shook as the man's wide back disappeared into the freshness of the outside. "The worst manners I have ever seen."

And that was the truth, reflected Two Rivers, making himself comfortable, as much as one could when offered a seat on the dirty earthen floor. He should have waited outside, should have been patient, should not have sent Tekeni and the girl away. What were they doing there by the boat? Quarrelling, as always?

He grinned. It was safer for them both to be here. He would go and fetch them the moment his host came back.

CHAPTER 10

The boat was gone!

Wide-eyed, Tekeni peered at the sunlit inlet they had left in the pre-dawn mist, his heart beating fast. For a moment, he considered the possibility of a mistake. Had they come upon another similar-looking place? Everything was there, their bags with food and spare clothing, both of the paddles, Two Rivers' club. But the small, whitish canoe was missing.

"What happened?" breathed the girl, nearing.

She had come here separately, choosing to make her own way from the strange man's hut. Anything but to follow Tekeni's lead. Which was a mercy. He didn't want her anywhere in his vicinity, either.

"Shut up," he hissed, grabbing her arm to make her stop. She seemed as though about to rush straight toward the small beach.

"Don't you dare to touch me!" Tearing her hand out of his grip, she turned to face him, her nostrils widening with every breath taken, eyes flashing.

He ground his teeth at her stupidity.

"Keep quiet," he repeated in a whisper, motioning in the direction of the river.

But, of course, it was too late. The bushes adorning the shoreline came to life with people springing out of them, heading in their direction. He might have been well concealed by his cluster of trees, but her indignant cry gave their presence away, impossible to miss.

He cursed, tearing the first arrow out of his quiver, his bow up and ready. But for Two Rivers' club! It was lying there vacant, inviting, almost within an easy reach. Yet, to do that he would need to run into the open, for those warriors to shoot him like a fleeing deer.

"Run back to the hut," he tossed at her, aiming as he counted their attackers. Only two men were crossing the shore, running up toward his trees, but he knew there would be more coming. There was no doubt about this being an ambush.

She said nothing, but he could feel her presence beside him, silent for a change, frozen. Stupid woman!

He shot at the nearing men, aiming not too carefully, then heard the others breaking through the bushes to their left. Damn it! He tore the whole quiver off his back, desperate to shoot the second man before the others reached him. One of the warriors upon the shore was on the ground, struggling with the feathered shaft that stuck out of his chest. But for the chance to take down his peer and run for the club!

The quiver fell off, slipping from his sweaty hands, as he whirled around to estimate the progress of their other attackers. They were closing up, running fast and without care judging by the noise they made, yet, he still couldn't see them through the trees.

His fingers fastened around an arrow that, miraculously, made its way into his hands. Not wasting his time on wondering about it, he turned back toward the shore, from the corner of his eye catching the glimpse of the girl as she stood beside him, his quiver in her hands, another arrow out and ready.

He shot with no time to aim, then grabbed the next offered missile. The man darted aside, then leaped up the incline, but the third shot pushed him back, to roll upon the ground, his screams bubbling, coming through the blood gushing out of his mouth.

As she thrust another arrow into his hands, he saw the other men bursting through the bushes.

"Get the club!" he shouted at her. "There, down the beach. Bring the club!"

The men hesitated for a heartbeat, three of them, sweat-covered and panting. Tearing his knife from his sash, Tekeni leaped forward, mainly to take their attention off the girl. She would sneak down the shore and would bring the club, of that he was certain now. This one was capable of doing this, having an admirable presence of mind, he was forced to admit.

A cudgel hissed, and he ducked out of its reach, stumbling over low bushes. Oh yes, he needed Two Rivers' club, and fast. Recovering his balance, he ducked another swish of the enemy club. Not that he had ever fought with this sort of a weapon, but clearly, his knife was useless against these people, and his bow had already served its purpose.

A spear flew by, scratching his arm, pushing him into the bushes to his left. Breathless, he rolled away from yet another attack, snatching a broken branch on his way. Without much of an aim, he struck out at the general direction of his attacker, just a muffled silhouette against the glow of the midday sun. Caught unprepared, the man wavered and paused to curse, allowing Tekeni a heartbeat of respite, to scramble to his feet and make his knife ready.

Ducking another onslaught, he plunged his knife out, feeling it sliding against some flesh, tearing skin. The man's gasp was music to his ears, but he didn't spend his time listening. A knife was no challenge against a club. It worked this one time, but only because his attacker clearly underestimated his victim, expecting nothing but more of the defensive thrashing about, more frantic attempts to avoid being squashed by the unrelenting pounding of the hard wood.

Not wasting his time on watching the man, who doubled all of a sudden, Tekeni darted toward the trail leading to the shore. He just needed to get that club, and anyway, the girl's screams had been coming from there for some time by now. He could hear that and the sounds of struggle, accompanied by shouting and cursing.

Pausing for only a heartbeat, to pick a large, sharp-edged stone, he raced down the incline, hoping the man with the spear would still be too busy recovering his weapon. A futile hope. Those people were warriors, not women. He barely managed to aim his improvised missile at the man upon the shore, who was busy dragging the girl by her hair as she struggled to get away, pressing Two Rivers' club to her chest with both hands.

His stone lurched into the air as someone crashed into him from behind, the heavy body of a man. Whatever his rival was trying to do, it sent them both rolling down the incline and onto the wet sand.

Trying to understand what happened, his senses in panic – *his knife, where was his knife?* – Tekeni kicked, desperate to squirm from under his heavy rival. The man pressed on, frustrating his attempts to break free. The sun sparkled from the ragged edges of the flint blade as it pounced toward his face, lethal, determined, impossible to stop. It was happening too fast.

His hand leapt up, pushing the blade away, grabbing it, his fingers wrapping around the cutting edges, the pain cascading down his stomach. He could smell the odor of the fresh blood as it trickled into his face, the struggle getting more difficult, the knife nearing but slower now, not reflecting the sun anymore.

Clenching his teeth, he put all his strength into this battle of wills, the knife getting closer, the blood dripping, stinging his eyes. It was hopeless. The razor-sharp flint was slipping through, cutting his palm, impossible to stop. He heard his teeth cracking, his jaw locked, to stay that way forever as it seemed, yet it gave his arm no additional power, with nothing to pit itself against, counting on his rapidly disappearing strength and nothing else.

The stench of the blood was overwhelming, so very close he could see it gathering around the sharp tip of the knife as it peeked through the reddish mess of his palm. He shut his eyes in the attempt to halt its progress, then heard the footsteps and the blow.

It was a strange sensation. He felt the blow clearly, resonating through his body, strong but bringing no pain. It was as though the man above him pushed himself forward all of a sudden, his face crushing into Tekeni's, blinding him with an additional bout of pain. Yet, the pressure of the knife disappeared.

Heart pounding, head dizzy, senses in turmoil, he pushed the limp body away, crawling from under it when it refused to move. The brilliance of the daylight pounced on him and he blinked, trying to clear his vision. The stinging in his eyes grew.

"Are you all right?"

The girl's whisper reached him, coming from above, trembling badly. He wiped his eyes with his other palm.

"Yes."

She was standing nearby, shaking so violently he thought she might fall. Incredulous, his gaze took in the club, dancing in her fluttering palms, its rounded, weighty tip glittering with wetness. His eyes slipped toward his attacker and the revolting mess of blood and wet hair on the back of the man's head. It was surely not her...

Blinking, he got to his feet, his limbs shaking, but not as badly as hers. The shore spread around, quiet, peaceful in the brilliance of the sunlight, the sprawling bodies not belonging to the pastoral noon of the mid autumn. He glanced at them quickly, then extracted the club from her trembling hands.

"Wait here. There was another man in the woods."

He bent to wrestle the knife out of his rival's lifeless hand, then turned to go.

"No!" She grabbed his arm with both palms, pressing, hurting the fresh scratches covering his skin. "I'll go with you." Her voice rang hollowly, too high to please the ear.

Taking in the wide-opened eyes with unnaturally enlarged pupils, set in the muddied paleness of her face, Tekeni nodded.

"Come. If this man is not there, we'll pick our things and run for Two Rivers as fast as we can." His palm pulsated with pain, and he shifted the knife into his other hand, eyeing the bloody mess.

"You need to wash it." This time her voice sounded calmer, almost normal. "Those cuts are deep. They can rot."

"First, we make sure no one attacks us. There was this man with the club back in the woods. I didn't kill him, and I don't think I harmed him seriously." He eyed the trees adorning the shoreline. They swayed peacefully, deserted. "Maybe he went to call for his friends. If these men were the party I saw yesterday on the other side of the lake, then there are more of them."

Her face turned yet paler as her eyes darted uphill.

"Come," he said. "Let us hurry." Unable to resist, he glanced at his attacker's broken head. "You killed him. With one single blow, too." He studied her, remembering the way she was handing him his arrows, the way she rushed to retrieve the club when he had told her to do so, the way she fought the man upon the shore, and now this. "You saved my life."

She shrugged, smiling weakly. "You saved my life too, when you threw the stone at that man, and when you fought them all." Her voice broke as her lips began trembling again. "I never killed anyone, never in my entire life."

He hesitated, wishing to reassure her but unwilling to touch her, even for a supportive pat on her back. It seemed inappropriate, somehow. "Well, you did it, and you saved my life. I will remember, always."

Her smile flashed out, small and atypically shy. "It was because of me they noticed us. I started to argue. I'm sorry about that." She shook her head, returning to her brisk, confident self all at once. "Go and wash your cuts, and I will collect our things."

He grinned against his will. "All right, War Chief."

Turning around, she laughed. "You did well, Warrior. But I hope Two Rivers did better than us."

CHAPTER 11

"How many were those men? The ones you saw on the other side of the lake?" asked Hionhwatha curtly.

Fascinated, Onheda watched the formidable man as he squatted beside the fire, seemingly calm and at ease, but she could see the tension in the wide shoulders, his squatting figure rigid, the large palms clutching the spoon, stirring the stew that was boiling in the pot.

"Ten men," she heard the scar-faced youth saying, obviously ill at ease. "Either hunters or warriors."

Hugging his knees, he sat there, leaning against the wall, tired, his face clean but ashen, his body covered with bruises, hand wrapped into a bandage of dry, brownish leaves. It was evident that his fall down the hill in the grip of the enemy warrior wasn't a smooth affair. Busy trying to escape the clutches of her own attacker, whose head had just been smashed by the hurled stone, Onheda was not too occupied to miss their fall. And the struggle that ensued.

She pressed her lips, fighting the terrible memory, the way the club felt heavy, slippery in her sweaty palms, the way her arms absorbed the recoil, resounding through her own body as it crushed against the man's head, the disgustingly smacking sound it made.

Shuddering, she pushed the memory away. It was in the past, and she should forget all about it. The scar-faced youth was an annoying, offensive piece of human being, and he was the enemy of her people, too, but he did not deserve to die. Not after he had fought so efficiently, so well, making such efforts to save them both. He was a good warrior. No wonder the

Crooked Tongues man trusted him, relying upon him entirely as it seemed.

She shifted her gaze back to the foreigner, seated opposite to her, on the other side of the fire. Another one looking as though he had been through a fight, his face sporting bruises and scratches, his ribs encircled by a bandage with more of healing leaves tucked against the bloodied side. How did he make formidable Hionhwatha listen? she wondered. Not by his foreign sounding words alone, that much was obvious.

"Hunters," she heard Hionhwatha saying as he stirred the stew. "Warriors don't travel in small groups." As the formidable man shook his head, the mane of his unkempt hair jumped. "You killed five of them. I wonder where the rest are."

"Four," corrected the young man, frowning. "The fifth was wounded, probably not badly. He wasn't there when we were on our way back."

"At least you bothered to make sure he wasn't waylaying you, although you didn't think to look for your boat." The older man's accusation was open, and she saw the youth pressing his lips, angered and shamed at the same time.

"He killed four men and got himself and the girl here safely," said Two Rivers, lifting his eyebrows. "I think it's a commendable deed in itself. The boat must be still there. We'll go and look for it after we eat."

"I'll go and look for it now," said the youth, jumping to his feet.

Two Rivers grinned lightly, but his voice brooked no argument. "Sit down, wolf cub. We'll go and look for it in a little while." The eyes resting upon the young man conveyed a message, of that Onheda was sure.

She watched him, admiring the way he was defending his young friend's honor. He was not about to allow their angry host to say bad things about any of them.

Earlier, when they had burst onto the clearing, panting and afraid that the rest of their pursuers might be hot on their heels, Two Rivers did not let the man throw them out. In his turn,

Hionhwatha, incensed by the fact that more people were to descend upon the privacy of his home, shot furious glances, talking about dirty enemies and the traitors among his own people. By the 'traitors,' of course, he meant her. It was too obvious to miss. Now he knew how the Crooked Tongue came to learn about him and his history, the man had said grimly, squashing her with a burning gaze. But Two Rivers told him flatly that he would leave if they were not allowed to enter and that she, Onheda, was a wise woman who recognized the plight of her country folk before anyone else, the brave woman that she was. She remembered the way he had looked at her, genuinely proud even though he still didn't know what she had done down there on the shore to save his young companion.

Shivering, she remembered the way he had said that, that she was a part of the new world already, a great woman to accept the Good Tiding of Peace. She didn't know if the former Onondaga leader understood all of the foreign-sounding words, but she hoped he did. Oh, but for a chance to understand the Crooked Tongues man as clearly as the scar-faced youth did! Back then the young man had been too exhausted, too busy dealing with his wounded hand, to translate. But now he did, grudgingly but accurately, as far as she could judge.

"I will see to our meal," she said, getting to her feet, disregarding Hionhwatha's once again disapproving glance. The man didn't like to have strangers poring through his possessions, that much was obvious, but she needed to do something. Two Rivers should see how efficient and good she was.

"The Onondaga People will never listen to you," Hionhwatha was saying, staring gloomily into the fire.

"If we start with the right people, they might."

"There are no right people to start with."

Two Rivers' eyebrows lifted slightly. "I started with you, and so far, you are listening."

The dark gaze shot at him might have disheartened another person, reflected Onheda, fishing two wooden bowls from behind the dusty cupboard.

"You broke into my house, damaged my possessions, fought me, and then simply refused to leave. I don't think you will go on living for long, trying to make people listen this way."

Two Rivers' grin widened, unabashed. "I apologize for this way of doing things. I had no choice. Yet, with your help, we will do it in a better way from now on. You will know the right people to approach, to start with. Our dealings with them will be simpler, swifter, more easily completed."

Glad to find another large wooden spoon – she didn't like the idea of asking their disagreeable host for the one that he held – she listened to the translation of the youth, anxious to understand every word this time.

"You tried to do this already, but you were alone, and your opposition was strong," Two Rivers was saying, leaning forward now, holding the man's hostile gaze. "You paid a terrible price, a price no man should be asked to pay. But it is in the past now. To live here all alone, hunting and weaving shell strings is not the solution. You need to finish what you have started."

Hionhwatha's snort could be heard by the lake shores, of that Onheda was sure.

"I wasn't trying to reach a peaceful agreement between us and the despicable enemy." The gaze shot at the scar-faced youth was startling in its darkness and intensity. "I wanted to unite my people so they would finish the enemy once and for all. People of the Flint or People of the Mountains, and all the small but annoying nations in between, they are all alike to me. They are the enemy of my people, with whom I had no intention of talking but on the ceremony of executing their captives." The thin lips twisted in a sort of a derisive grin. "You've been misinformed. You spent your time in vain, journeying here." Now it was Onheda's turn to receive a dark gaze.

As though noticing none of this, Two Rivers reached for the bag they had brought back from the shore.

"I have not been misinformed," he said, fishing out a smaller package that contained their stacks of tobacco leaves, pulling a few out and beginning to crush them, his fingers nimble, hands steady. "I heard your story, repeated by different people. I know what you intended to do. And I know what happened. You tried to achieve what I am trying to achieve, but for different reasons. We think more alike than differently, and who knows? You may still see beyond the obvious." A calm gaze rose, boring into their host, glowing eerily, suddenly full of power and meaning. "You have a destiny to fulfill and it is time."

Slowing her step, Onheda lingered beside the entrance, reluctant to go out in order to wash the dirty utensils. She should have remained in her place, sitting beside the fire. It was silly of her to volunteer to serve their food.

"Why you?" asked Hionhwatha darkly. "Why should I listen to you, of all people, a stranger from the lands of the Crooked Tongues? Why do you think you can see my destiny?"

"Because I was sent to do so."

The silence prevailed, heavy, difficult to bear. Even the wind seemed to pause. No sound came in through the gaping door, and she felt her hair rising, her skin prickling. Eyes glued to his face, she saw it taking a different glow, bright and powerful, impossible not to look at. He did have a wonderful strength behind his eyes, a strange, unsettling power. That's why they all listened to him. He *was* the messenger of the Great Spirits.

Her insides fluttering, she took a hesitant step, then another, desperate to reach the light and the freshness of the outside. The birds were chirping in the softly rustling bushes, calming. She took a deep breath, then peeked back through the gaping doorway. They still sat there motionless, appearing as mere silhouettes rather than real people in the dimness of the rancid-smelling hut. Just silhouettes. The vision was gone.

Was he or wasn't he? she wondered, pouring the water over the dirty bowls, trying to scratch remnants of old food. Her mouth was dry, and she drank from the wooden cistern, although its contents were not as fresh as spring liquid should be. They would need to find a source of fresh water before the darkness fell. Also they would need to go and search for their boat, then make sure the people who attacked them were alone and not a part of a larger group. Hunters or warriors, it didn't matter. They would be incensed and blood-thirsty now, not about to let even the recluse old leader shelter the culprits.

Was he or was he not?

The question kept nagging, despite her attempts to think about practical, necessary things. He came out of nowhere, from the distant lands of the Crooked Tongues. He could not speak their tongues properly. He needed his young companion to speak for him, to explain. And yet, they all listened – her, Jikonsahseh, and now the powerful, deranged Onondaga leader. They all listened to his wild, impossible idea of making peace with their avowed enemies; people like this youth, the young, violent man, the perfect representative of his Flint savages.

What was his story? she wondered. Why did he follow the Crooked Tongues man, going after him and doing anything required with no questions asked? With no hatred clouding her mind, she had looked at him this afternoon time after time, curious. Brave and resourceful, the scar-faced youth had saved them this morning, fighting like a true warrior. But wasn't he too young to be such? And what were these long, twisted scars covering his face and his chest? Such a strange-looking pattern. As though he had been a captive warrior once upon a time, having gone through some alien ceremony of torture? Was this how he and the Crooked Tongues man met? Had Two Rivers done the unspeakable, saving a captive from a traditional death?

"I'm going to look for our boat." The voice of the Flint youth jerked her from her reverie, making her jump. "Before it gets dark."

"He needs you to translate, doesn't he?" She looked at him, taking in the stubborn frown and the club grasped tightly in the unharmed arm.

"They are too busy arguing, not stopping for enough time to translate anything." He grinned. "I suppose they understand each other well enough. And anyway, I think Two Rivers wants to be left alone with that man now. Our presence makes the old leader irritable. I think he fights the urge to grab his pretty flint-spiked club every time his eyes are resting on me."

She grinned back, piling the clean bowls one on top of another. "You do this to people, you know? I feel the same most of the time."

The twinkle in his eyes was too obvious to miss. "Onondaga People are intolerable snobs."

"Yet, you don't look as though in a hurry to head for your own lands," she said, balancing the plates on one hand. "Why?"

He frowned. "Two Rivers needs me. I will not leave him running all over the enemy countryside alone and unprotected."

"If Hionhwatha decides to join him, he won't be alone anymore."

"Oh, please!" His snort was loud, full of doubt. "He can't trust the crazy old man. He needs a companion, a partner, a friend who will be there for no other reason than to help, with no hidden motives. A person he can trust."

She watched him, surprised by the passion his words radiated. In the soft afternoon light he looked handsome, a perfect warrior, the scars not marring the clearness of his face and his masculine chest, but adding to it, like a war paint.

"Why are you with him?" she asked, feeling as though in a dream, strangely comfortable, not caring that he was the enemy of her people anymore.

He peered at her, puzzled. "I told you why."

"You told me how you feel about him, but what I want to know is why? Why did you follow him in the first place?"

His face darkened all of a sudden, losing much of the magical attraction it held before.

"It's a long story and it's unimportant. I believe in him and in what he is doing. I will stay with him and help him all I can." Shifting his gaze, he shrugged, but she saw a glimpse of misery peeking out of the large eyes. "I will leave him only one time, when I'll cross the Great Sparkling Water once again. But I do hope it won't take me long to come back."

"Back to the Crooked Tongues? Why would you do this?"

"I made a promise." His voice was nothing but a whisper, hardly audible in the strengthening breeze. "And I will keep it, even if I die doing this."

That didn't make much sense, either. "A promise? You promised him to go back?"

"No, it's something else, something different." He began turning away. "Another long story." Suddenly, his gaze was back upon her, full of bewilderment and a painful expectation. "Will you help me if I ask you for help one day?"

Taken aback, she stared at him, her stomach twisting. "Yes, I will help you. Well, maybe. In what way?"

"Will you shelter a girl?" He hesitated. "A foreign girl. Will you take care of her if I can't, make her feel at home?"

"A girl? What girl? And where would I shelter her? At Jikonsahseh's hut?"

He shook his head vigorously. "No, it won't happen that soon. You will be back in your town by then." He shifted uneasily, dropping his gaze. "I thought... Maybe... If Two Rivers made a good progress by then..." His face twisted with pain as his free hand strayed for his hair, forgetting the bloodied bandage. "Forget it! I don't know what I'm talking about."

Involuntarily, she caught his arm as he began turning away.

"I will help you," she said, peering into the darkness of his eyes, willing the desperation away. "Whenever it happens, wherever I am by then, I will help you with that girl of yours."

His gaze clung to hers, as hopeful as that of a child. "I will never forget if you do. I will repay you your kindness. Always..." His voice broke as he turned his head away with a suspicious haste.

"It is for her you have to cross back," she said, making it a statement.

He just nodded.

"When?"

"I don't know. When we are more established, when I have a place for her to live." He shook his head, his shoulders sagging.

"A long time from now. Too long."

"Will she wait?"

"Yes, I think she will." A convulsive sigh. "But who knows? Many things may happen, things that would cause her not to wait."

"Then go and bring her now. I will take care of her. We will put her at Jikonsahseh's until you are advised of your plans better."

He turned back so abruptly, they almost bumped into each other. "Do you think?" The intensity of his gaze seemed to burn her skin. "Do you think it would be wise to do that, to bring her here now? Oh, Mighty Spirits!" Once again, he ran his hands through his hair, not wincing with the pain even. "If I go now, I can do it in less than a moon. Well before the first snow. I can do it so quickly. We are close to the usual crossing point here, anyway. Just a day of sail, really. Oh, all the great and small spirits!" His eyes focused back on her, sparkling, making him look irresistibly attractive again. "Oh, I will repay you for all of it, I swear. Anytime, anywhere, anything you will want, I'll do for you."

Warmed by such ardently open gratitude, she laughed. "I did nothing yet. After I have taken care of your girl, feel grateful all you like." Grinning, she raised her eyebrows. "You are still my enemy, don't forget this. Even if I will help you with your Crooked Tongues beauty. Two Rivers is yet to make us into allies."

His grin matched hers. "He already did, Onondaga girl. We are already allies, and we didn't even notice. And that man, your formidable old leader," a light wave indicated the hut behind their backs, "he is with us, too, even if he still tries to maintain his dignity by arguing. He is no match for Two Rivers. No one is." Another beaming look. "And he will manage to do it to all our people. All of them, Onondaga girl. He can do everything. The Right-Handed Twin himself and all the sky spirits and the good *uki* are watching over him, helping him along, eager to see him succeeding."

She caught her breath. "Is he the messenger of the Great Spirits? Was he sent here by the Right-Handed Twin himself?"

Holding her breath, she peered into his eyes, afraid of his answer. Whatever he said would make her feel bad, she knew. A mysterious person from the mists of the Great Lake, or just the regular man with irregular thinking – she wanted him to be both.

His smile beamed at her, surprisingly open. "I think he is. But I can't tell you for sure. I'm not a man with visions and dreams. I just see what I see. But I wish I could see what he sees." Shaking his head, as though trying to get rid of a vision he claimed he never saw, he let out a deep breath. "But I can tell you that in his homelands there was a prophecy. Crooked Tongues feared him. They looked up to him, with expectation and fear. And there were those who mistrusted him, too. He was surrounded by stories, and he had powerful dreams. I know that for certain. One dream included Little Falls. That's why we were heading this way. Little Falls has a part in all this, and I just happened to be from there. Or maybe it was the part of the prophecy, too. Maybe the Great Spirits brought me to the Crooked Tongues' lands for a reason." His face darkened, closed. "In Little Falls there was the prophecy too, about me and my brother. Well, maybe…"

She listened, drinking in every word, fascinated, but his voice trailed off, as his face turned yet darker, his features again twisted by anger, or more likely, with anguish.

"What clan did you belong to back at Little Falls?" she asked, wishing to bring the cheerful youth back. "I've been to your town, remember? I spent two long, annoying moons there." She grinned into his eyes, challenging. "I hated every man and woman in that place, but I do remember many of them. I can tell you about your family."

But the shadows did not disperse, obscuring his eyes, making him look older, just a scar-faced warrior, dangerous and fierce.

"They are not there," he said quietly. "None of them."

Oh, Mighty Spirits! She let her breath out, understanding

now too well.

"Even your mother?" she whispered.

"Her before all the rest." His words were hardly audible, no more than the rustling in the bushes. She wasn't sure he had said it at all.

The anguish was too visible now, lurking too near the surface. Or maybe it was always there, but she had been too angry at him to notice before.

Unable not to do so, she touched his arm. *"Wipe away the tears, cleanse—"*

"Don't!" He jerked away, shrinking from her touch. "I don't want to hear that. Not these words!" Breathing heavily, he turned away. "The accursed prophecy!" The words seeped with difficulty through his clenched teeth. "Living among the Crooked Tongues, I used to think that the prophecy was nothing, a mistake, someone's silly, misinterpreted dream. But now, now I understand. The prophecy was right, but oh Mighty Spirits, sometimes I wish it had never existed."

"What did it say?" she asked quietly. "What did his prophecy say? And what was yours? Was it the same thing?"

He shook his head. "I don't know. I had never been told about mine. It's just that the people were always whispering, looking at us, me and my brother. And Father was always proud and expectant. He thought we were destined to destroy our enemies." His grin twisted as he shook his head again. "Speaking of wrong interpretation, this one, apparently, went as wrong as it can go."

"And his prophecy?" She motioned back toward the hut.

"I don't know exactly what it is, either. He didn't like to talk about it. He hated that prophecy." Frowning, he let out a reluctant grin. "It feels like gossiping, to talk about him in this way. Ask him, maybe he'll tell you. He obviously likes to talk to you."

She felt the warmth spreading into her face, making her cheeks burn. "He likes to talk to anyone who is prepared to listen. He talks a lot." His widening smile and narrowing eyes made the burning in her face worse. "Stop staring at me like that. There is nothing going on between him and me. I just like to hear what he says."

"Speaking of gossip," he said, laughing into her face, openly amused now, his previous gloom receding, but not disappearing, not entirely. "In the Crooked Tongues lands, women used to make fools of themselves when it came to him. Half of the female population of the town was dancing through the social parts of the ceremonies, drinking him in with their gazes, hoping to catch his eye. They say he had his share of lovemaking, too. But usually, he was too busy to pay attention." He beamed into her eyes, not deterred by her direful frown, as it seemed. "Well, he doesn't seem too busy to spend his time with you, even though now he should be occupied by his mission and nothing else. He finds time to talk to you. He brought you here with us, to help us find the way, allegedly, but I'm sure he wouldn't have dragged anyone else to help us find your formidable old leader. We would have managed to find him all by ourselves. Think about it, pretty Onondaga girl."

"Oh, stop this nonsense! You don't understand what you are talking about." She stomped her foot. "I can't believe you are telling me this now. It is not what you are thinking it is. It is not!"

But his eyes lost their spark all of a sudden, darkening, concentrating.

"Hush," he whispered, grabbing her arm and pressing it lightly, signaling her to keep quiet.

With the morning events still fresh in her mind, she didn't argue this time, didn't try to take her hand away. Following his gaze, she looked at the trees, already darkening in the dimming light. She could feel him as tense as an overstretched bowstring beside her, and as dangerous. The laughing youth was gone again, replaced by the fierce warrior.

"What is it?" she whispered, but he pressed her arm again, listening. The rustling in the trees was that of the wind, she knew, and yet...

"Get down!"

His scream echoed in her ears as his arm pushed her hard, sending her sprawling into the damp earth beside the wooden cistern. She hit it with her shoulder, but the heavy container did not topple on top of them as their bodies met the ground. Out of instinct, she threw her arms forward, so her elbows absorbed the painful impact, her face brushing against the uneven surface but lightly, scratching her cheek. Desperate to roll away from the reach of his arm, she pushed him away, but he kept pressing her down, uncompromising.

"Don't move. Stay behind that thing," he breathed, crouching above her, squeezing behind the hard wood. "Stop wriggling!"

She paused, trying to understand what he said. The cistern shook, and now her mind absorbed other sound. The dim hiss. One more time, and an arrow swished, flying above their improvised shelter.

"What in the name…"

"Don't move, not yet," he repeated, and she raised her head carefully, to see his strained, ashen face, his eyes narrow and concentrated, the pattern of scars reassuring, somehow. "The moment I tell you, run for the house. As fast as you can."

"And you?" she breathed.

"I'll do it, too. In a good time."

The cistern shook once again, absorbing another arrow, probably. Then it turned quiet.

"Now!" he whispered, pushing her again.

Struggling to get back to her feet, cursing the stupid dress that kept hindering her progress, she wanted to tell him to stop pushing her, or giving her orders for that matter – *who did he think he was?* – but the urgency in his face stopped her words.

"Come with me," she whispered, instead. "Don't stay here to fight—"

"Go!" he hissed, and if not for the club clutched now tightly in both hands, she knew he would shove her again, harder now. Self-assured skunk!

Giving him a look that was supposed to convey her opinion of him, she rushed into the open, her heart beating fast. Just a few paces, ten at the most. The screen covering the entrance was already pushed aside, with both older men there, clutching their weapons, ready to fight.

Their sight reassured her, and she doubled her efforts, but another hiss made her stumble, pushing her forward, in the silliest of ways. The earth jumped into her face once again, and for a moment, she suspected that her scar-faced companion was running after her, pushing her again to make her run faster.

This time the fall was more painful, because her right arm did not react properly to stop the collusion. Blinded with pain, mud filling her eyes, she spat the earth from her mouth, revolted by the salty taste. She needed to get up in order to reach the entrance, she knew. He had told her to do so. But pressing her palms against the earth in order to push herself up didn't help for some reason. It just made the pain in her shoulder explode like a thunderbolt, piercing her whole body. *What was happening?*

Through the wild pounding of her heart, she could hear the hurried footsteps, and then she was lifted off the earth, the grip of the arms around her making her pain worse, the swaying of the movement unbearable, nauseating. However, she didn't care, because she knew it was the Crooked Tongues man carrying her now. She could feel his smell and the warmth of his body, and it reassured her, made her heart slow down. Whatever happened, he would make it right again, she knew, relaxing and closing her eyes, giving in to the nauseating sensation.

CHAPTER 12

Stumbling into the safety of the dim entrance, Two Rivers rushed toward the pile of hides, his worry mounting. He needed to get back and see that the wolf cub was all right, but the girl was bleeding in his arms. He could feel the warm flow trickling down his arm, could feel her clinging to him, stiff with pain.

"Don't move," he told her, laying her on the soft blanket, careless of the stains. Hionhwatha would be furious, he knew, at this further damage to his house and its possessions.

"What happened?" she mumbled, trying to get up.

"Stop wriggling. I want to see your wound."

No shaft fluttered out of the fleshy part of her upper arm, but the cut was wide enough, seeping with blood. No more damage as far as he could see, no broken bones. Good!

"Stay here until I come back," he told her, jumping to his feet. There was no time to talk to her, to reassure her, but she didn't argue and this pleased him, too. A brave little thing.

"Is the youth still out there?" he asked the Onondaga man, who towered near the entrance, clutching a spear. The man had a whole arsenal of different weapons, apparently.

"Yes, the stupid Flint boy has no sense to follow your woman. He is still behind the water bin. They will shoot him the moment they circumvent my clearing." The man frowned direfully. "Or when they decide to charge."

Two Rivers bit his lips. "They won't charge that fast. Their vantage point is good, judging by the accuracy of their shooting. They are probably four, five people. No more than that." He shrugged. "Otherwise they would have circumvented it from the beginning."

"They will come out the moment your stupid companion is here. Whether he makes it here or not."

"He should stay where he is." Coming closer, Two Rivers cupped his mouth with his palms. "Don't come out," he shouted, hoping that his people's tongue would confuse their attackers into misunderstanding his words if they could hear him. "Stay there for now."

He could see the youth nodding, shifting into a better position, ready to fight.

"I guess they are the rest of the party that attacked them this morning," he said, glancing at their host, feeling guilty.

The man shrugged. "What does it matter? No one came to attack me in this place before you appeared. Some tidings of peace you bring."

Two Rivers shook his head, grinning, relieved. The man seemed to be more alive now, vigorous, even excited. There was no real anger in his words.

"We'll have to fight for this peace, yes. But it will be worth it."

"Will it?" Hionhwatha turned to glance at the girl, who had stifled a groan as she tried to sit up. "Keep an eye on the clearing while I see to your wild fox."

"She is not a wild—" he began hotly, but the man was already on his way, waving his hand in dismissal.

"Yes, I heard all about it. Wise woman, plight of our people, tidings of peace again. Spare your oratory for quieter times."

He tensed as more arrows swished around the clearing. Pressing against the pole supporting the doorway, he peeked out carefully. No figure crouched behind the wooden cistern anymore, and he scanned the rest of the open space, worried. What was the wolf cub up to?

"What are you doing?" he breathed, not daring to shout it out, but gesturing forcefully when he spotted Tekeni rolling to reach the nearby cluster of bushes, avoiding the touch of another flying missile by a miracle, as it seemed.

The youth pressed against the ground, trying to minimize his visibility. Twisting his body, he seemed to be studying the way the shafts were stuck in the cistern, now behind his back.

"Good thinking," commented Hionhwatha, coming back and standing beside Two Rivers. "He wants to know where exactly they came from and how far from here."

"I see." Against his will, he felt proud. Oh, the wolf cub was a born warrior. "What do we do to help him?"

The large man snorted. "To help him? Nothing. To help us? Quite a lot." Adjusting the quiver of arrows behind his back, the man picked up his bow and placed it beside the flint-spiked club. Only now did Two Rivers notice that the spear was gone, replaced by more convenient weaponry. "Where is his bow?"

"In the bag."

"Tell him to come here or wait on the other side of the house. Behind the back wall," said Hionhwatha curtly, heading for their pack of belongings.

By now he knew the man too well to ask questions.

"Tekeni!"

The youth turned his head carefully.

"Get behind that hut." He didn't dare to gesture, still hoping that the yells in his people's tongue would not be understandable to their attackers. "Meet that man there. Do whatever he says."

After a heartbeat of hesitation, the youth nodded, then began crawling along the bushes, trying to avoid an open ground.

"Do you have another means of getting out?" he asked, as their host straightened up, holding Tekeni's bow. The Onondaga girl, he noticed, was standing too, swaying a little, but holding on. A stubborn fox.

"What do you think?" The man grinned, kicking the bag away from his path. "If your young companion is worthy of something, we will surprise the disgusting pieces of rotten meat. Circumvent them and fall on them from behind."

"I'm coming with you." He reached for the bag, snatching his bow. With Tekeni having his club, this was the only worthwhile weaponry he had been left with, aside from his knife, of course.

"No." The older man was already behind the fireplace, pulling one of the rectangular bark sheets out of the wall, making no visible effort. "Stay and make yourself useful here. Shoot an arrow or two. Maybe roll around the clearing the way he did. Make them think we are still here." Another sheet of bark came out, letting some of the afternoon light into the dimness of the room. "The girl can help. She can make noise, scream or cry. No matter how, you two keep their attention here."

"I will." Resigned to the necessity of receiving orders from the former Onondaga leader, Two Rivers rushed back toward the doorway, relieved to see Tekeni already out of sight, safely behind the back wall of this hut, he hoped.

Adjusting his own quiver, he made sure his knife was within an easy reach, then picked an arrow and rushed outside, lingering for long enough to shoot in the general direction of the swaying trees to announce his presence. Satisfied, he listened to the familiar swish as he dived into the bushes Tekeni had crouched behind earlier. Now what?

He peeked out carefully. By the way the feathered shafts fluttered in the bark of the water bin, he could tell that their attackers were at some distance, shooting upwards and not straight away. They could see their clearing but not very well. *How many of them?*

Judging by the volleys of shooting they must have been at least five or more. Maybe he should have been more insistent on coming along with their irritable host? But then…

He shrugged. Those people were not exceptionally smart, if all they did was waylay this dwelling and take a good shooting position. A smarter move would have included a well organized attack timed to come from two different directions. He would have done this, and he had never been held to be a brilliant warrior. Anyone would think about it. And if anyone…

He looked around again, his senses honed, tuned to the sounds of the deepening dusk. No, it was not wise to leave a wounded girl here all alone. It was good that he stayed. Involuntarily, he glanced at the house. Sure enough, she was standing at the doorway, silhouetted against the darkness of the inside. Leaning on one of the poles with her wounded shoulder, she clutched a spear in another hand, looking so wild he wanted to laugh. A female warrior.

"Go back," he whispered loudly, gesturing her to get in.

"I can bring you the spear," she shouted, looking as though about to do just that.

"No! Go back, go inside."

Their exchange brought another volley of arrows, three at once. So maybe there were only three shooters. Yet, weren't they supposed to run out of ammunition by now?

He measured the way to the water bin. The large container offered a better protection and more opportunities to observe the other side of the clearing. *Were these people truly so dense as to just lie there and shoot for the whole afternoon?*

A zigzagged dash saw him to his new position still unharmed, but the wound in his side, the reminder of the earlier encounter with their formidable host, began bleeding again, and he was hungry and dead tired. The damn ambushers! How long would it take Hionhwatha and Tekeni to reach them? And would they manage, two warriors, one old and not at his best and one way too young?

No sound came from the small trail leading toward the lake, still, his nerves prickled and he sat leaning against the warm wood of the cistern, watching the trees. The afternoon breeze made them rustle softly, but sometimes an occasional branch would creak a little too abruptly for his peace of mind. The clearing behind his improvised shelter was too quiet. He cursed and took his eyes off the silent trees.

"Throw something," he called, peering out carefully and seeing her still lingering at the doorway.

She needed no explanation. Amused, he watched her diving back into the darkness. Shortly thereafter, a large wooden bowl came flying out. It drew a small volley, consisting of merely a pair of arrows. Maybe he should run out, back toward the bushes, he thought. What if one or two of the shooters went away, to try to circumvent this place? Hionhwatha counted on him to keep their attention.

Glancing again at the woods surrounding the trail, he began getting up, pulling an arrow out of his quiver. Just another mad dash, accompanied by a quick shooting. Nothing challenging. He'd be crouching behind the low bushes before he knew it—

Two figures sprang into his view as he began straightening up, prepared to race. Having taken his eyes off the trees already, he caught just a glimpse of a fast movement. But one glimpse was enough. In less than a heartbeat, he was on his knee, shooting at the first moving silhouette, his heart throbbing in his ears.

It was a good shot. The man was thrown back into the bushes, the feathered shaft wavering in his chest, its colorfulness not a part of the surrounding green. Not spending his time on watching, Two Rivers jumped onto his feet, tearing his knife out of its sheath, but the second man was already upon him, nimble and forceful, his club swishing, his face clear of paint, glistening with sweat.

Abandoning the attempt to get to his knife, Two Rivers threw himself backwards, stumbling over the cistern. It toppled with a loud smack, taking the attention of his attacker away.

Grateful for the moment of respite, he scrambled back to his feet, seeking any sort of an improvised weapon to meet the next onslaught, which didn't make him wait. As the man leapt forward, he pushed the overturned bin with all his might, making the invader waver as it crashed against his lower body. Heedless of the arrows, he rushed back toward the house, needing to reach a weapon, any weapon, the touch of the knife in his palm reassuring.

He could hear the hurried footsteps behind his back, and his body threw itself sideways, out of an instinct as much as a thoughtful reaction. His senses in panic, he slashed out without aiming, feeling the proximity of the man more than seeing it, eyes catching the last of the sun sparkling off the vicious spike that adorned his attacker's club. It swished so close, yet somehow he still managed to tilt out of its reach as his knife felt a familiar sensation of the tearing flesh. Obviously not enough to make his enemy fall, the cut made the man, at least, pause.

He calculated fast. To throw himself at the man and try to best him in the close hand-to-hand seemed to be, as always, the best opportunity under such circumstances. And yet, he was wounded already, and not at his best, with the way to the house and its stocks of weapons looking temptingly open.

The man clutched his club with both hands, bringing it up, pressing his lips, obviously in pain. He felt the pain pulsating in his own side, too. No, he was in no condition to gamble on his rival's lowered guard. The moment he pounced, the club would be waiting for him, to meet him half way.

Glancing at the clearing but still keeping his rival in sight, his eyes caught a movement of a nearing figure, running in an uneven gait. Before his mind absorbed this new information, his instincts told him that it was her, disheveled, pale and smeared with mud, but her, a friendly presence.

He didn't pause to think about it. It was not an enemy, and nothing else mattered. Ducking another onslaught of the club, not as well directed as the previous ones, he felt the rough shaft of a spear being thrust into his hands, his eyes catching a glimpse of her huge, wide opened, gaping eyes, feeling the trembling of her hands. Oh, the best of timing. She was sent to him by the Great Spirits themselves!

He didn't try to cast his newly acquired treasure. The advantage of the longer-reaching weapon was too good to miss. A few loosely directed thrusts and the man lost half of his previously aggressive confidence, lingering before each sway of his club now, careful of his advances.

She was still there, keeping close, distracting. Swinging his spear out of the heavy club's reach – those were not the weapons to pit one against another – Two Rivers narrowed his eyes, trying to find the opportunity to thrust it toward the man's exposed torso.

"Go back," he tossed toward her, not daring to shift his gaze off the once-again-rising club. "They'll start shooting any moment."

And then it dawned upon him. No arrows crossed the clearing since the beginning of their fight, not a single shot. Hionhwatha and the wolf cub must have found their targets. And they must have been successful.

His excitement welling, he feigned an offensive toward his rival's right arm, lingering, letting the man think he was losing his patience. The bait was promptly taken. He saw the club leaping into the air, intending to crush the spear in two at the very last.

Another heartbeat of hesitation, and he saw the flint of the sturdy cudgel sparkling, descending rapidly, just as his spear slashed downwards, cutting through the man's loincloth and the exposed thigh as it went.

The blood spouted out spectacularly, in a wild gush. For a heartbeat, they all stared, fascinated. The world seemed to stop. Then the man let out a strange sort of a gasp, collapsing all at once, like a cut down tree; one moment alive and dangerous, the next – just a heap of muddied limbs, with his life forces escaping rapidly, pulsating in a magnificent flow, so powerful, so rich in color. A breathtaking sight.

Shaking his head to make it work, Two Rivers looked around, taking in the mess of the previously cozy enclosure, now littered with utensils, studded with arrows, the overturned water cistern creating a muddy puddle, the sprawling bodies adding to the effect. Hionhwatha will be furious, he reflected again, finding the thought amusing. What a wreck!

Her gasp was soft and he felt rather than saw her swaying, waving her hands in the air. To catch her was easy, although he didn't feel too powerful himself at the moment.

"Come," he said, pressing her tightly, enjoying the warmth of her body, although it hurt his wounded side. "I told you to stay in the house and rest. How many times did I tell you that, eh?"

Her trembling was bad, still he wanted to smile as she leaned against him, drained of the last of her strength.

"You never do what you are told, do you?"

"I helped," she whispered, her face tucked into his chest, making it warm with the softness of her breath.

"Yes, you did. And I'm grateful." He stroked her hair, damp and disheveled, full of leaves, but still as pleasant to touch as he expected it to be. "You are a brave woman. I knew it all along. But you're a fighter, too. A warrior. A partner."

He could feel her smile spreading, soft against his chest, and it pleased him, but his senses shouted danger, aware of the unwelcome reactions of his body, battered and exhausted but, apparently, still full of desires.

"I did nothing," she said, squirming to look up at him, her eyes glittering in the muddied paleness of her face, sparkling, expectant. "I just brought you the spear."

"It was enough. It saved us both."

He stared at the dark, glittering depths, seeing the gentle curve of her cheeks and the bold outline of the full lips, slightly opened now, as though expectant. He pressed his own lips tight, but it did not help to fight the magic off. A distance might have helped, he knew, but in order to step aside he would need to unlock his arms, and it was proving impossible, beyond the limits of his strength.

Her gaze deepened, and she seemed to contemplate breaking away too, but evidently, she had not much strength left, either. A heartbeat of staring and he saw her lips quivering, curving into a sort of an inverted smile, a typically female daring kind of a grin. That was too much. His willpower snapped.

Pressing her tightly, he sought her lips with his, feeling them dry and cracked but pleasing, sending rays of excitement down his chest, all the way to his stomach, setting his body on fire. It was like a swirling current before the waterfalls, determined to drag him along.

He felt her shuddering in his arms, then pressing closer, opening her lips, receiving his with an ardent welcome. The sounds of the clearing receded, disappeared, with nothing left but the feel of her body against his, the stiff, blood-soaked material of their clothes getting in his way.

His palms sought frantically, craving the feel of her skin, but as they pushed through the open part of her dress, she winced and cried out, and he remembered her wound, and the sounds returned all at once, the chirping of the late birds and the buzzing of the mosquitoes, and the wind rustling in the treetops and the bushes all around them; *and the possibility of more enemies lurking.* It was not the time, nor the place, and he let her go, embarrassed, supporting her and taking her weight just in case, but with his arms only now.

"I'm sorry," he muttered, clearing his throat. She was leaning heavily against his arm, shivering. "Come."

Another scan of the clearing and the trees all around. How damn reckless! Had he lost his mind entirely? The men he'd just killed might have been a part of a larger group, advancing faster than the rest. And the people who were shooting at them might have been heading here too, in case Hionhwatha and Tekeni didn't succeed in catching them off guard. And what had he been doing? Lusting after a woman. Losing his mind to a mindless spell of desire. The silliest youngster of no experience would not have behaved this way.

"Come," he said, avoiding her gaze.

Supporting her, taking most of her weight, although his arm had gone numb, trembling with an effort, he hurried her across the open space, ready to duck should a familiar hiss tear the silence. Did Hionhwatha and the wolf cub manage to get rid of the attackers? He felt a stab of anxiety. *Oh, Great Spirits, please keep them both safe.*

She protested when he led her toward the cluster of hides at the far corner of the darkening hut. "I'm feeling better now," she said, but he made her lie down, still avoiding her gaze.

"You need to rest and gather your strength." He looked around. "You also need to put more of those leaves upon your wound. It's bleeding again."

"You are bleeding, too," she said, frowning, peering at his side.

"We'll take care of our wounds when Hionhwatha is back. He knows his way with herbs. I don't." He shrugged. "But you need to rest now and stop running around. Rest, Onondaga girl. For real. Lie down here and do nothing. That's what rest means."

She met his gaze, for the first time since what happened back on the edge of the clearing, a frown and a smile fighting each other across her face. It glimmered softly in the deepening dusk, a beautifully painted, exquisitely carved wooden mask. He clenched his fists, fighting the urge to touch it, to run his fingers alongside the soft line of her cheek.

Her eyes narrowed, the uncertainty in them too obvious to miss.

"I'm sorry about what happened," he said, clearing his throat again. "It was rotten of me to do that."

The smile won, and its sudden appearance took his breath away. It was like a rainbow in the brightening, drops-sprinkled sky.

"It was not entirely your fault." Her smile widened, turned mischievous. "It was as rotten of me to do this to you."

He narrowed his eyes, feeling his own grin peeking out against his will. "It's always the man's fault, isn't it?"

"Not always. But usually, yes." She laughed, then winced again and shifted her wounded shoulder with an effort. "Usually yes, it would be the man's fault."

"But with you, nothing is usual, is it? You are an unusual woman."

The twinkle in her eyes deepened. "Oh well, of course. I'm the woman who had accepted the Good Tiding of Peace, a brave woman who had seen the plight of her people before anyone else, am I not?"

This he could understand with almost no difficulty, having heard this same phrase only half a day ago, translated by Tekeni in exactly the same words.

"Oh, you are, you are that. But there is a problem. You are beautiful." Unable to fight the urge anymore, he let his finger slide over the curve of her cheek. "Sometimes I wish you were old and ugly."

Her eyes clung to his face, expectant and afraid at the same time.

"Why?" Her question rang strangely in the dimness of the closed up space.

He felt the rays of excitement running down his palms, like flashes of lightning in the thunderstorm, shooting through his stomach, making it tighten.

"I can't concentrate with you around. I can't think of my mission." Gaining confidence, his fingers lingered around her lips, feeling them out, remembering how they had felt against his only a short while ago, this frightening sensation of losing control. "That's why I sent you back to the boat this morning. I wanted to be fully there when meeting your former leader. I didn't want to be distracted."

His hand slipped toward her neck, marveling at its softness. Her skin was creamy and smooth, delicately tender, hidden in the depths of her dress, where no sun and no elements could have reached it. Again his body was proving impossible to control, demanding more, to taste these lips, to have this perfect creation of the Right-Handed Twin all for himself. The way her eyes peered at him, enthralled and as though spellbound, didn't help.

Then his ears picked up the sound of people coming down through the bushes, picking their way carelessly, sure of themselves. Grabbing the spear, he leaped toward the doorway, in time to see the figures of Hionhwatha and Tekeni spilling into the clearing, walking in perfect unison.

His relief was vast, pushing his disappointment away. Oh, their timing could not have been better, he knew, rushing outside, his heart still pounding, not in unison with what his mind was telling him.

CHAPTER 13

It was good to be back at the rancid smelling hut. Contented, Tekeni stretched, then made himself comfortable, half sitting half lying upon a hide he had been offered, albeit reluctantly, by their formidable host.

What a man, he thought, admiring the former Onondaga leader against his will, the memories of their afternoon forage in the woods surfacing; the way the man had led their way, sure and confident, picking his step in the thickest of the trees, unerring, following the invisible trail, closing on their ambushers, turning the hunters into a hunted prey.

The archers, three of them, had no time to even get an idea of what came over them, before it was over. There was no need to employ Two Rivers' club even. Quick, well-coordinated shooting put an end to the crouching men, leaving them sprawling or thrashing about in agony, their end near.

Muttering quiet prayers to see the departing spirits off, Hionhwatha had picked up their weapons, then straightened up.

"You shoot well," he said curtly, giving Tekeni a look slightly less cold than his usual ones, with a flicker of appreciation sparkling in the dark depths. "Take the rest of their bows, and their knives. Tomorrow we'll come back and give them proper rites."

Not making sure if his orders were followed, the man turned around and stalked off. Still, the words had been uttered, making Tekeni's heart swell with pride. He had, indeed, done well, and not only while shooting. He gave the old leader no trouble, following the silent gesturing, interpreting those in a correct way, helping the man to implement his plan, which might prove more difficult to do if alone. Oh yes, he had done well, and he knew that the fierce old warrior appreciated his help. Somehow, he was sure of that, and it made him feel good.

He watched both men sitting beside the small fire, poring over elaborately woven strings of shells, talking quietly. Their words floated in the darkness, not touching him. He would be required to translate any moment, he knew, not minding this newfound duty of his. Yet, to just lie in the semidarkness, drifting between the sleep and the reality was good, relaxing. It was as though they were still on the other side of the Great Lake, enjoying a little peace and quiet before plunging into the dangers of their projected mission.

He sighed. Maybe Two Rivers had enjoyed himself back then, loitering upon the deserted shores of the Great Sparkling Water, but he, Tekeni, felt nothing of the sort. Recovering from the wounds was bad enough, but coping with his anger, his frustration with being dragged around and yet again decided upon, and on top of it all, his desperate longing for Seketa – no, the restful days on the other side of the Great Lake were anything but pleasant.

Squinting against the fire, he tried to see the pictures it drew. What was she doing now? Was she calm and asleep on her bunk in the Beaver Clan's longhouse, or was she wandering about, thinking, remembering maybe? How long would it take her to forget all about him, the troublesome foreigner who did nothing but complicate her life?

He ground his teeth. She would give up on waiting, unless he hurried. Even though loving him the way she said she did, she would not wait forever. The Onondaga girl thought he should go and fetch her right away, and this woman would know.

Turning his head, he sought her dark silhouette, spread upon a small blanket, half sleeping half awake, or maybe just drifting the way he did. She should have been resting, he knew, sleeping inside, comfortable upon the pile of hides. Her wound was not dangerous, yet she had lost a considerable amount of life forces, bleeding for long enough to make her look frighteningly pale, unable to walk without support. She should have been resting, but of course, she did not. This girl was a law unto herself. And what can one do with such a thing?

"Do you need something?" he asked, catching her eyes resting upon him, reflecting the light of the fire.

"No." She shook her head quietly. "I think I fell asleep before."

"You should sleep. Want me to help you to the corner with the hides?"

"No, I want to listen." As her gaze shifted toward the dark figures, he followed it, eyeing the conversing men, curious now too. "Why aren't you translating?"

"I haven't been asked to."

"Oh, I thought you were already fast asleep, wolf cub," called Two Rivers from across the fire. "Actually, I thought you both were wandering the worlds of the spirits just now. You should, if you ask me."

"And so are all of us," muttered the girl under her breath.

Two Rivers didn't seem to notice, his attention back on the wide string he held.

"So, actually, every one of these *wampum* strings is commemorating an event," he said, addressing their host again.

Hionhwatha narrowed his eyes, but when Tekeni translated, he nodded, his face sealed.

"Tell him that yes, he can put it this way," said the former leader, grimacing direfully. "Each pattern is dedicated to one person, or event, if he likes to think about it in these terms."

Curious, Tekeni came closer, crouching beside them, disregarding yet another dark look of their disagreeable host. Back in the woods the old warrior had been stern but not hostile, while the hut seemed to bring the worst out of him again. Tekeni shrugged. If he was asked to translate, he could very well see what they were talking about.

Two Rivers picked another, longer and thinner, strip of white shells, dotted with only occasional purple.

"This can be a good way," he muttered, as though talking to

himself.

"A good way to do what?" This time the Onondaga leader seemed to understand without Tekeni's explanation.

"To commemorate more than a person's personal memories." Still immersed in studying the string, Two Rivers frowned. "If we are to reach an agreement, you and I, for example, we could make a string to reflect on the nature of it. It would help us remember. It would make us more committed to what was agreed upon."

Hionhwatha's eyes flickered. "It's plenty of work. You should train your memory to remember your agreements rather than rely on others to weave your strings for you."

"I don't doubt my memory." Two Rivers nodded in his turn, acknowledging Tekeni's translation. "But if many people were involved in the meeting and the agreement they reached was complicated, then such a string would help if woven in a special manner and approved by all the leaders involved."

"What are you thinking?"

From the corner of his eyes, Tekeni saw the girl leaning forward, trying to hear better.

"In the sort of a meeting you held two summers ago," went on Two Rivers, oblivious of their piquing attention. "If you were to reach people's consent, a string commemorating it would help to make the agreement more… lawful."

"Those meetings achieved nothing," grunted Hionhwatha, his face turning into stone.

"We will hold another one in the not-very-far future."

"I wish you luck."

Two Rivers' grin was wide, his eyes holding the gaze of the grieving man, their warmth wonderful. "We will do it together."

"We will never succeed. Maybe his people," a curt nod indicated Tekeni. "Maybe they would be prepared to let you talk. Well, for a short while, at least. I doubt the fierce savages would let you live long enough to sound half of your far-fetched ideas." The pursed lips pressed tighter. "But my people? My people will not listen to you at all. They are led by Tadodaho, the most despicable man our earthly world has ever seen. You will never succeed in gathering my people and making them listen. They are too afraid after... after what happened."

"What sort of a man is he?" Two Rivers eyes didn't waver from the darkening face of their host, and Tekeni stopped translating, afraid to miss a word of what had been said. Neither of the men seemed to notice.

"He is an able man. Good warrior, good leader." Hionhwatha's gaze was firm upon his hands that toyed with a thin string they held. "He knows no fear, and no misgivings. He listens to no one. His opinions are strong and unwavering, and his temper frays most easily." A pause. "He is a strange person. Many people are afraid of him." The dispassionate voice began trailing off. "His right hand is short and withered. Many think he has some of the power of the Left-Handed Twin and his minions."

"You think that, too." Two Rivers' voice rang clearly, his words a statement.

Hionhwatha shrugged.

"Since you left, this man's grip on the Onondaga People tightened. No one dares to sound his opinion if it contradicts those of Tadodaho. Many settlements are suffering quietly, not even squirming in his firm grip. Many people would welcome the change. Many would welcome your coming back. It is true, isn't it?"

Now the Crooked Tongues man's gaze rested upon the girl, who straightened up abruptly, as though awakening from a dream. Tekeni translated hastily.

"Yes, yes, it's true." Shyly, she looked at the old leader, whose eyes were now upon her as well. "I haven't been to our towns for the past season or so, but I remember what happened since..." She cleared her throat. "Since you left."

"Where are you coming from?" asked the man curtly, voice low.

"The town of High Springs. It's just two days' walk from Onondaga Town."

"I know where High Springs is!" The old irritability was there, bringing the violent recluse back. "Did you attend any of the meetings?"

She swallowed visibly. "My man went to attend both of them." Another painful pause. "He was greatly impressed. He loved your ideas. He said you were talking a plain good sense."

"Who was he?"

"Just a young warrior. No one of importance."

Glancing at Two Rivers, Tekeni saw the man leaning forward, listening avidly, his gaze glued to her face, intent, boring into her, its expression strange. There was something anxious in those eyes, something painfully expectant, as though he was trying to understand her and not her words. It was as though he needed her to say the right things but not because of the old leader.

Contemplating a quick translation, Tekeni decided against it. Whatever Two Rivers' problem was, this dialogue was important, and his whispering might serve as a distraction, making their host dive back into his hostile, uncommunicative shell.

"What did he tell you about these meetings?" The interrogation went on without interruptions.

"He told me you wanted to unite our people, to organize a council of the entire nation. He said it was a good idea. He was angry with the people who disrupted the first gathering."

"Pity he didn't come to talk to me," muttered Hionhwatha. "I could have used young men such as him." The large eyes narrowed. "What happened to him?"

"He was killed. Later... on one of the raids." Her voice was still clear, but there was a strident note to it.

"And you?" The stony gaze turned stonier. "Why did you leave your people?"

The defiant frown brought back the girl Tekeni had come to know well through their journey and their stay at Jikonsahseh. "I didn't leave. I was captured."

"Oh." Hionhwatha's nod and half a grin held a measure of a

grim amusement. "That explains your present-day company. Not very well, but better than if you still belonged to High Springs."

"I will return to High Springs," she said, her frown deepening. "I just needed to do something, to pay a debt."

All of a sudden, she glanced at Two Rivers, her gaze wary and questioning, dropping back toward the fire with an indecent haste. Puzzled, Tekeni watched the Crooked Tongues man frowning, leaning back, thrown out of balance, too, somehow.

"High Springs may be a good place to start." Hionhwatha shrugged, oblivious of his guests' sudden discomfort. "This place and the surrounding villages might listen more readily if you start talking to the right people."

"Yes, I agree," Two Rivers nodded thoughtfully, back to his calm, confident self. The girl, noticed Tekeni, looked up, her face bright and expectant. "Tadodaho and his town should be left until we have a strong following."

"We?" repeated Hionhwatha, his eyebrows lifted high.

"Yes, we," said Two Rivers firmly, standing the direful glare. "You start to talk to High Springs and its people, while I do the same in Little Falls and its surroundings."

"Still want to test the Flint People and their patience, don't you?"

"Yes, I do. I have no choice but to do this. Your people will listen more readily when I come to join you, backed up by the agreement of the Flint People." He shrugged. "And maybe even their neighbors to the west."

"The People of the Standing Stone?" The old leader's laughter rolled between the hut's walls. "And they thought me to be out of my mind."

"Your neighbors to the west will be the next," said Two Rivers, unperturbed.

"And then?"

"And then the People of the Mountains."

Hionhwatha's grin was sudden, full of gloomy amusement. "And then your Crooked Tongues, I presume."

"Maybe. Maybe my people, too."

Two Rivers' darkening face made Tekeni remember the bay and the high cliff facing the lake. Would they agree to listen to this man, if he returned, backed by the united people of this side of the Great Lake? Somehow, he doubted that. This man's country folk were set against him, no matter what he said or did. But maybe when he went there to fetch Seketa, maybe through her…

He shook his head. No! They would never listen, not to the murderers who had fled the town only two short moons ago. But for Seketa, he would rather never cross the Great Sparkling Water again.

He shivered, thinking about the projected journey. The Onondaga girl advised against making Seketa wait. She said he should go and bring her now, to put her in Jikonsahseh's care, until they were done and he, Tekeni, could settle, somehow. And if Two Rivers were to go to High Springs now, instead of Little Falls…

"Why don't you go to High Springs together?" The girl's voice tore the silence that momentarily prevailed.

Tekeni glanced at her, startled by the way she stared at Two Rivers, the hurt in her eyes too obvious to miss.

Two Rivers smiled at her softly. "It has to be done this way."

"Why?"

"Both peoples would listen more readily when the other side is already approached and made willing to talk. This way no one does the first move."

Hionhwatha nodded, shooting a disapproving glance at the girl, who didn't seem to care.

"You will endanger your life for nothing but a slight possibility of being listened to." She peered at the Crooked Tongues man, leaning forward, as though anxious to make him listen. "I do understand why you wanted to go to Little Falls before. This young man was your only ally and his town seemed as good as any to start. But it's changed now. It changed! You have a powerful ally among the Onondagas, a respectable man who knows how best to approach it and what people to talk to. While in Little Falls you have nothing but fierce enemies eager to shed your blood." She drew a deep breath. "Why not talk to our people, and then, only then, backed by a strong nation, go to the east and try to talk to them?"

Two Rivers' smile faded as he watched her, his eyes thoughtful, full of strange softness. He pitied her, realized Tekeni. He didn't wish to hurt her in this way.

"Stop talking nonsense," said Hionhwatha sharply. "Our people will not listen, unless he has something more tangible then his wild idea of the great peace. He needs to make sure both sides are willing to listen before anyone would commit to anything. Why do you break into your elders' discussion with nothing but silly talk?"

But now Tekeni had had enough. "She is not silly. She talked plain good sense. I know we should not interrupt your discussion, but this is not a town council's meeting place. We are in an unusual situation, and so all of us are entitled to sound our opinions."

"And what do you think, wolf cub?" asked Two Rivers, grinning. "Should we go with our original plan or should we change it and make your people wait?"

Tekeni bit his lips, disregarding the squashing gaze coming from Hionhwatha. "Well, I don't know. I suppose... maybe..."

For the life of him, he could not meet the penetrating gaze of his most trusted friend. The man had always been able to see through him, to expect his reactions and read his thoughts. Easily. Too easily for Tekeni's peace of mind. He didn't want to face his own half formulated hopes, let alone chance the perceptive man's ability of deciphering them. If Two Rivers went to High Springs, accompanied by the strong, clearly still influential leader and the girl, then he, Tekeni, would be free to cross the Great Lake now, before the coming of the Freezing Moons. The decision to go to Little Falls would see this plan of his ruined.

He clasped his lips tight. "I don't know. It's up to you to

decide."

"At least one of your followers has some sense," muttered Hionhwatha, but Two Rivers said nothing, studying Tekeni, the smile upon his lips kind, not unlike the smile he had bestowed upon the girl earlier. *Had he pitied him, too?*

"I know, wolf cub. I know what you think, and it will happen. But maybe after the Freezing Moons."

Tekeni felt his heart pausing, sliding down into the emptiness of his stomach.

"I didn't think about that," he muttered. "I will do whatever you do, go wherever you go."

"I know that too, old friend." The penetrating gaze held his, glowing warmly, radiating power. "And I will not let you down, either. I promised to help, and help you I will. We'll make it happen. We'll do it together and in the not-very-far away future."

The silence enveloped them, wondering, uncomfortable silence. He felt the questioning gazes of the other two, and he swallowed hard, trying to calm the wild pounding of his heart.

"Yes," he muttered, shifting his gaze to the safety of the glittering fire. "Yes, I trust you. I always have."

For a while they said nothing, each lapsing into their own uncomfortable thoughts. He wouldn't cross the Great Lake, not before the Awakening Season, thought Tekeni, his stomach heavy, mind empty, indifferent in a strange way. He would go to his hometown, instead. Little Falls, the town of his childhood.

He thought about the people he knew, boys he used to play with, snotty girls they used to tease, he and his brother and their best friend Anowara, a thin, quick, mischievous boy. And there was this pretty little thing from the neighboring longhouse, Father's closest friend's daughter, Kahontsi. They used to play together, and he used to envy her brother for being older and stronger. Also, at some point, he remembered thinking that it was too bad that she belonged to the same clan and, therefore, could not be thought about in any other way but as a sister, a member of his family.

He shrugged. Now her brother was dead, killed at the same ill-omened raid he was taken prisoner, and Father was no more but a spirit, residing safely in the Sky World. But the girl might still be there, and so was her father, Atiron, the member of the Town Council. Would this man be prepared to listen? He doubted that. The People of the Flint, the dwellers of such an influential town as Little Falls in particular, had little patience for strangely speaking foreigners. The Onondaga girl was right. It was not the best of the solutions, but what choice did they have?

CHAPTER 14

Jikonsahseh's mushroom-like cabins greeted them warmly, bright in the soft afternoon sun. Leaning against the wall of the larger hut, Onheda smiled, enjoying the peacefulness of the light breeze. She was dead tired, and her wounded arm itched, now uncovered and open to the touch of the fresh air. Jikonsahseh insisted that it was the best thing to do, and the old woman would know.

It was as though they had been away for a whole span of seasons, and not only five dawns had passed since they had left the sanctuary of the small clearing.

Five dawns! She shook her head, desperate to collect her thoughts, to arrive at the decision. The beans and squash were already harvested and stored, the maize ground, wild berries and firewood collected. In their absence the old woman had completed the chores, wasting no time on idleness as it seemed. She did not need Onheda's help anymore. The debt was paid.

Narrowing her eyes against the glow of the setting sun, she watched the tall figure of the Crooked Tongues man as he spoke to their hostess, standing easily, displaying no signs of tiredness, his shoulders straight, legs wide apart, arms folded upon his bare chest. Imposing, pleasant, sure of himself. Annoyingly handsome.

She pursed her lips. This man, *this foreigner*, was of no consequence to her. When they left, she would leave, too. She would go back to her town and her people, just like she intended to do from the very beginning, and she would forget all about this span of seasons, all the good and all the bad. She would resume a normal life of the Hills People's woman, and if she heard about the further exploits of the Crooked Tongue man, she would smile and pay it no attention. He was not a man to think about in more than a fleeting manner, to admire and respect, maybe, because even though his ideas were strange and far-fetched, his drive, his conviction, his courage, his firm belief in what he thought was right to do were admirable, worthy of respect.

As for that breathtaking kiss and the memory of his arms pressing her, enveloping in his warmth and this masculine smell of his, powerful, attractive, impossible to resist, despite the sweat and the blood, well, she would forget all about it, too.

Clenching her teeth, she pushed the memory away, hating the way her stomach tightened and her skin began prickling in small waves of warm agitation. He was not the man to feel this way about him. He was too busy with his mission. He could have come to High Springs, accompanied by formidable Hionhwatha and her, the member of this very town, but he chose not to. He may have praised her company; he may have liked talking to her; he may have rushed to save her when that arrow had taken her down; he may have even enjoyed kissing her, still, she was no more than another companion to him, another person to listen and help. Like his scar-faced follower whom he had been clearly very fond of. Nothing more. He would not change his plans for a chance of spending more time in her company. He would not even hesitate.

"Nothing beats the chance to just sit and do nothing." The scar-faced youth neared, smiling broadly, his face ashen and pale in the last of the sunlight, but his eyes glittering cheerfully.

"Yes, Jikonsahseh's clearing is a wonder to behold." She smiled back, forcing her face into lightness, glad to have his company. "When are you leaving?"

"With dawn." He squatted beside her, uttering a sigh of relief. "One misses this peacefulness at times."

"If he had chosen to go with Hionhwatha, you two would not need to endanger yourself more than necessary."

"Yes, I know." He glanced at her fleetingly, then returned his gaze toward the conversing figures. "But they both are right, you know? Your people will not listen, unless the other side has been approached, softened and prepared."

"And, of course, he is ready to endanger his life, do whatever is necessary, to make it work."

"Of course. He wouldn't have crossed the Great Lake in the first place, if he wasn't prepared to sacrifice his life for that purpose."

"And yours, too."

He shrugged lightly. "I go wherever he goes. I owe him my life, my dignity, my pride. I owe him everything." From the corner of her eyes, she could see the shyness of his smile. "Also, I do believe in him. I'm not going after him blindly. He is the wisest man I have ever met. His spirit is the brightest, as appropriate for the Messenger of the Right-Handed Twin."

"He is just a man," she said, annoyed. "Man, like anyone of us."

"If he is just a man, then he has the blessing of the Great Spirits. He will achieve what he strives to achieve. Our people *will* live in peace."

"I'm yet to see him surviving Little Falls," she muttered, staring ahead. "When you come back, followed by the hordes of your people eager to make peace, then I may listen to any of you again."

He laughed. "It will be a challenge, yes. But we will come back. You just wait and see."

Shrugging, she shifted to make herself more comfortable, wincing at the pain in her arm. "I will not wait, but you are welcome to come back any time."

"Will you not stay here with Jikonsahseh?"

"No, I'm done here. I will go home now."

"To High Springs?"

"Yes."

"To help Hionhwatha?"

"No," she said sharply. "I'm going home to live my life, with no strange people and no strange ideas."

She felt him turning his head, measuring her with a wondering glance.

"You are angry with him because he is not going to High Springs," he said, making it a statement. "I know why you are feeling this way. But even your old leader agreed that Two Rivers must go and secure my people's willingness, while he is working on convincing your people. He is not being stubborn about it. He is doing what is right." Picking a small stone, he studied it thoughtfully, then threw it into the bushes. "He is not willing to leave you behind. I can assure you, he came to appreciate your company. He would have taken you to Little Falls with us if not for your previous stay there." His chuckle rolled softly in the deepening dusk. "And I would get angry with him, because under similar circumstances he refused to let my girl join us." Another stone went flying into the bushes. "She is as brave as you are, and as beautiful. But he said women are not to be risked on dubious missions, and I was wounded badly back then and in no condition to argue for real." He shrugged lightly, shaking his head as though trying to get rid of the bad feelings. "So if he tried to bring you with us to Little Falls, I would argue and make it difficult for him. But honestly, I would love to have you along. You are a worthwhile partner. And a worthy woman for someone like him." The third stone cut the air, flying farther than the other two. "He will come back, Onondaga girl, and he will seek your company. I'm prepared to bet my necklace on that."

She felt the warmth washing her face, making her cheeks burn.

"Not your necklace, surely," she muttered, trying to cover her embarrassment. "This is too high of a bet."

"Of course. But it's a sure thing. I know I will not lose any of my precious bear claws."

She watched his fingers running along the shiny row, caressing the fangs lovingly.

"You killed the huge grizzled bear?" she asked, mainly to change the subject.

"Yes, I did." He grinned lightly. "It was a wild affair. I still don't understand how it happened."

"How old are you?"

"I've seen close to eighteen summers."

"So young!" she exclaimed, surprised. "With all the scars and the bear's claws, I thought you were older."

He grinned again. "I think that, too. Maybe I lost count, or maybe the summers in the lands of the Crooked Tongues count for more. I certainly had too many adventures on their side of the Great Lake."

"Including this brave, beautiful girl, eh?"

But his face closed, turned to stone. "No. She was not among my adventures." The words came out muffled, seeping through his pressed lips. She could feel his sadness coming in waves, like a wind upon the lake's surface. "I found her and lost her on the same day. On the day we left."

"But she was willing to leave with you?" asked Onheda, puzzled. His story was strange. Like everything about him. And about the Crooked Tongues man.

"Yes, I think she was. I could feel her excitement. It was dark, and I couldn't see well, but she was in my arms, and by the way she caught her breath, I could tell she wanted to leave with us." The air hissed as he took a breath through his clenched teeth. "But Two Rivers said no, we can't drag a girl along. We were fleeing, you see. They might have caught us and, well, I was in no condition to fight if they did. And so she stayed. And now it's been two moons, and I will not be able to come back to her before the end of the Frozen Season. All because of one rotten, jealousy-eaten lowlife! May the Evil Twin take him into his realm and make him suffer for all times to come."

She caught her breath, startled by the intensity of his rage. "Will you kill this man when you are back there?" she whispered, shivering.

His mirthless chuckle shook the air. "He is already dead. Two Rivers killed him, and maybe it's for the best. If I could lay my hands on him now, I would turn into a person as despicable as he was."

Taken with compassion, she touched his arm, feeling him shivering, as though awakening from a dream. "You will come for her. I know you will. And when you bring her here, I'll help you all I can. We will make her very comfortable, and she will never regret leaving her people for the sake of being with you."

His gaze leaped to her, so full of hope her heart twisted. "Do you think it will happen? Oh, I will make so many offerings. I will never forget your help, never. As long as I live." He swallowed, and turned away, and she paused to watch the thickening dusk too, allowing him the privacy to cope with his feelings. What was his Crooked Tongues' girl like? she wondered. Was she anything like Two Rivers, her countryfolk – forceful, courageous, strange?

She sought him with her gaze again, but he was nowhere to be seen now, with Jikonsahseh alone, stirring her pot, preparing their evening meal in this unusual time for the meal to be prepared. Oh, but the old woman was glad to see them back!

Onheda smiled, remembering their warm reception this morning as they stumbled into the clearing, dirty, wounded, exhausted, just as the rain stopped and the high-morning sun broke free through the puffy clouds. Oh, how Jikonsahseh rushed toward them, taking the matters into her hands with a purposeful, businesslike manner typical to her, so obviously relieved to see them alive and in high spirits. And now the best of the food stocks were rummaged through, producing wonderful smells coming from the bubbling pot.

"I'll go and help her with our meal," she said, getting to her feet.

The Flint youth's smile flashed at her, as he nodded without moving or even opening his half-shut eyes, at peace for a change. He'll be all right, she thought, smiling in her turn. He'll get his girl, eventually. With Two Rivers' promise to help, he cannot but succeed, can he?

Her stomach twisted. And what about the Crooked Tongues

man? Did he leave a lost love in his cold, distant lands, too? Was that why he was so busy avoiding her company through their day-and-a-half-long journey back here? Was that why he preferred to go to Little Falls?

"You should be resting, girl," said Jikonsahseh, her hands busy, adding a handful of berries into the dough she was mashing, eyes on the stack of corn leaves beside her, the smaller, second fire almost extinguished, glowing with embers.

"I'm not tired. I want to help."

"Oh, yes you are, you stubborn little thing." The smile bestowed on her was so full of affection, Onheda's chest filled with warmth. "Look at your wound. It's still open, still oozing things. I shall tie a new bandage of healing leaves on it after we eat. But for now, go and rest. Be sensible." The old woman's chuckle rolled softly, caressing the afternoon air. "Like our guests."

"The Crooked Tongues man is not resting, and he has been wounded, too."

"Men cope with wounds differently. He doesn't think that cut on his ribs should hinder his activities, and something tells me he is right about that, too. Pain is nothing to the warriors like these two."

"Where is he?"

"I sent him to bring in more firewood. He was talking too much."

Against her will, Onheda felt her grin spreading. "He does that."

"But he talks sensibly, doesn't he?" Stirring the glowing embers with a stick, the old woman began fishing out bundles of corn leaves wrapped around the baked rolls of bread. "He makes people listen, even with no embellishment in the translation of his young companion. He has it all worked out in his head, I suspect. How to make our people live together, and not only why."

"Do you think he will succeed?"

"Oh yes, he will. With so much courage, good sense, and

determination, he cannot but succeed, girl."

Concentrated on what she had been doing, Onheda picked one of the yet-to-be-baked balls of dough and began wrapping it in the corn leaves. "Is he the Messenger of the Great Spirits?"

The woman's chuckle rustled softly, caressing the thickening dusk. "Maybe, girl, maybe. Until I met this pair, I thought I had seen everything an old woman like me could have seen on this earth. But oh Mighty Spirits, was I wrong!" A penetrating, well meaning gaze slid up, lingering upon Onheda's face, making her uncomfortable. "Don't let your heart grow attached to him, though. He is not for this, girl. He is a man with a mission, whether of Great Spirits or of his own. He has much work to do. He'll always be too busy to give himself to a woman."

She felt the wet leaves slipping from her hands, and fought to recapture them, damaging the bun in the process. "I do not feel about him this way! I'm just curious. He talks well. I like hearing him talking, even though his accent is dreadful and his ways are strange at times. Like the Flint youth, I want to help, maybe. You are not suspecting this young man of having inappropriate feelings for the foreigner, are you? Then why me?"

"Oh, but you do fit your name, oh spiky porcupine girl. I apologize for giving you unwelcomed advice. No, I do not suspect you of having inappropriate feelings. In fact, I think that all the feelings you have are appropriate, but some of them may hurt you." The woman's grin was wide again. "Now stop ruining my cornbread. The way you mash it, it'll make the poor dough go flat. Go. Go and rest, or clean some dishes or bring more firewood. Make yourself useful, you rebellious thing."

But the openly encouraging smile did not make Onheda feel better. So they all thought she had feelings for the strange foreigner. Jikonsahseh, the scar-faced youth, and even unapproachable Hionhwatha, they all assumed she was in love with this man.

Kicking angrily at small stones, she began ascending the path that led toward the spring and the small field, now neglected and abandoned with the maize harvested, ground, and stored. Well, they were wrong, plain wrong. She was not in love with this man. He was a fascinating person, an interesting company to spend one's time with, to listen and argue and ask questions. Truly the Messenger of the Great Spirits, maybe. But messengers of the divine powers were not to be treated in the same way as regular earthly dwellers. And they were not to kiss with so much passion that the mere memory of it, even now, two dawns later, would make her knees weak.

Yet, still it said nothing, she decided, passing carefully between the conical hills of the abandoned field. It was just a normal reaction of two people who had almost taken a step toward the Sky Journey. She was wounded and needed his support, and one action brought out another, but then Hionhwatha and the Flint youth came back and what might have happened didn't. Which was for the best, she had decided back then, reading the same disappointed relief in his handsomely sharp, well-defined face. He was as afraid, as wary, as dismayed at the face of this powerful urge, although there was nothing wrong with the act itself, with this simple gratification of their senses.

The thought about what might have happened made her knees tremble again. No, she needed to find him and talk to him about that. They did nothing wrong, yet his behavior had changed through the night spent in the old leader's hut and then through their day-and-a-half-long journey back. For two long dawns, he had barely spoken to her, avoiding her gaze and her company, talking to the former Onondaga leader all the time. It was understandable too, she decided, as the two men had much to talk about, many details of their projected plans to coordinate.

Hionhwatha was heading for High Springs and other smaller settlements, hopeful to make them listen by the time the Awakening Season came. It was worth a try, the old leader had declared, his lips smiling, eyes sparkling, the change in him pleasing, as though the turbulent day and the fight in the woods had awakened him, bringing back the formidable but also well-meaning, pleasant man he obviously used to be. The violent, ill-mannered recluse was gone. Just like the Flint youth, he was grinning readily now, talking in an unreserved manner. What an influence this Crooked Tongues' man had on people, she wondered, shaking her head, awed.

However, when they crossed Onondaga Lake, parting their way with Hionhwatha, Two Rivers' behavior toward her did not change. If anything, it got worse. He made such visible efforts not to spend any time in her company, preferring to row, navigating their canoe along the strengthening current, peering ahead, happy to let his young companion take care of her. It was as though he was not interested in her company anymore, having found a better, more valuable ally among her people. The thought that made her grind her teeth in anger. No! Whatever brought the change in his attitude, she would have to talk to him before parting their ways and forgetting all about him and his strange ideas.

Disregarding her tiredness, she climbed the path leading toward the spring, knowing where one would go to gather firewood. There were plenty of good, dry logs to be found around this higher ground.

Sure enough he was there, poised on the head of the path, his arms loaded with branches and beams, his eyes staring at her, surprised and wary, as though she had caught him doing something wrong. She stared back, her rage bubbling, threatening to spill out.

"What are you doing here?" he asked finally, not moving, frozen in the pose of a hunter waiting for the opening move of the dangerous beast.

"Me? I came to gather some firewood at the request of Jikonsahseh. And even if I did not, am I to justify my going around before you?"

His gaze relaxed as he took a deep breath, making a visible effort to collect himself. "No, of course not. You don't have to tell me... to tell me what you do." For her sake, he was trying to speak in her people's tongue, and against her will, she appreciated that. "But it's getting dark, so you better, better make hurry."

"You don't have to wait for me," she said, not making an attempt to resume her walk. It would force her to push herself past him, and it would make the awkwardness even worse.

"Of course I'll wait." His smile flashed out, surprising her, making her knees weak again. The knot in her stomach was so tight she didn't think she would manage to take a deep breath in her turn. "In fact, I think what I bring might be just enough. She wanted to make one more large fire for the last round of this delicious bread with berries. So just pick these two logs and let us go."

Difficult to understand as he switched back to the Crooked Tongues' way of talking, she took her eyes off him and headed up the path, catching the general gist of his suggestion. Yet, as she came closer he moved away, pressing against the bushes, as though a mere touch of her would burn his skin. Or maybe contaminate him in some way. She clenched her teeth.

"So will you stay with Jikonsahseh for the winter?" he asked, as she picked her logs and proceeded after him, at a respectable distance.

"No."

That made him stop and turn around.

"No? Why?"

"I have a home, remember? High Springs? My clan? My people?" She glared at him, her heart beating fast, welcoming the confrontation. "I've had enough dealings with strange people. And with foreigners, too. I'm going home!"

He narrowed his eyes, studying her in a somewhat frustrated way, his lips pressed tight. "I see."

"And I will not help Hionhwatha, either. I will forget all about you and your Flint People companion and your strange ideas." She felt like hitting him, the way he looked at her, his eyes mere slits in the ashen tiredness of his face. Still so annoyingly attractive. "I don't believe you will succeed. And I don't believe you are the Messenger of the Great Spirits. And I don't want to be part of your plans. I wish I never came to Jikonsahseh in the first place. This way I would never have met you, would never have heard your stupid, annoying ideas." Her voice shook badly, and it served to make her yet angrier. It sounded as though she was yelling, but she didn't care. He was listening now, shattered or angered, his previous indifference gone. "I wish you had stayed on your side of the Great Sparkling Water! I wish you had never come to preach to my people."

There was a sound of logs hitting the ground, and suddenly his arms were upon her shoulders, pressing her tightly between them, his eyes close again, like back then, but holding no desire.

"Stop it, Onheda. Stop screaming," he breathed into her face, his eyes sparkling. "Are you out of your mind? What's gotten into you?"

She tried to break free, her mad wriggling hurting her wounded arm, although he was careful to hold her beneath the cut.

"Let go of me!" she hissed into his face, hitting his chest with her fists. "How dare you to touch me? Let me go!"

"When you stop screaming and acting mad, I'll let you go." His face was calmer now, very close, his eyes concentrated, the grip of his arms as firm as before. "Calm down, woman. Calm down now!"

Although he looked composed again, she could feel the wild pounding of his heart as it resonated through her fists that were pressed against his chest, not beating but pushing into him, as though trying to leave a print. Fighting the tears, she made an effort to get a grip of her senses.

"I'm calm. I'm all right. I'm calm…" Frustrated with the way her voice vibrated, she swallowed, aware of the tears. If only he wouldn't hold her so firmly, in such a detached way, she would have been able to wipe them away. If only he would envelope her in his arms, the way he did back then, after killing that man with the spear she had brought to him. "I'm good. Let me go.

I'm..." It was of no use. Her voice refused to work.

And then she was in his embrace, and the way he held her had changed, bringing the memories back. She could feel his warmth, and his scent, and the loud thumping of his heart, now pressed against her cheek, easier to hear. And it didn't matter that her arm hurt now, and that she had made a complete fool of herself with her stupid insults and the silly crying, because he was not reserved, not indifferent anymore.

"I'm sorry," he was whispering into her hair, pressing her hard. "I didn't want to hurt you. I think... I don't think we should. Because... because I can't give you what you deserve to have. I can offer you nothing. I can't..."

His voice trailed off, as his lips brushed against her hair, sliding down toward her face, seeking her lips, forceful, demanding, as full of desire as back then. It took her breath away, leaving her legs powerless to support her.

Leaning heavily against him, she closed her eyes, to savor the feeling, but also ashamed of the tears. He should not see her so ugly, so disgustingly weak. He would turn away, disappointed. But then his lips parted hers, and she forgot all about these other misgivings, giving in to the wonderful sensation, caring for nothing but the powerful waves washing her whole body, making it strong and as demanding as his kisses were.

The world swayed, and she clung to him, realizing that he picked her up and was carrying her somewhere, she didn't care where. The sound of the trickling water and the softness of the muddy grass told her that they were back beside the spring, but she gave it no passing thought, enveloped in his warmth, her body welcoming his, eager to have him all for herself, clenching him tight with her limbs, savoring every vibration, every pulse of his being.

He was whispering something, stroking her face, kissing her neck, but she didn't listen, too absorbed to try to understand his words. What he did mattered more, all the wonderful, beautiful things that she didn't think one human could do to another. It was as though she had known no man before, so different was the sensation, so fulfilling.

Breathing heavily, they lay beside each other, resting, spent, their limbs entwined, impossible to unclench. To stay like that forever, she hoped dreamily, her spirit floating, not connected to her body, riding the clouds of euphoria.

He raised his head and was watching her through the thickening darkness. "You are no woman," he said. "You are an *uki*, a beautiful spirit of those local forests. There is no other explanation."

"Am I?" She returned his gaze, too spent to raise her head, although she wanted to see him better. All she could pick in the deepening dusk was the outline of his prominent cheekbones and those wonderfully large, almond-shaped eyes of his.

"Yes, you are." Smiling, he leaned closer, and now she could see what his eyes held. An open admiration. A wondering inquiry. "I can find no other reason."

"And what does it tell you?" she asked idly, satisfied. Oh yes, she was not a regular woman. He should realize that. He had known many women, too many, according to his young companion.

"It tells me that the local spirits are favoring… in favor. They want me to succeed with my mission."

She smiled, pleased that again he was making an effort to talk in her tongue. Or was he trying to make the local spirits listen?

"What if I get angry with you? What if I go to my other fellow spirits and tell them you are no good for us?"

His finger drifted alongside her face, outlining her cheek, sliding down her chin, to make its way up the other side, as though drawing its silhouette.

"You will not do this. You are too beautiful, and your magic is good."

She shivered, enjoying this light, almost reverent touch.

"You trust people too readily," she whispered.

He laughed and the magic broke. "What choice do I have?"

"Not many." She rose on her elbow, grimacing from the pain in her arm. "So what now?"

His face closed all of a sudden. "What do you mean?"

She grinned, amused but not in a mirthful way. "Don't get that frightened. I didn't expect you to forget all about the Good Tidings of Peace for the sake of coming to live with me in my clan's longhouse."

His eyes narrowed again, as defensive and wary as back on the trail. "It's not like that, Onheda. What happened between us is anything but a simple lying around. I suppose it should not have happened at all, but rest assured you are important to me and not only as a person who helps us so tremendously. I tried to fight it, those other feelings. I wish I were stronger."

She peered at him, frustrated. Again he was talking in his tongue and just as she needed to understand every word.

"I can't ask you to accompany us to Little Falls, but I wish you could."

Oh, this one she understood well, feeling her heart skipping a beat, then beginning to pound wildly.

"What do you want me to do while you are gone?"

"Stay here with Jikonsahseh until we are back. It should not take us too long. Maybe we'll be able to come back before the snow." His smile was wonderful, flashing at her, making her stomach flutter. "When I come back, we'll go to High Springs together, to help Hionhwatha. His mission will not prove easy, I can promise you that. Judging by you and that formidable former leader, Onondagas are headstrong and stubborn. He'll need help."

She laughed and pushed his encircling arm away.

"Oh yes, we are that," she said, climbing on top of him, sure of herself all of a sudden, feeling him stirring, tensing against her touch.

You are so self-assured, she thought, *and you can think about nothing but your mission. And yet, you can't help but to feel strongly about me. You fought it and you failed. You admitted that yourself. And by all the spirits who inhabit these woods, I will make sure you remain powerless against this particular magic. You will want no other woman.*

"Yes, we are headstrong and stubborn," she said, moving

along with the pulses of his body, letting her own needs guide her. "And we are very strong, too. Our desires are powerful, our needs great, and we will not settle for anything but a full partnership in your proposed league of nations. Or maybe even more. We will demand a leading role, and you will have to give it to us, too."

His eyes were huge, staring at her, mesmerized, full of expectation, but as her own delight began taking over, interfering with her ability to talk, she saw them clouding too, giving in to the most divine pleasure the Great Spirits had given to their human creations.

"You are magic," he was murmuring, his hands wandering her body, guiding it, helping it climb the peaks of delight. "I will not let you down, never. You are the gift of the Great Spirits."

Oh yes, I am that, she thought, swept with the powerful wave, comfortable in losing control now. *I am that, and you will not let me go, ever.*

CHAPTER 15

With the rain ceasing during the second part of the day, Atiron felt his mood improving, climbing up of its own accord. Squinting, he watched the sun breaking through the grayish clouds, filling the muddy alleys of Little Falls with cheerful people eager to catch the last of the warmth.

"Trying to warm your old bones, aren't you?"

"Oh, yes." Not bothering to take his eyes off the brightening sky, Atiron grinned, recognizing his friend's voice. Tsinoweh was a good man from the neighboring Wolf Clan's longhouse, an old friend, although they argued and disagreed more often than not. "Let the Father Sun favor our hunters for a little longer."

"And our warriors, too."

"Our warriors can stay home safely. There is no urgency in their mission. While with no more hunting parties we would be forced to count every bite of food through the Freezing Moons."

The Wolf Clan's man shifted his weight from one foot to another. "There is urgency in our warriors' mission, too. The People of the Standing Stone should be punished for their brazenness. They should be taught a lesson."

"The People of the Standing Stone learned a bitter lesson themselves this time, while attacking that small village and failing on even this accord." Taking his eyes off the sky, Atiron shrugged, his peacefulness gone. "They sneaked back with their tails between their legs, shamed. They have punished themselves, and Little Falls should not starve in order to drive the lesson further." He frowned at his friend's darkening face.

"If our crops were plentiful, I may have seen the reason for one more raid. But our storage rooms are half empty, so every available man must be out there, hunting and fishing. Not running about, waving their clubs."

The stormy glance was his answer. "If I hadn't known you for a very long time, old friend, I would be telling some harsh words to you now." The man shrugged, his face clearing. "But anyway, the War Chief has called a meeting of the other war leaders. They don't need yours and the Town Council's agreement to do that."

"But he needs the agreement of the Clans Mothers."

"And he may get it as well."

Atiron turned so abruptly, he needed to grab the nearest pole to steady himself. "Not the Turtle Clan's Mothers, surely."

"I don't know. I just heard that they all might have reached an agreement. One last raid before the snows. And why not?"

"Oh, I want to know what they promised the silly women. I bet it is something good."

Tsinoweh's laughter rolled down the alley. "I'm sure it is." Turning away, he beckoned Atiron to follow. "Come, old friend. Let us find out what the War Council is up to."

The open grounds beside the tobacco plots were bubbling with life, with people of all ages walking around, gesturing, talking agitatedly. Purposeful and busy, young men were checking the central pole, drawing glances of giggling girls. The War Dance was in the air, a sure thing.

"Father!" Kahontsi brushed past them, her face flushed, eyes sparkling.

"Where are you going?" Eyeing his daughter's pleasantly fresh, shining face Atiron smiled. It was impossible to stay gloomy in her company.

"To the ceremonial grounds."

"What? No more chores for today?"

"Oh no, we are almost finished, and anyway, the Clans Mothers are busy with the councils." Her smile beamed at him, unconcerned. "Too busy to pay attention to us and our chores."

"And why would they do any of it without being supervised, eh?" The Wolf Clan man's grin was wide, as unconcerned as that of Kahontsi. "Girls!"

"Yes." Watching his daughter's happy gait as she rushed off down the incline, Atiron shrugged. "When the leading women are busy with war more than they are concerned with the wellbeing of this town, what would you expect the young people to do?"

"We'll survive. Don't we always?"

"Some of us probably will. But not all. If we are not to eat well through the winter, some of our people will not live to see the Awakening Moons." Squinting, he watched a group of men that hurried up the path. "I think we are going to find out if there is a War Dance or not."

"Yes, sooner or later."

The leading man was waving his hand, bearing upon them.

"The Town Council is gathering at the ceremonial ground," he said, panting. "Please, come."

"Sooner, it seems." Atiron shot a meaningful glance at his friend, then concentrated on the newcomer. "What is the news?"

"Quite a lot." The man rolled his eyes, agitated. "The warriors were on their way to the gathering of the War Council when they spotted foreign men camping upon our shore."

"What?"

"Yes, foreigners. Would you believe that? Maybe our warriors will not have to spend their energy rowing against the current to kill some enemy."

"On our shore?" Atiron and Tsinoweh exchanged wondering glances, their differences forgotten. "They are getting bold."

"How many warriors?"

"I don't know. The Head of the Town Council just sent us to fetch you and the other members."

"Oh well." Atiron glanced at his friend, knowing how badly he wanted to be in the Town Council. "Come with me. They may make it open to a wider audience this time."

But Tsinoweh just shrugged. "No, you go. I'll sniff around and hear what people say. Through gossip, I may learn more than you, anyway."

Grinning, Atiron shook his head. "It can happen."

So the enemies were as foolish, as desperate to prove their superiority as his people were, he thought, heading down the incline, following the path where his daughter's swirling skirt disappeared only a few heartbeats earlier. Was it good? Well, of course it was. Little Falls was always prepared, always ready to defend itself. People who tried to attack a town of such importance were foolish. And yet... He shook his head, feeling his own rage rising. What a brazenness, indeed!

The six of the Town Council's members were already there, squatting in the sun, enjoying its soft touch. Their nods acknowledged his greeting.

"The Father Sun is wonderful to us," said the Head of the Council, shifting to make himself more comfortable. "I hope Heno the Thunderer waits for a few more days before sending his blissful storms our way again."

"Yes, let us hope he takes a rest," agreed Atiron, squatting beside them, holding his curiosity at bay. The custom bade no straight away broaching of the subject. His questions would have to wait to be answered. Indeed, his friend might learn the news sooner than he.

"The War Chief and his advisers were reported heading back to the town," said someone.

"Good."

More comfortable silence. He saw representatives of two more longhouses nearing.

"All longhouses of our clan seemed to be done with their winter preparations," said one of the two Wolf Clan representatives.

"Until more meat is brought to Little Falls."

"Yes, until then."

More silence.

"You've been summoned here on such a short notice,"

began the Head of the Town Council, counting them with his eyes, satisfied, "because of the strange happening reported to us by our warriors." The man paused, encircling them with yet another thoughtful gaze. "Foreign men were seen camping on our shore, making no effort to conceal their presence."

"How many?"

"Two."

"Two men?" They all stared, taken by surprise.

"Then it is no raiding party!" exclaimed Atiron, curiously relieved.

"No, it is not." The Head of the Council nodded thoughtfully. "They are being watched until we decide what to do with them. The War Chief and his men will join our discussion shortly."

"We should send a delegation and enquire what their purpose is. If they are just sitting and waiting, then they obviously came to talk."

"Unless they are just two stupid people who lost their way," said Ohonte, another representative of Atiron's clan.

"They would be anxious to hide their presence in that case. No one would camp openly before a settlement as large and as important as Little Falls."

"Yes, I agree," said the Wolf Clan man. "We can always kill these men, but there is no harm in enquiring for the purpose of their coming here before we decide."

"Maybe they are no foreigners but our people from this or that distant village," suggested a thickset man from the Bear Clan.

"They would have come straight away to the town if that was the case," insisted Ohonte.

"They are evidently polite and well-versed in good manners." The Head of the Council shrugged. "It might be wise to hear them out, whether foreigners or not."

"Their timing could not have been worse. They interrupted the Warriors' Council. The War Chief will be furious."

They all nodded. Polite and well meaning or not, the visitors would have done better appearing earlier or later, not today.

"We will wait to hear out the War Chief and then we decide."

The sun was rolling down the sky, threatening to disappear behind the trees that were lining up the curve of the shore. Glowering, Tekeni watched its progress, willing it to slow its movement, the roaring of the falls calming and upsetting him at the same time. So many memories!

"Why aren't they coming out?" he muttered, unable to keep quiet. "Did they go back and forget all about us?"

"Maybe." Two Rivers' light grin seemed to be forced, lacking its usual spark.

Tekeni restrained himself from kicking a stone that was jutting against the side of his moccasin. "What will we do after the darkness falls?"

"We'll go on sitting here, smoking and waiting."

"And tomorrow? What if they don't come to meet us tomorrow, either?"

This time the amusement crept into his older companion's gaze. "Tomorrow we'll have a good breakfast first, before resuming our waiting."

"Oh, good. I'm hungry." Clenching his teeth, Tekeni sighed. "I'm sorry. I should have more patience. I just… well, I apologize. I'm not a good company of late."

The amusement intensified, sparkling out of the large eyes, so very familiar by now. "Well, yes, wolf cub. You are losing your patience and just as we need it the most. But it's all good. They have seen us, and they went back to deliberate as to what to do with us. It's an appropriate thing to do." The full lips twisted in a provocative grin. "They didn't shoot at us right away, and it's a good thing. Your people may have more sense than their neighbors are crediting them with. They know we are here to talk, but they need time to decide whether we are worth listening to or not."

"Or maybe they think we are so stupid as to miss their warriors watching us from behind the trees!"

Biting his lips, Tekeni busied himself with feeding the fire, angry beyond measure. Since leaving Jikonsahseh's clearing four dawns ago, he had been all nerves. The oh-so-long-awaited homecoming was not turning out to be the journey he had expected it to be. To dream about it while living among the Crooked Tongues was one thing; to have it actually happening, apparently, was quite another. Or maybe it was he who had changed.

Back in his captors' town, a possibility to sail the Great River, following the current, seemed like a wonderful fulfillment, a triumph, the ultimate achievement. To be back among his own countryfolk, his town, his tongue! To see the alleys of Little Falls, the people he knew since being a child, the forest trails he used to run and play around, his extended family and his childhood friends – a wonderful dream straight away from the realm of the Sky World.

Yet now, with all this actually happening, he felt nothing but anxiety, even fear. What if his people turned out unheeding, inattentive to reason? What if they refused to listen? What if they killed Two Rivers without giving it a second thought, the despised foreigner from across the Great Lake, the Crooked Tongue?

Shuddering, he clenched his fists. He would not let it happen, even if his life had to be sacrificed to prevent that. But would he be listened to? A mere youth of no importance. Two Rivers valued his courage, his spirit, his abilities and talents. Jikonsahseh and the Onondaga girl came to appreciate him and his skills. Even the fierce, austere Onondaga leader was impressed. But Tekeni's own people knew nothing but the mischievous boy who had left almost three summers ago. They must have remembered his father, but they would not appreciate the strange company and ideas the lost son of the dead War Chief had brought along. They would shrug and turn away, killing the Crooked Tongues foreigner, forcing him to run the gauntlet on the carpet of glowing embers.

If only Father were alive! But even Father would not listen, he realized, a bitter taste in his mouth revolting, making him want to spit. The War Chief would be the last person willing to listen to a strange suggestion of making peace with their people's enemies. And neither would the current Warriors' Leader be more attentive, whoever had been chosen to replace the dead one.

"If they hurried, we could have sailed back before Frozen Moons," said Two Rivers thoughtfully, sucking on his pipe.

"Oh, yes, if they invite you to speak before the Town Council right away, tomorrow with dawn at the latest, listen to your every word, receive your directions as to what they should do in your absence, give us plenty of supplies and a better canoe, and send us back with their gratitude and offerings to the Great Spirits, then, yes, in this case we can be back among the Onondagas before Frozen Moons." Feeling ridiculous with being upset over a mere comment, Tekeni kicked away the stone. "And why would you be in a hurry to go back?"

"To see how Hionhwatha is faring?" Two Rivers' eyebrows climbed high, his eyes sparkling coldly, relating to Tekeni that he had taken it too far now. "He might be facing a bigger challenge than ours."

Or maybe to see how the Onondaga girl was faring, thought Tekeni, turning away to watch the river, knowing that there was much going on between these two, although they made an effort to behave as though nothing happened on the last evening of their stay at Jikonsahseh. He suppressed a snort. Of course, it was anything but nothing, while those two spent what seemed to be half an evening somewhere in the woods, coming back all amiable, their faces shining, gleaming with an indecent euphoria. And not that he grudged them their feeling of well being, but if he, Tekeni, had to put his love aside in favor of their important mission, Two Rivers had no right to make haste now, in a hurry to get back to his girl. No right whatsoever.

"Calm down, wolf cub. Just calm down." Two Rivers' voice rang calmly, back to his old, confident self. "Go and take a dip in the river if you must."

"If they are watching us, as I'm sure they are, my going to take a leisurely swim might confuse them into attacking us."

"Then calm down without swimming. Sit and take a grip of yourself, before you start yelling and running around like a coyote with a thorn in its paw." The man sucked on his pipe again, so strongly it made the tip of the beautifully carved object glow.

He was not as calm as he tried to appear, realized Tekeni, glancing at the familiar face, noting the signs of the obvious agitation, expressed in the pressed lips, the overly concentrated gaze, the way the wide palm clutched at the pipe.

For a while they said nothing, watching the sun.

"It's good that the rain stopped."

"Yes, it is." Two Rivers' grin returned, flashing lightly. "We must have been looking pitiful this morning, soaked and so hopelessly tired. While now, all dry and presentable, we're bound to make a good impression."

"I'm still tired. And I'm hungry. And I wish those people would do something already."

"Your people, you mean."

"Yes, my people." He felt like stomping his foot. "They can deliberate for days, the Town Council. I remember it now. My father was always frustrated with them talking and talking, reaching no decisions."

"Your father would have already reached the decision, eh?" Two Rivers' face darkened all of a sudden. "Maybe it's good that they are deliberating for so long."

"They must know we saw their people staring at us from behind the trees. So they know that we know. And if so, why won't they invite us in and start talking already?" He shook his head, refusing the offered pipe. With all his hunger and tiredness, the strong tobacco would make his head reel, he knew. "As for my father, yes, he may have been entertaining the idea of getting rid of us right away. But he also may have become curious. You don't know what he would decide."

"Yes, of course. I'm sure your father was an outstanding man." Two Rivers shrugged, then threw another log into the fire. "We'll run out of firewood soon."

"I'll go and fetch more." Jumping to his feet, Tekeni welcomed the chance to do something, but Two Rivers shook his head.

"Stay, wolf cub. We are being watched, and running around, in and out of the bushes, will bring nothing but confusion into our projected hosts' minds. No less than the swimming in the river. We made our move, and now all we can do is to wait for them to make theirs." Another branch went in, to catch fire and turn into a charred arch. "Be patient. They won't make us wait until nightfall."

"I hope so." Tekeni kicked at another stone, then cursed silently. "It's worse than to wait for the bear to come. Back then I had to crouch without moving for a long time, too, but at least I knew what I would be required to do when the time came. At least I knew what I was waiting for. But here?" He snatched a branch out of their diminishing pile, breaking it in two. "What should we do if they attack us? Do we fight like back at Hionhwatha's place? And what if they talk to us first and then decide to kill us? We will need to fight together, but how do we coordinate our actions?"

"We are not fighting them, you wild thing," said Two Rivers, shaking his head. The smile was lurking in the depths of the dark eyes, but the man's lips did not twist. "We came here to talk, and talk to them we will."

"And what if they refuse to listen? What if they start shooting right now?"

"They will not. If they wanted to shoot at us, they would have done so when the sun was still high, when first spotting us. They will come to enquire as to the nature of our mission before the sun will be kissing the treetops on the other side of that impressive river of yours." The grin that finally flashed was calm, even if mirthless. "These are your people, wolf cub. You will not be fighting your people. And you will not be hurt by them, either. I'll make sure of that."

Tekeni caught his breath. "If they try to hurt you, I'll fight them. We are together in this, my former people or not. I will not go on living happily in Little Falls if my people kill you. It will not happen."

The eyes peering at him softened, filled with light. "I know that, old friend. And we will succeed. Little Falls will listen. You just wait and see."

There was a sound of people walking down the hill, coming from the town, not trying to conceal their progress. Tensing, they turned to watch, although the tall trees blocked the view of the trail.

"I wish those falls were not roaring so loudly," muttered Two Rivers, his face darkening all of sudden. "That's one noise I can do without."

Too tense to respond, Tekeni found it impossible to tear his gaze off the head of the trail. Still, the words of his companion puzzled him. Why would Two Rivers complain about the silly noise that had nothing to do with the danger they were in?

□-□◆□-□

They were coming down the trail slowly, calmly, not in a hurry. A group of people, numerous enough to make the thought of resistance die away, yet not large enough to relate any serious interest. Mainly warriors of various ages, with only a few elders leading the procession.

Impressed they were not, reflected Two Rivers, ice piling in his stomach, making it heavy with disappointment. The strategy that worked so far, failed. He would not be addressing them from a slightly superior stance of the initiator, the mysterious man from the mists of the Great Lake, the Messenger of the Great Spirits. These people came to enquire as to his purpose out of sheer, slightly bored politeness. They were not impressed with his unwarranted coming to their lands. If anything, they seemed to be already irritated by it, put out with his audacity at interfering with their regular daily activities.

He fought the urge to rise to his feet, his hand itching to crawl closer to his sash and his knife. Instead, he remained still, watching them nearing. From the corner of his eye, he could see Tekeni freezing, turning into stone, ceasing to breathe, maybe. The youth had been too nervous upon this last stretch of their journey, but now he seemed to calm down, and it was a good thing. He needed his most trusted ally calm enough to make no rash decisions.

The delegation was very close now, proceeding slowly, in an even gait. He counted the feathers upon the headdress of the leading warrior. Was it the War Chief? Not likely. The man looked not old enough, about Two Rivers' age maybe, too young to hold such a leading position. And his headdress was barely decorated. Just a few feathers and some beads. One of the minor leaders, most probably. If not anything else, it proclaimed their contempt.

The two elder men wore no special insignia, their faces impartial, indifferent, not colored by even the slightest curiosity. Why did they bother to come out at all?

The silence hung, an uncomfortable, hostile silence. He returned their gazes, measuring them with all the calmness he could muster, disregarding the roaring of the falls behind the curve of the river. If it was his time to die, to crash against the sharp rocks under the mass of the gushing water, he would do it proudly. Now he knew that for certain, his misgivings gone. Maybe his death was the required sacrifice, to make them listen to one of their own, the brave, outstanding youth he knew he had saved once upon a time for a reason.

"What is the purpose of your coming here?" asked one of the elderly men curtly, disregarding any sort of polite greeting.

Two Rivers stood the penetrating gaze. "I came from the west, and I'm going eastward. I bring Good Tidings of Peace," he said, pleased to hear his voice ringing firmly in the deepening dusk.

Their eyes narrowed, but Tekeni was already speaking, translating promptly, embellishing his words judging by the length of his speech. He didn't mind. He trusted the youth's judgment. Also with their attention shifting, he had a moment of respite to study them, to prepare his further claims.

Their gazes came back, wondering.

"Where did you come from?" asked the leading warrior, when neither of the two elders spoke.

"The lands of the Crooked Tongues. I crossed the Great Sparkling Water in order to proclaim the tidings of the Great Peace."

The warrior's eyes narrowed. "It sounds as though you presume to patronize our people."

Grateful for Tekeni's quiet translation brushing past his ear, Two Rivers stood the stern glare.

"I presume nothing. The Great Spirits directed me to come here. I've been acting as the Right-Handed Twin's messenger. It was not of my choosing."

"Or so you say." The man did not move, did not change his pose, but the air of danger surrounded him now, radiated by his pose as much as by his words.

"If I'm allowed to address the town's council, I might be able to explain better."

"You can talk to us," said one of the elder men, taking the lead. "We are here to determine if your words are worthy of our Town Council's attention."

Two Rivers suppressed a sigh. "Very well."

He nodded thoughtfully, desperate to convey a confidence he didn't feel. They were not predisposed to listen, that much was clear. He had been too familiar with the signs.

"I came to bring accord between the peoples of this side of the Great Sparkling Water. To plant the Great Tree of Peace. The warfare between your brother-nations has to stop. The Right-Handed Twin is displeased, watching his children destroying one another, destroying the world of his creation. The bloodshed must stop."

It was no oratory. How could one talk with his audience hostile and unable to listen to one's direct words? He tried to collect his thoughts, but they refused to organize, the roaring of the falls distracting, making his stomach heave. *How would it feel, that fall into the gushing current studded with sharp rocks?*

He tried to concentrate, but the proper thoughts didn't come. Would his sacrifice help? Would Tekeni be able to make it all work? There was so much to do yet. Making these people listen was only the first step.

Tekeni's voice flowed calmly behind his back, talking on and on, sometimes rising, sometimes lowering to almost a whisper. *Full of confidence.* What was the youth talking about? To translate the short, artless speech he just made should have taken a few heartbeats, no more than that. Still, the youth pressed on, and the eyes of their interrogators were on him now, suspicious but attentive too, captivated.

He tried to listen to the foreign words. The prophecy, he was talking about the prophecy now, telling about the floating stone canoe and the willingness of the Onondaga People to listen. Where did the wolf cub learn to orate like that?

He wished he could see what the youth's face held, but standing half a step ahead made it impossible. He could not turn his head and look because they were glancing at him every now and then, their gazes holding a wonder. So he kept his back straight and his face unreadable, full of calm dignity. Or so he hoped. *What was wrong with him?*

Again, the stone canoe was mentioned. He suppressed a grin, remembering what Jikonsahseh had told them upon their return. Apparently, a group of Onondaga warriors passed her clearing when they had been away on their quest to find Hionhwatha. The hunters didn't stay for a night, but spent enough time enjoying her wonderful hospitality, and what they said made the old woman pause. Stranger had been reported to cross the Great Lake, said the Onondaga men, arriving in a canoe made out of white stone; stranger that brought an unusual message, promising to solve all the troubles of the Onondaga people.

He remembered how he and Tekeni looked at each other and laughed, recalling their first encounter with that hunter on the day of their crossing. They had bluffed mightily back then, afraid and anxious to get away. But from the 'Messenger of the Great Spirits' to the canoe made out of white stone it was a long way. How these people arrived at that conclusion, they'd never known. Although, indeed, their canoe was unusually bright, almost white, really. But made out of solid bark.

Tekeni's voice kept rolling on, gaining power. He could feel that himself, understanding only a part of what the youth said, but captivated nevertheless. Oh, the wolf cub was a good orator. They drank his words in, enthralled now, the elders and the warriors, even the younger ones. Especially the two of them, young men of a little more than twenty summers old, staring, wide-eyed.

"So Little Falls was the first to receive his message?" asked one of the elders thoughtfully, when the gush of the words stopped, coming to a natural halt.

"Of all the important settlements, yes." He felt Tekeni nodding solemnly, but he wished he could see what his face held. "However, as I said, the important Onondaga leaders have been approached, indicating their willingness to listen to the words of the Messenger."

The warriors' leader narrowed his eyes, studying the youth suspiciously, impressed by the scars, of that Two Rivers had no doubt.

"And you? Who are you? You talk our tongue too well not to be one of us, and you do remind me of someone."

Now he truly wished to see Tekeni's eyes.

"I was born and raised in Little Falls," said the youth calmly, perfectly composed.

"I knew it!" cried out one of the younger warriors, breaking into the speech of his elders, apparently unable to hold his tongue. "You are the twin, the late War Chief's son."

Temporarily forgotten, Two Rivers saw their eyes widening along with their gaping mouths.

"It can't be!" muttered one of the elders.

"Yes, I'm the surviving son of my great father, your former War Chief." Tekeni's voice did not shake, but there was a strained tone to it now.

"But how?" The leading warrior's frown was almost painful, thrown out of his composure at long last. "Where did you come from? Where have you been?"

Unable to fight the temptation anymore, Two Rivers turned his head slightly, in the corner of his eyes catching the handsome, well familiar face, seeing it losing some color, closing up.

"I didn't die on that ill-omened raid because… because I was destined to join the Messenger, to follow him as he brings his message of Great Peace, to help him along." He hesitated. "It was the part of my prophecy. I know it now."

The elders exchanged glances, while the leading warrior's face darkened.

"Some of us heard of your prophecy, yes, and most of us remember you well. We do not know what sort of a person you turned out to be, but we all admired and respected your great father." The man shook his head. "Yet your companion, the man whom you presume to represent so ardently, is nothing but a stranger to us. How do we know that what he says, what you translate, is not just words? How can we determine that this man is, indeed, the messenger of the Right-Handed Twin?" A wide gesture indicated the river. "Your canoe seems to be of a regular sort now, and the prophecies may be misinterpreted."

The dark gaze shifted, meeting that of Two Rivers, challenging, daring him to reply, to provide the proof. He saw the doubt, the defiance, the open suspicion. Yet, the hesitation, too. They wanted to believe in what the youth said, they needed someone to come and make the change.

Taking a deep breath, he stood the defying glare, calm and

not afraid anymore.

"I'm willing to prove the divine nature of my mission. I'm willing to stand any test you would like me to undertake." A slight nod indicated the curve of the river. "Your roaring falls are here and waiting."

The silence prevailed, accompanied by their narrowing gazes. Tekeni did not translate, but they seemed to understand him well enough.

"Very well." One of the elders nodded. "Let us go to Little Falls now. The Town Council might be willing to meet you. As for the test," the man shook his head. "This will remain the prerogative of the council members to decide upon."

As they turned to go, he could see Tekeni struggling to compose himself, biting his lips, his scowl deep. *Why*, shouted the youth's gaze, its glow dark and full of desperation. *Why?*

CHAPTER 16

The rain was pounding against the bark walls, tugging at the rectangular sheet that shut the opening in the roof, keeping the corridor of the Turtle Clan longhouse cozy and warm.

Shifting closer to the fire, Atiron grinned. "It's good you reached Little Falls before nightfall."

The foreigner grinned back. "Yes. We… we wet last night, but tonight, tonight would see us drown, drown in the rain." Talking slowly, careful to pronounce every word, the man made a tremendous effort to be understood, still it was a challenge to talk to him without Tekeni's helpful translation. His accent was dreadful and, but for the miraculously returned son of the dead War Chief, no one would listen to this man, the message of the Great Spirits or not.

"The Hunting Moon will yet see quite a few clear days," said Atiron. "I heard in your lands the cold is fiercer."

"Yes." The man nodded, reaching for the fire and holding his palms close to it, enjoying the warmth. "We call this time, this moon, the First Cold Moon, and we keep, keep our expectation low. Not many warm days."

"I see."

Studying the strong, alien-looking face, Atiron took in the light frown, the tension, the tiredness behind the large eyes. It had been a long evening for the Crooked Tongues man, talking to all sorts of people who came to pay a visit under this or that pretext, curious about the stranger. Not the people the visitor hoped to see, of course. Persons of importance did not deign to come. Aside from Atiron himself, who insisted on hosting Tekeni and his companion, being the closest friend of the youth's father and the man of the same clan, no member of the Town or the War Council came. Their chance of interviewing the foreigner would come on the morrow, and it would be an official event. Tomorrow would seal this man's fate.

"If you want to take a rest, you are more than welcome," he said, with a light nod indicating the nearest bunk. "You made a long journey."

"Oh no, no." The foreigner shook his head, his smile flashing, surprisingly light, captivating beam. "I would want, would like, to talk more, unless you are tired." His grin widened. "My young companion rowed for most of today, and I don't see him sleeping here."

Finding it difficult to understand the foreign speech, Atiron grinned against his will, thinking about Tekeni, the impressive twin, the boy of the prophecy, the favorite son of his best friend, coming back from the dead, and in the most spectacular fashion. Weathered, tall, broad-shouldered, *unrecognizable*. Not a mischievous boy, but a young warrior, with his eyes wary and reserved and the scars making a strange pattern, not spoiling the natural attractiveness of his face but setting it apart, making one stop and wonder. Or maybe those were not the scars but the general air the youth's whole being radiated, the air of alertness and danger, of not-too-deeply hidden violence. A walking image of his father, and yet… There was something about this young man, something that set Atiron's nerves on edge.

"Tell me about him," he said, trying not to let his anxiety show.

"Oh." The man nodded, his gaze sincere. "He is a remarkable young man. I didn't notice him at first, but then, there was an incident, and I was able to help. Then I started watching him. He has great courage and quick thinking. His abilities are impressive. He is smart and observant, and he is learning fast." The man hesitated. "He is loyal. An invaluable companion. One could not wish for a better partner."

It was difficult again to follow, although the man evidently tried to talk in a simple manner. Atiron watched the fire, seeing it flickering with a draft, drawing pictures, bringing memories back in force.

"Did he suffer?"

"Yes."

"The scars?" He swallowed. "Was he put through some ceremony?"

"No." The man seemed to be concentrated on the fire too, his eyes clouded, wandering unknown distances. "It was, well, it was ugly, what happened, and we fled because of that. But no, when he was captured, he was not harmed. He was adopted very quickly." A shrug. "He is an impressive-looking youth. Quite a few families wanted him."

The thought hit him like a punch in his stomach. "Were there other warriors? Did someone else survive that raid?"

"No, there were no other survivors." The man's gaze focused, resting upon his host, concentrated. "Neither adoptees, nor captives."

Atiron clenched his palms together, feeling them sweaty, unpleasantly slick. No, of course not. But the twin was back now and he knew, even if this foreigner did not. He would ask the youth about his son's death. And no later than tonight, the moment he came back. With an effort, he concentrated on his guest, seeing the understanding reflecting in the dark eyes. And the compassion.

"War," he said, pleased to hear his own voice low but firm. "What can one do?"

The man's grin was surprisingly open, flashing out without warning. "We can do something. We can stop the war."

"Yes, I hear that it is why you came to our lands."

He remembered the conviction with which Tekeni had spoken earlier, when those two had just been brought to the town. The youth's ability to make a speech was not a bad one. Speaking simply, his phrases short and uncanny, presenting his claims in a logical way, the twin did not leave his audience indifferent. Not a classic oratory, but a good way of speaking, impressively simple. With his eyes meeting the gazes of the people he talked to, firm and unwavering, radiating conviction, the lips of the young man had told them that his companion was sent by the Great Spirits to make their lives better. This was the will of the Right-Handed Twin himself that this man should be listened to and assisted. A claim that should have made people laugh, or maybe argue, but for some reason, it did not. Instead they listened, patient with the ceaseless translation, their eyes suspicious but thoughtful, their minds absorbing the words.

"Tekeni believes you to be the Messenger of the Right-Handed Twin."

The man's eyes flickered with what seemed to be a mirthless amusement. "My mission does have a blessing of the Great Spirits. There was a prophecy. It was interpreted wrongly, for too long. I was blind. I couldn't see. I had dreams, but I did not want to accept them. But now, now I know better." The same mirthless grin stretched the generous lips. "So, yes, he believes that, and I believe that too, now. I shied away from my destiny for too long. But I will ignore my purpose no longer."

Fascinated, Atiron took a deep breath. "What *is* your purpose?"

"Our people should not war on each other. It's a war among brothers." The luminous eyes sparkled. "We are no different. Especially your people, and by your people I mean all the people from your side of the Great Lake. I've conversed with the People of the Hills, I've enjoyed the hospitality of a wonderful woman belonging to the People of the Standing Stone. I now warm by the Flint People's fire. All these people are not different from each other. They live in the same way, they follow the same customs, they speak similar tongues. They are brothers that should not war on one another. Their hatred is destructive and fruitless. It must stop. Time to bury the weapons has come."

Sighing, Atiron wished Tekeni had stayed instead of sneaking away the moment he could. Oh, how he needed the youth's translation now!

"You say we are no different," he said, nodding. "This is a strange argument, coming from a foreigner. No matter how much Tekeni had told you about us, no matter how many people you met, you did not spend enough time on our side of the Great Lake to form a worthwhile opinion." He raised his hand, when the man began saying something. "But this argument aside, how will you make it work in case the people were willing to listen." Seeing the painful frown of his guest, he sighed, simplifying. "How will it work? Who decide? Who say how to do things?"

The man's face brightened. "Oh, how work? The councils, of course. The council of the whole people. Like Town Council, but of all people. Flint People council, Onondaga People council. See? We will need to organize those, and it will work, as it will be no different from the way we manage our towns and villages. The same thing." Now it was his guest's turn to stop Atiron's words with a polite gesture. "The council of the whole people would decide the matters of the nation, but not these of their neighbors, of course. Not the matters concerning the whole, err, union."

"How would the problems between the nations be solved, then?"

Another bout of simplifying and his guest smiled triumphantly. "Another council, of course. But of a different kind. The Great Council of the Nations." His smile widened. "Five nations, or maybe more. Who knows? More people may want to join us with the passing of time."

Atiron felt his head reeling from the effort to understand the foreign-sounding words intermitted into the attempts to use the Flint People's tongue; the grand scale plans that, at least in the privacy of his home and the cozy warmth of the flickering fire, actually sounded not that impossible. Or were they?

"The Great Council that would work like our towns' councils?" he said, shaking his head, watching the pictures the dancing fire drew. There were too many drafts. The cracks in the walls needed to be located and patched before the winter

moons came. "Who will be the representatives? How many?"
Again, the frustrated frown of his guest made him simplify his
words. "Who decide which people are going to your Great
Council?"

"The Clans Mothers, of course." The foreigner looked up,
satisfied. "It will work because nothing would change. Same as
the regular councils, the regular way of managing our towns'
affairs, but on a greater scale." The grin disappeared, replaced
by a thoughtful frown. "Some changes would have to be made,
of course. Changes, adjustments. In the way the Great Council
would be conducted."

"Like what?"

"The decisions. The way they would reach the decisions. It
can't be the majority, like with town councils." The man paused,
standing Atiron's questioning gaze. "Each decision would have
to be reached by mutual agreement. Every, err, representative
would have to agree, otherwise they would not be able to
proceed."

Thunder growled in the distance.

"They will get nowhere if they strive to reach the consent of
each member. You can know the laws and the customs, but
unless you've been a member of your town's council, you
cannot truly know how it works. So many arguments!" Bringing
his palms up, Atiron drew a breath. "I've been a member of our
Town Council for more than five summers. No council would
get anywhere if their decision would require the unanimous
voting."

The foreigner nodded, his forehead glittering with sweat at
the effort to understand.

"And yet, no nation, no town would agree to be the part of
the union which is not respecting its views and opinions," he
said quietly, narrowing his eyes against the glimmering of the
fire. "One member whose protest had been overlooked would
represent one nation, one town, ready to leave in anger, never to
return. Ready to go back to the old ways."

For a while they said nothing, each sinking into his thoughts.

Yes, the foreigner was right, thought Atiron, his head aching. While Town Councils could argue and get angry with each other, with the Clans Mothers having their own scores to settle, such conduct could not be allowed at the Great Council of a newly organized union. The temptation to spit in anger and leave would be too near, within an easy reach. With the memories of the old wrongs still fresh in everyone's heart, the representatives whose opinions were not listened to would be prompted to do just that.

"The Great Council would have to function in a different way," he said, sensing more than seeing his guest's gaze, clinging to him, expectant. "Their way of deliberating should be more complex, involving more directions than just sitting across the fire and talking." He looked up, meeting the narrowing eyes. "How many representatives?"

"Same as the amount of towns," said the man instantly, not pausing to think. He had thought it all out already, realized Atiron, a stab of excitement rushing through his chest. It was more than just prophecies and dreams. "How many important settlements do People of the Flint have?"

"Eight large towns."

"Then eight representatives. A man from each town."

Looking up, Atiron glimpsed his daughter coming down the corridor, proceeding quietly, trying not to disturb the sleep of their longhouse's dwellers, her dress soaked, her braids sparkling droplets of water.

"The People of the Hills have more towns," he said, taking his mind off the girl, fighting the urge to scold her for running around at night and in such weather. "We will never agree for the other nation to have more representatives."

The foreigner's eyes followed the girl's progress absently, not registering her presence to its full extent, of that Atiron was sure. Yet, as Kahontsi's gaze lingered, studying the man with unconcealed curiosity, his eyes focused and he grinned at her, his smile reflecting a pure masculine appreciation, sliding down the delicate curves of her body where the wet dress clung to it, revealing more than it concealed.

"Why were you out there in such weather?" asked Atiron, more curtly than he intended to. "Take dry clothes and go to your mother. She is at your sister's now."

Kahontsi's cheeks took a darker shade. "I was out there with the twin, helping him around, introducing him to his old friends. You told me to do this!"

"But not through the whole night!" Feeling ridiculous at being so angry, Atiron drew a deep breath. "Go to your mother now. Take dry clothes and go. Where is the twin, anyway?"

"Still out there," tossed the girl, offended, her eyes drawing again to the foreigner, who, to Atiron's unexplained relief, sank back into his thoughts, staring into the fire.

Pursing her lips, the girl turned around, heading in the wrong direction again, back toward the entrance and the beating rain. Atiron stifled a curse.

"The amount of representatives should not matter if the…" The man frowned, searching for a right word. "If the unanimous vote is required."

"Oh, well, yes, this is true." Surprised by the truthfulness of this claim, Atiron took his thoughts off his daughter. "Still, why would the smaller nation be represented by more people?" He shook his head. "Our people won't like it, unanimous voting or not."

The foreigner shrugged. "Yes, it was just a thought. We may find a better way to… to nominate representatives." His grin was again thin and mirthless. "We will deal with it when the time comes."

"So this is what you will be suggesting to our Town Council tomorrow, when it will gather to listen to you?"

"Yes, more or less. I will talk about the general agreement between your people and the others. Less in the detail we discussed, I suppose."

Atiron suppressed a grin. "Yes, if they listened, in general or in detail, it would be a miracle."

The foreigner's eyes sparkled strangely. "They will."

"Why?" Unsettled, he watched the thoughtful expression, the firm jaw, the dark, glowing gaze. What did the man know that they all did not? Had he the blessing and the outright support of the Great Spirits, after all?

The pursed lips twisted lightly. "I came that far, and there is no way back. It won't be easy to convince them, but convince them I will. By all means."

Oh, if only he was not switching to that horrible sounding tongue of his people all the time. Atiron pressed his lips in his turn.

"They won't be inclined to listen," he said, catching the general gist. "On that account I'm in minority. The insults of the past are too fresh to forget. Our Town Council is more violently inclined than the War Chief for a change."

"If the War Chief listens it's good," said the man eagerly, his gaze losing its ethereal glow. "Also, you listen. That is good, make two people."

"Which leaves you with many more influential townsfolk to deal with." Stirring the fire to make it come back to life, Atiron sighed. "Tekeni will be translating, which will be of a great help. My head is aching from our conversation already. At times, it was tempting to stop listening."

"Oh, I regret that!" The man laughed loudly, taking the last of the strange sensation away. He was just a man, a wise, enterprising, impressively strong-willed person, a creation of the Right-Handed Twin, yes, but not his messenger. "My head is no better. I wish I could speak my tongue for a day or two without feeling guilty. Trough our journey here, we tried to speak in your people's tongue only, to make me learn faster. Tekeni was very insistent."

Atiron could not suppress a smile. "He was always like that, such a strong-spirited, willful creature. His brother was just the opposite." His mood darkening, he remembered the other twin. "They completed each other so well, this pair. So different, always together. The twins of the prophecy."

"The twins?" The eyes of his guest widened. "They were

twins?"

"Yes, they were twins. Impossible to tell apart as babies, but very different once children. Tekeni was the stronger of the two, and it showed, always taller and broader, so vital. His brother was small and thin. It was a strange pair. They looked as different as they looked alike."

The man's eyes clung to Atiron's face. "What did the prophecy say?"

"Well, the prophecy was not clear. It said that the twins were destined to help Little Falls gain the most prominent place in the land. More power maybe. More influence among our people. No one knew for certain. They were twins, a miracle in itself, born to a very prominent man. People were ready to believe in their destiny." Shrugging, Atiron busied himself with the fire, wishing to conceal his expression now. "When the other twin died, the people of Little Falls were shattered. It was not a part of the prophecy. They were expected to do the changes together. It was always about Tekeni, the stronger twin, but never alone." Suddenly, he caught his breath, staring at the man in front of him. *No, it could not be!*

"He never told me about the prophecy," muttered the foreigner, frowning. "Did he know?"

"Oh, yes, he did. It was no secret. Maybe not the details, but both twins knew the general gist. Their father was too proud to keep it to himself."

For a while they kept silent, each deep in his thoughts. But no, it could not be about this man, thought Atiron, his heart beating fast. The most prominent place in the land? To make Little Falls the leading town of the Flint People? But the foreigner suggested something completely different, something strange, unacceptable. It could not be a part of Tekeni's prophecy.

And yet, if the peace with their neighbors was to be reached and the Great Council of this man's vision organized, Little Falls would gain the most prominent place, being the first to back the innovative foreigner up.

The light of the fire danced, reflecting in the face of his silent guest, sliding down the sharp cheekbones, bouncing off the strong jaw. This man had made such a long way, going against the currents and against the better judgment, following his vision. He believed in it, enough to endanger his life and be ready to sacrifice it even. Was he truly the Messenger of the Great Spirits?

Atiron sighed. "If the storm continues into tomorrow, you may be able to talk to our council sooner than you think."

If the storm continues...

CHAPTER 17

Huddling under the platform encircling the upper part of the inner fence, Tekeni winced as another wave of thunder rolled above, drowning their voices in its mighty roar. Heno the Thunderer was not in the most pleasant of moods, he reflected, watching the small torrents raging around his moccasins, covering them up to his ankles. No wonder, truly. He felt as angry, as frustrated as the thundering deity. More so, come to think of it. If he were Heno, he might have directed one of the thunderbolts straight into the roof of this or that longhouse, setting it on fire.

Disquieted with this thought, he frowned. This was his town, his people. How could he wish them so much harm?

"If it goes on raining like that, there will be no jumping falls tomorrow," said Anowara, pressing closer to the wooden poles, trying to escape the slashing rain.

"I hope so," muttered Tekeni. "But we can't count on it. It might get as clear as the midsummer with dawn." He narrowed his eyes, trying to see through the hazy darkness. "Are you sure it will work? We have so little time!"

The tall youth snorted loudly. "Yes, I'm sure, oh honorable visitor from the lands of the savages. My plans are always good. Or have you forgotten even this?"

"Oh yes, they are always good. Like this plan to keep the bees busy so we could get to the honey with no trouble. That was one good plan."

Against his will, he laughed, remembering the way they had literally rolled down that tree, three silly boys in panic, seeing the clouds of angry bees nearing, buzzing so loudly they could be heard in the realm of the Sky Deities, of that they were sure. Anowara had maintained that if one of them lured the busy insects away, the other two could gorge on the honey with no trouble. He was a lanky boy back then, thin and angular, not especially impressive, but his mind was bursting with brilliant ideas, and reinforced by the twins, his closest of friends, he brought them into all sorts of trouble more times than not.

"Oh, so the scar-faced warrior remembers his past. How touching." The youth's laughter rolled in perfect accord with the next thundering. "The people of Little Falls are honored, I can tell you that."

"Shut up." Shielding his eyes, Tekeni peeked out, trying to see through the darkness. "Where is Kahontsi? Why does it take her so long?"

"What do you want? Her longhouse is on the other side of the town, and it's dark now." The youth's shrug was clearly visible in the next flash of lightning. "You made the poor girl run in the storm, and now you are complaining!"

"I couldn't go myself. They would make me stay and translate again."

"But you do it well." There was a trace of appreciation in Anowara's voice. "I still can't believe you speak the way the Crooked Tongues do, and so easily."

"If you lived among them for two summers you would speak their way, too."

The pair of the wide-opened eyes neared, peering at him. "How was it to live among the savages? I mean, it must have been strange and, oh, disgusting too, no? They are ugly and fierce, and so, well, crooked-tongued."

Tekeni suppressed the familiar wave of irritation. "It was strange, yes. They have different customs. But they are no savages, and their tongue is all right. You've seen Two Rivers. He is not strange and not ugly, and what he says should be listened to. He knows what he is talking about."

"Or so you keep saying, but without you, no one would listen to him at all. And if no one listened, then the test of the falls would look like a bright summer day compared to what they would have done to him."

The falls! Tekeni ground his teeth. "Why do they have to test him? Why can't they just believe him?"

"He said he is the Messenger of the Great Spirits. We can't take this claim lightly."

"I said that, not him!" cried out Tekeni, frustrated. "I said it because I do believe in him and his destiny, but it's not that simple. He is a man, and he can get wounded or killed. We've been to battles. He gets wounded like any other person." He flapped his hands in the air, pushing the rain away. "But he *is* the Messenger of the Great Spirits all the same! It has nothing to do with the abilities of the Sky Deities. He is a mortal man with a mission of immortal deities."

"Well, if the Right-Handed Twin needs this man, then maybe he is using you and me now to save him. And we are doing this, so stop screaming and beating at the rain. Concentrate on our planning." The dark eyes flickered again. "You were always wild, but the stay among the savages turned you into a complete beast."

"They are no savages," muttered Tekeni stubbornly, trying to get hold of his temper. It was fraying too easily these days, he knew. Since they set out toward Little Falls and its people, *his people*, sailing with the current, he'd known not a heartbeat of peace. "If the rain continues they may decide to let him speak before the council first, and by the time he finished, they would have changed their minds."

"What does he want, anyway?"

He took a deep breath. "He wants us to make peace with our neighbors. He wants us to stop warring with each other."

The skeptical grin and the lifted eyebrows were his answer. "Yes, I know that. They've been talking about nothing else this evening, nothing but your strange foreigner and his strange ideas of negotiating with the dirty enemies who happen to be our neighbors. Oh, and your miraculous reappearance, of course! Back from the dead and straight away into the action."

The flicker in the dark eyes was unmistakable. "Not bad, old friend, not bad at all. A spectacular appearance, I say. Someone else might have just come home and said *she:kon*. Someone else but not you! Why would you return without stirring a trouble, eh?"

The hurried footsteps cut the darkness as Kahontsi's slender silhouette slipped in under their shelter, her dress soaking, hair askew, wet tendrils plastered to the glittering, exquisitely shaped, gentle face of hers.

"Oh, Mighty Spirits, but Heno is in the fiercest of his moods tonight!" she exclaimed, pressing against the poles, shivering with cold. "I can't believe I came back."

"You should have stayed in your longhouse." Pulling his shirt off, Anowara wrapped it around the girl's shoulders, protective in too obvious of a way. "It can wait until tomorrow. I'll take you home now."

Having no shirt to offer, Tekeni eyed the girl guiltily.

"What did you find out?" he asked, unable to keep his anxiety at bay.

"Oh, well, quite a lot." Her eyes were wide-open as she leaned forward, trying to see him better. "I was in the Wolf Clan's dwelling, and then I went to the Bear Clan's longhouse, to visit my friends. Or so I claimed. They were talking about your foreigner, of course. The entire longhouse, huddling together, speaking all at once. No one listened to the other. Their Clan Mothers were furious." She giggled. "And they talked about you, too. It's difficult to overcome the shock of your coming back from the dead, you know?"

Anowara laughed loudly. "He is a spirit, I'm telling you. We should run away from him instead of listening to his wild schemes here in the darkness."

"Are you?" asked the girl, eyes glittering, teasing.

"Yes, I am. And I'm an evil spirit, too. I resided in the meanest, sickness-stricken coyote of the northern woods. So you better be nice to me and do everything I ask."

"*Everything* you ask?"

Her laughter made him uncomfortable, but it also served to ease his tension, his nerves less taut now, enjoying her presence under their improvised shelter. She was full of mischief, this playful cousin of his, and yet the similarities to Seketa were there, too obvious not to notice, in her beauty, her kindness, and this readily trilling laughter of hers.

Anowara frowned. "Go on, tell him fast. We have to bring you home. Your mother will be furious."

"She is at my sister's," said the girl, unconcerned. "I've been there before I came here."

Tekeni caught his breath. "Are they still talking?"

"Yes, oh yes! My father and your foreigner are talking, and a lot. When I came they were deeply immersed, although both seemed to be having a hard time understanding each other. Still, they went back to councils and representatives the moment I left."

"Oh, it's good. Your father is listening!"

But the girl frowned. "My father is not a problem. He was always inclined this way. Even back in the days of your father he was arguing against some of the raids and their necessity." Her shrug was a brief lighthearted affair. "He hasn't changed."

"But if Two Rivers made him listen, then he will turn into an ally. He may even talk against the stupid testing-powers ideas in the council tomorrow."

"Oh well, I wouldn't go that far. They are determined to see him doing something wonderful, or dying in a spectacular fashion. That's what I gathered while running around the other longhouses. They talked about his jumping the falls as much as about the other thing."

Tekeni clenched his fists. "Bloodthirsty beasts." They both stared at him, aghast, so he moderated his tone. "Well, I'm sorry. I didn't mean it that way. But they should not make him do anything dangerous. They should just listen to him and do as he suggests. The other people listened. Why does Little Falls need proof?"

"The others were silly to just listen," said Anowara, clearly deeming it high time to contribute to the conversation. Now that the girl was back, the youth seemed to lose some of his bantering lightness, turning serious, desperate to impress. "They should have demanded proof of his powers, too."

"He is an interesting-looking man," said the girl thoughtfully. "Strange, outlandish. But interesting. Impressive. And he has beautiful eyes." They both stared at her now, so she shook her head. "Anyway, how do we go about making sure your foreigner doesn't die in the falls? The way Anowara suggested?"

"Yes. I'll go and see that tree in the morning." Frowning at the diminishing roaring of yet another thunder, Tekeni peeked out. "The storm is going away. Damn it."

They listened to the soft beating of the rain, relatively dry in their small hide-away, the oblique sprays getting scarcer, not reaching them anymore.

"You don't have to check on that tree. I know what I'm talking about," said Anowara impatiently. "It's inclined just the right way, to go straight into the pool if cut. You don't have to get all leading-like, you know? You are not the War Chief yet."

"What if they see through our ploy?" asked the girl thoughtfully, brushing wet tendrils off her face.

Fighting the urge to glare his former friend down, Tekeni shrugged. "They won't, because we'll make this offer sound like more of a challenge than just a simple jump into the falls." He glanced at the tall youth. "I'm not trying to tell you what to do. I do appreciate your help. Your idea is good and I'm grateful."

"Then it is something," Anowara's pressed lips twisted into a sort of a grin. "I hope your foreigner is worthy of our trouble."

"He is! He is worthy of our trouble and more. You'll see. So just make sure to organize your canoe to be down there and ready the moment they decide."

A mere trickling greeted them as they ventured into the open, huddled together, mainly for warmth.

"I'll go and see Tsitsho," said Anowara, slowing his step beside the longhouse with a huge turtle engraved upon its façade. "He is still awake. I'm ready to bet my bow on this."

"Why?" Glancing at the sky once again, Tekeni scowled. The sprinkles came down weak, disgustingly scattered.

"He'll help us, that's why."

"But can we trust him? I say we should do this all by ourselves. Less people involved, less chances of our ploy being discovered." Impatiently, he waved his hands in the air. "How difficult is it to bring that stupid canoe down there, into the quietest pool ever, and just sit and wait for someone to fall into one's lap, eh? Why do you need someone else's help?"

"Because Tsitsho is good in navigating through the rapids, you stupid lump of meat. Did you think about it, eh? How to bring that canoe down there? Have you happened to think of the details, you grand strategist, or all you do is demand to be helped like the spoiled brat that you are?"

"Oh, stop arguing," exclaimed Kahontsi, as her companions glared at each other, going dangerously silent all of a sudden. "We have something important to do. To save Tekeni's foreigner, the messenger of the Great Spirits or not, we have to be quick and enterprising, and we have to behave like the grownup people we are. Not like two angry boys, ready to punch each other!"

She glowered at them in her turn, genuinely enraged, and again Tekeni reflected how Seketa-like she looked, fierce and unafraid, full of righteousness. His stomach twisted as he made an effort to control his anger. Yes, Two Rivers' life was more important than the silly rivalry of his childhood friend.

"I just think that if less people know of our scheme, it has less chances of being discovered. Even if it worked and all went according to our plan, we don't want anyone discovering what happened, not even summers from now. They will be furious, and with a good cause. And it may spoil Two Rivers' mission, somehow."

"All you worry about is your foreigner and his stupid mission," muttered Anowara, but there was no challenge in his voice anymore, and his eyes were firm upon the tips of his water-soaked moccasins.

"Tsitsho can be trusted as much as any of us." The girl's smile was sudden, startling in its glamorous lightness. "Of course, we don't want anyone learning of what happened, even summers from now. But first of all, we need to succeed, and this is what must be our main concern. So if Anowara enlists Tsitsho's support, we are good. I'll be down there too, but you," she peered at Tekeni, her forehead creasing. "You will have to be here, among the people who would come to watch. You will be forced to be among the elders and the members of the council, so you will be of no help to us down there." Her smile was small, full of concern. "It will be difficult for you. I know that."

"I'll manage, as long as this ordeal will be over with no one killed or drowned." He smiled at the girl, then touched Anowara's arm. "I'm grateful, I truly am. You two are great friends. So much has changed and still you are ready to help me with the strangest request possible. I will repay you, both of you." He grinned. "And Tsitsho too, if he can navigate that well."

Their laughter tore the darkness.

"Well, this is your first time coming back from the dead." Anowara's grin was free of shadows as well. "Maybe next time we will not be as nice. I'll come to fetch you first thing in the morning," he added, addressing the girl. "So be ready." A light wave at Tekeni. "Sleep well, Crooked Tongues boy."

The way to the Turtles Clan's largest longhouse was clear now, brightened lightly by the fresh moon.

"I wish your brother was still with us," said Tekeni quietly. "He would have helped us."

He felt the girl tensing by his side, and it made him regret the spontaneous words.

"Yes, he would have solved this whole thing with no trouble." Her whisper was hoarse, cutting the darkness. "Many things would be different if he and you and your father did not go on that raid."

"Yes." Now it was his turn to fight the violent squeeze in his stomach.

"How did he die?" she asked, after a while. "I know Father will ask you that too, but I want to hear it from you and not from him."

Tekeni held his breath, afraid to invite the memories he was careful to push away for more than two summers. "He was very brave. He fought like a mountain lion. There were so many of them, and more were coming from among the trees. He shot all his arrows, and then he charged with his club, waving it in the way that made the enemy hesitate, retreat a little." He swallowed. "Father was dead already, and our people lost their spirit, but when your brother charged, they went after him, ready to die with honor and not to be captured."

It was difficult to talk now, so he paused, seeing the distant northern woods in his mind's eye, the slashing wind and the glowering sky, the swaying trees and the blood-freezing cries rolling from all around, filling the world with the heavy stench of gore and worse; that and the terrible, mindless sense of horror that tasted like vomit in his mouth, the memory of it never going away.

"I didn't see how he died, because a warrior hit me, and I was upon the ground, trying to get up." Another knot in his throat swallowed. "I should have fought on, died like they did. They were brave. I was not."

The squeeze of her palm upon his arm brought him back to the damp chilliness of the night and the colorful leaves piling before her longhouse, swept by the wind.

"You were a mere boy back then. You were not a warrior yet," she said firmly, holding his gaze. "And I'm glad you didn't die like they did. You have your destiny to fulfill. You were not destined to die in the Crooked Tongues lands, but I understand now that you were supposed to be there, to bring us your wondrous foreigner, to make our lives better, like your prophecy foretold. Look at you!" Shorter than him, she stood on her tiptoes, peering into his face, making him shiver as he hung on her every word. "You are a warrior now. An impressive warrior with no fear in your face, with no hesitation. You have a bear-claw necklace, and it means only one thing. You slew a huge brown bear while seeing less than twenty summers of your life. You have scars to prove you fought a human enemy, too. And, most importantly, you have an important mission. Without you your foreigner would not be heard, not here, not among our people; and not among the other peoples of our side of the Great Lake, I suspect. Have you translated for him when he talked to the Onondagas? Thought so!" Taking in his hesitant nod, she pursed her lips, her eyes narrow and attentive. "You have your destiny, and it is a glorious one. So stop thinking about the past and the people we lost. We should let their spirits rest. Your father, my brother, all of them. And your brother, too. They are in the Sky World, looking upon us, proud and happy at what we are doing. I know that now."

Resuming her walk, she let his arm go, but he felt the warmth of her touch lingering, encircling his wrist.

"This is the first time I feel glad to be home," he said, when able to talk. "You are a wonderful person, Kahontsi. You were always this way. When I remembered Little Falls, I always remembered you and your father. The other people were just blurred silhouettes in my mind's eyes, but you two were always bright, distinct, wonderfully vivid. And now I know why."

"Why?" she asked quietly, slowing her step once again.

"I can't explain it. But now I know that you are like him, in a way. Strong and determined, but never prejudiced or narrow-minded. You have a beautiful spirit that is able to see beyond the obvious."

And you are like her too, he thought, the stony fist back, gripping his insides. *Oh yes, just like her, beautiful, fierce, brave, oh-so-very kind. And yet, you are nothing but a naive young girl, floating happily in your cloud of innocent confidence, trusting life to be just and kind to you, always. While she had known suffering already, learning the lesson, discovering that life would not always offer a fair judgment, and even if you were to follow the rules it could all get out of hand, force you to go against the convention, force you to pay the price while doing it. A heavy price, and she was paying it now. Unless...*

He clenched his fists tight. Unless she chose to forget, after all.

"Tell me about him." Slowing her step in front of the wooden partition, shut tight because of the rain, Kahontsi peered at him, bringing him back from his dark reverie.

"Oh, him, well, he is an outstanding man." Glad to escape his unhappy thoughts, Tekeni shook his head. "Of a sort you never met. There are simply no people like him. He is fierce and courageous like the best of the warriors, and he is a great hunter, too. He was the one to help me track that bear of mine. Without his guidance, his way of teaching me, I would have been lost, dead most certainly. He has been so kind to me, on so many occasions!" He frowned. "But of course, there are quite a few great warriors, great hunters and kind people out there. So no, it is not where his special strength lies. It is something else. I don't know what it is, but he thinks most clearly, and he plans for long summers to come, as though he can see the future. He knows so much! I don't think there is something in our earthly world that he doesn't know, nothing that he didn't think most thoroughly about already. Do you see what I mean?"

She nodded, fascinated, her eyes wide open and round, her mouth almost gaping.

"I think he can see people's minds and what they hold. Many times I saw the proof of it. He knows what should be done with our people, and I'm telling you, it is the right thing no matter how you look at it. He knows." He clenched his teeth. "And he knew that Little Falls was a dangerous place for him to go. I could see it most clearly, through this last part of our journey and before, too. He knew it would be dangerous, but he also knew that our town is important and could not be avoided." He shut his eyes for a heartbeat, frustrated. "I fear for him. I wish they asked me to jump into the falls, instead of him."

She gasped. "Would you do this for him?"

"Yes, yes, I would! I would do anything for him." He hesitated. "Anything but one thing."

"What?" she whispered, holding her breath.

"I will not break a promise that I made. Not even for him." The black wave of desperation was back, threatening to drown him again. "But I postponed even that, for his sake. If he chose not to go to Little Falls before the Freezing Moons, I might have been able to keep my promise this span of seasons and not the next."

She eyed him thoughtfully, her eyes shining with excitement. "It's a promise to a woman," she said, making it a statement.

"Yes."

"Does she live in the Onondaga lands?"

"No. She is a Wyandot girl." He saw her frown, and the blank expression in her eyes. "Crooked Tongues, she is Crooked Tongues girl."

"Oh." She let out a breath, her face agog with excitement. "You fell in love with the woman of your captors!"

"I was adopted," he said, shrugging. "I was one of theirs. Well, officially, if not otherwise."

"But you didn't mean to leave?"

"I did, yes, I planned to run away in all sorts of ways. And then it all got complicated. And well… I left with Two Rivers in the end." He eyed the wooden partition, wishing the storm to return. It would keep Two Rivers safe tomorrow, and it would also stop this flood of questioning. "We should go in. We need to rest, gather our strength for tomorrow. Also, your family will be angry with you."

"Why did he leave?" she asked, watching him as though he had not spoken at all. "Was there a reason, besides his mission and the prophecies?" Her high forehead creased as her eyebrows met each other. "Why didn't he start with his own people? Don't they deserve to live in peace, too?"

He sighed. "They didn't want to listen to him. They were blind, blind with hatred and prejudice. Good, decent people loved and admired him, but there were more of those who did not." Shrugging, he shifted his weight from one foot to another. "They are foolish, and they will be made sorry for their mistakes. They will pay the price, eventually."

"But not the girl you love?"

"She will not stay with her people. She will leave when I return for her." He swallowed. "She promised."

"Oh, I can't wait to see her," exclaimed Kahontsi, eyes shining. "She must be beautiful, this mysterious Crooked Tongues girl who captured your spirit and who is holding it so firmly until you can think of nothing else, not even the mission of the man you admire the most. Not even your own people."

"That is not true," he protested. "I help Two Rivers all I can. I do everything that is in my power to do." He glared at her, very put out. "And I do care about my people. I'm here, am I not? Aiding in every way, speaking until my throat hurts, trying to make them listen."

"But you think of her," she insisted. "You think about her so much, you told me all about her on our first evening together, before you told me anything of significance." Her laughter trilled, shattering the darkness of his mood. "Oh, don't look at me like that. I'm not teasing you. It is the most beautiful feeling, the heart of many stories. Remember the death song of the falls? You would do this for her too, wouldn't you? Take your canoe and sail straight into the worst of the cascades? And she would do this for you, I'm sure of that." She sighed, her smile beautiful. "And it will happen to me, too, one day. I'm yet to feel what you feel, and I can't wait to meet the man who will do this to me." The beauty of her smile faded, turned mischievous. "And your foreigner, the Crooked Tongues man, did he leave a beautiful woman behind, too? He isn't young; he must have left a family behind."

"No," said Tekeni, relieved to stir from the musings concerning his feelings. That old story with the girl and the waterfalls. How stupid. She was so silly at times, this vital, sparkling Kahontsi. "He never settled with a woman. They just kept making fools of themselves over him and his affection. But he was too busy, of course."

"Too busy, eh?" Her smile deepened, turning so feminine he felt like taking a step back. She was a beautiful girl, and in the almost three summers of his absence she had definitely turned into a woman.

"Don't think silly thoughts," he said, reaching for the wooden screen, feeling awkward. "He is busier than ever now. And also, there is this Onondaga girl."

Her eyes narrowed. "What Onondaga girl?"

But that was just too much. "Listen, if you want to know things about his private, err, interests, go and ask him. If you two speak slowly you can do without me translating. But I would advise you against entertaining this kind of ideas. He is not into silly things, surely not in the town of people who are suspicious of him and his motives. He is not one of us, and he may never be that, too. He belongs to no people." He shook his head, furious with himself for getting into such discussion, her challenging gaze irritating, making him feel silly, out of his depth. "Let us go in and forget about this conversation. Just help me make sure he survives tomorrow, for you to entertain more silly thoughts about him."

Pulling the heavy screen aside, trying to make as little noise as possible, he heard the air hissing behind his back as she drew a deep breath.

"You are talking so much nonsense, one's head reels," she exclaimed, stomping her foot. "What a wonderful faith-keeper you will make, advising people on the proper behavior. I wish you would keep your silly advice to yourself, you know?"

"Come in and stop screaming. You'll wake up your entire longhouse."

Hiding his grin, he slipped into the darkness of the storage room, enjoying its smells, his hunger rising. He should grab something edible before going to sleep, he thought. A freshly baked cornbread with berries could be wonderful, but a strip of dried meat would do just as well. Tomorrow there might be a feast thrown in their honor, to celebrate his, Tekeni's, miraculous coming back and to welcome Two Rivers into the town.

His stomach twisted again, with hunger this time. It would be wonderful to eat well, and to meet all the people he knew, and to start implementing their plans. There was so much to do, so much to accomplish, so many matters to attend to. Plenty of work, but plenty of enjoyment, too.

He could picture the surprise on Hionhwatha's face, and the twisted grin of the Onondaga girl, and the deep, satisfied smile upon Jikonsahseh's face. They would be surprised, all of them. And they would be pleased too, even if they'd make an effort not to show it. *If Two Rivers survives tomorrow!*

He took a deep breath, his hopeful mood gone. Not touching the food, he proceeded down the darkly lit corridor, following the angry swirls of Kahontsi's skirt. *Oh, Mighty Spirits*, he thought, sick with worry. *Please, let our plan succeed. Please, keep him safe and in good health. Please!*

CHAPTER 18

The wind tore at the treetops, rushing the clouds across the scowling sky. The storm was gone, but its sights were still there, with the sunlight hesitant, not eager to break through the grayish mass.

Was he to receive no blessing of Father Sun, wondered Two Rivers, his mind numb, dizzy with lack of sleep, heavy with foreboding? Was he to seek his Sky Path in this gloomy unfriendly haze?

He stood upon the top of the cliff, the effort to keep his shoulders straight difficult, taking more of the remnants of his strength. If only there weren't so many people around, silent or talking quietly, their gazes upon him, consumed with curiosity. Not cruel or bloodthirsty. Expectant. Like children offered something fascinating to watch. *Like back in his dream.*

He suppressed a shiver. Since crossing the Great Sparkling Water more than two moons ago, the vision did not visit his sleep. The last time it happened was on the bear hunt, when he came to know that the savage youth has a part in it all. The dream had not returned since then, but here it was, happening all the same – the foreign faces peering at him, some friendly, some wary, some indifferent, drowning in the dreadful roaring of the falls. Oh, but for the terrible growling he might have felt a little better. It was worse than the thundering of the last night's storm, worse than the wild thumping of his heart. He could not hear his own thoughts even. No wonder they were dashing around his head like a bunch of panicked squirrels.

"Are you certain you wish to do it in the way you suggested?" asked the square, middle-aged man, his gaze piercing, his face long and impassive, giving nothing away. The Head of the Town Council, followed by other prominent people of the town. At long last, he had been honored with proper introductions.

"Yes, I wish to do it this way," he said, surprised to hear his own voice steady and calm, carrying clearly above the deafening noise. It was as though someone else were talking. "I will climb this tree, and you will cut it and let it fall into the worst of the falls."

Tekeni translated rapidly, standing beside him, his presence reassuring. Again, it took the youth longer to finish his speech, making it sound more flowery, more daring and challenging, of that Two Rivers was sure.

He didn't mind. It was this young man's idea from the very beginning, his planning, his executing. The wolf cub seemed as though knowing what to do, just like back in the dream. A ridiculously simple solution. But not that simple at all!

He remembered the previous day, the difficult evening, the endless talking and translating, the need to keep his back straight and his face impassive, standing the people's gazes and the enquiring nature of their questioning, coated with only a thin layer of politeness. They were curious, but mainly by his bravery at coming here. They were not prepared to listen, not to a foreigner. But if he survived the fall into the cascading mass of furious water, they might.

As though anyone can survive the dreadful falls, the wild torrents and the sharp rocks lining its bottom.

And yet, there was a quiet pool just a little way behind the first rapids, Tekeni had whispered, when they lay on their mats beside the dying fire, waiting for the night to dissolve. Satisfactorily large and deep, it offered a chance of survival. With some preparation and a benevolence of the Great Spirits, the test of the falls might be overcome.

He remembered the youth's eyes, peering at him through the smoke-filled darkness, anxious, their fear unconcealed. Careful to keep his voice low, Two Rivers questioned him all about it, and about the plan. A precarious, desperate solution, but they had no better one. The people of Little Falls were no fools.

"But they will not see through our ploy, if we will challenge them, will make this jump to seem even more impossible," whispered the youth, his words gushing like the rapids themselves, anxious to be said. "There is nothing mysterious, or spectacular, about a simple jump. But if you demand to climb the tree for it to be cut and fall into the falls, well, this might give their storytellers a tale to retell through the long winter moons to come."

"And the tree will help me to reach the pool somehow?" he asked, warmed by the youth's open concern.

"Yes, it will. Anowara, this boy who used to be my friend, says it's inclined just the right way to start falling into the direction we want." Tekeni's eyes glittered, their tension obvious. "So you will have to be careful to climb it from its eastern side, to add your weight and make it fall in a right way for sure." He frowned. "I will check that tree first thing in the morning, of course. Just to make sure Anowara knows what he is talking about."

"And then?"

"And then, well, it'll fall as close to the pool as possible, and you better jump when it's half way down, directing yourself into the deepest of the water." His frown deepening, the youth shifted, leaning on his elbow, trying to keep still. "And Anowara and another boy will be there, in their canoe, ready to fish you out should you not make your way down there smoothly enough to just swim to the other side of the rocks."

"And what will the town folk see? The divine messenger jumping aside half way down the road, to be fished out by a few youths?" He forced a grin. "I'm not sure it'll be their idea of the miraculous survival."

"They will see nothing. Midway through the jump it will be all swirling mist of drizzle and sprays. One can't see the bottom of the falls from the cliff you will be jumping off of."

He remembered his stomach twisting so violently, he was

afraid he would vomit right there, in the compartment of his kind, open-minded host. Breathing deeply, he made the spasm subdue.

"It will work. I'm sure it will," he said, however Tekeni's sigh sounded anything but encouraging, so he smiled at the youth, doing his best to reassure him. "Our mission is in its early, beginning stage. There is much work to be done, and I will not leave you to do it all alone."

"You better not." The handsome face contorted, making the scars upon it shift in a strange manner. "I still can't understand why you had to give them the idea in the first place. They were ready to invite us into the town, the suspicion of that warriors' leader notwithstanding. No one thought of the falls until you pointed them out, challenging them to challenge you."

He sighed. "It had to happen this way."

"Why?"

Holding the stormy gaze, Two Rivers remembered the calm flowing through his body, making his limbs relax at long last.

"It was foretold, all of it. Remember back in my town, our conversation on the cliff, when I asked you to talk in your people's tongue? The dream was always there, haunting me, but I could not understand its meaning until we talked on that eventful day. It was all in the dream, the falls and this town and your people, crowding around, talking in your tongue. And you were there, also, and so was your solution. Not what you suggested now in particular, but some solution, brought up by you, not me." He shook his head, relishing the memory. "On the night before you killed your bear, I had this dream for the last time, more vivid than ever. Only then did I know you were to be a part of it. Only then, I understood." Shrugging, he took his gaze off, staring at the fire instead. "I still didn't know what to do, but then, on our last evening among my people, you told me the story of the falls, and then I realized where the dream was happening. Here, in Little Falls. I asked you to leave me alone back then because I needed to think it all over." He grinned. "I didn't expect you to get into so much trouble in the short span of time I needed to decide."

He could see Tekeni's face darkening. "I thought we left because we killed Yeentso and the others."

"Yes, we left because of that. When your girl came running, crying for help, I had not arrived at the decision, yet."

"I wish this filthy lowlife had not died that fast!"

"Oh, yes. He died an undeservedly easy death."

The handsome face looked now as though chiseled out of lifeless stone. "In your dream, did you survive the test of the falls?"

He sighed. "I don't know. The dream never went past the moment upon the cliff. It always ended before the actual happening." The embers glowed warmly, inviting to near the fire, but he remained on his mat, shutting his eyes, instead. "The last time it ended with the realization that you were there, having a ridiculously easy solution to the whole problem."

He could hear Tekeni shifting again. "Well, it's not ridiculously easy at all. It's dreadfully complicated, and it still puts your life in a grave danger."

"I know, old friend. I know. But like I told you before, I will not leave you alone to do all the work. We'll do it together, you and me."

Oh, but back in the warmth and the tranquility of the night, in the safety of the longhouse with a symbol of a turtle engraved upon its facade, it was easy to give this promise; easy to tell the words, easy to believe them himself. Yet now?

He eyed the surrounding faces, some friendly, some expectant, some indifferent. Just like in the dream, but painfully real, with angry drops spraying the air, and the thundering of the falls drowning any other sound.

He tried not to shiver as the wind cut into his skin, keeping his back straight and his head high. No, under the ferocious wind and the grey, mournful sky he was not so sure Tekeni would not be left alone to do all the work.

"I'm ready and most willingly accede to your request," he said, meeting their gazes. "Because the Good Tidings of Peace has come upon us, I now confidently place myself in your hands."

It came out well. He heard Tekeni translating in a rush, impressed, not embellishing his words for a change. Their faces were thawing, he could see that, their eyes filling with hope. It gave him strength to walk toward the edge and the indicated tree, seeing it leaning toward the chasm below, old and wobbly, easy to cut.

He fought the urge to look down, his stomach churning. The pool Tekeni had told him about was supposed to be to his right, somewhere behind the roaring mist. He found himself staring into the abyss, his limbs going numb. After the tree would be cut, plummeting into the thundering void, he would have to jump, trying to make it as far eastward as he could.

Forcing his gaze off the howling haze, he tried to calm the mad pounding of his heart. The tree, he was supposed to climb it. He sought a comfortable branch to place his foot on. How ridiculous. He hadn't climbed trees since he had been a youth! Did he climb gracefully enough for their taste? Or did they expect him to fly straight toward the top? Well, in that case, they would be disappointed. He could not fly, and he could not survive the fall into the cascades. It was hopeless. Come to think of it, the Little Falls' dwellers could have done better things with their morning. They would not get the value for the time spent in the cold wind and the near-rain. They would go home soon, disappointed.

The Head of the Town Council was talking. He forced his mind, finding it truly difficult to hear with the rumbling of the furious water. Had they not said it all already?

"We made this proposal, and therefore, you will now climb this tree so it will be a sign of proof, and the people may see your power." Tekeni's translation rang clearly, the only one to overcome the roaring. "If you live to see tomorrow's sunrise, then we will accept your message."

The young man's eyes sparkled, as he translated, not daring to add a word of his own, not with their full attention upon them, listening avidly, but his eyes related it all, his elation, his hope, his belief, boring at Two Rivers, glowing like embers of yesterday's fire. He smiled back with his eyes only, feeling a little better, his limbs lighter, catching the branches, pulling his body up, making it look like an easy work. If he lived to see tomorrow's sunrise, they would accept his message. It was a clear promise. There was no way back from it.

And even if not, he thought, grinning to himself, now out of their sight and able to relax his facial muscles. Even if he died, they would listen to Tekeni, and they would talk to Hionhwatha and his people. The courageous boy he had saved once upon a time lived up to his expectations, growing into a remarkable, outstanding man.

Up on the higher branches, making himself as comfortable as he could between the old wobbly sprigs, he glanced at the gloomy sky, squinting against the wind. It would be difficult to find his path in this clouded vastness. It was always better to go at night, when the dark sky was clear and studded with stars. Like at the night of Iraquas' death. He remembered the anguished face of his friend, twisted and coated with sweat, clinging to his, Two Rivers', hand, whispering with desperation. Still, Iraquas left peacefully, surrounded by love and mourning. He had found his Sky Path with no difficulty, of that he was sure now. But it wouldn't be as easy for him, to find the right path in the bleak, gloomy morning of this distant foreign land, with his shattered, broken body tossed by the swirling currents, crushed against sharp rocks.

The wave of panic splashed again and he fought it, clenching onto the thin branches, feeling them swaying under the monotonous thuds of the axes down below. One, then another. He remembered himself cutting trees, many, many trees, clearing the fields mostly, but sometimes for the firewood, too. It was a difficult task that could take a long time to accomplish. But this tree was old and tottering. It would not take them long to cut the last cord tying him to life.

Stop it, he admonished himself as the tree shook, swaying

madly in the strengthening wind, less and less stable with each strike. *You do whatever you can to make it to the pool, and you leave yourself at the hands of the Right-Handed Twin and the good uki who inhabit these woods and these waters. You came so far, and if it's your time, you will meet your fate with dignity and pride, as a courageous person should. You will not think of the fall anymore. You will think about your mission.*

Clutching to the creaking branches, he crouched upon his precarious perch, ready to jump the moment the tree would go plummeting down. If he survived this fall, they would listen. If he survived this fall, he had won.

He took a deep breath, his excitement welling. It would be good to return to the lands of the Onondagas, backed by the Flint People's agreement, just like he promised. Hionhwatha would be impressed, and the Onondaga girl would be waiting for him at Jikonsahseh's, expectant and proud, challenging, offering more of her delightful companionship, sensible advice, and the most exciting lovemaking he had ever experienced. Oh, what a lover this woman turned out to be, wild, demanding, unrestrained, but sensitive to his needs too, a perfect partner.

But for this alone he would make an effort to stay alive, he decided, fighting his grin, his body ready, as tense as an overstretched bow, his instincts honed. He had promised her to return, and he would have to keep this promise. She would be furious if he did not.

CHAPTER 19

Kahontsi was the first to see the tree coming down. The thundering of the falls above their heads did not let them hear a thing, but she saw the shadow flying across the spraying mist, saw the dark silhouette cutting the air.

"It's coming down," she screamed, but the boys needed none of her warning, paddling vigorously in order to avoid the crushing touch should the tree make it all the way toward their relatively calm hideaway.

"It's not coming our way," called Tsitsho, ceasing to paddle, but just stroking the water now, making sure their canoe did not sweep into the second rapids.

Relieved, they watched the old tree hitting a rock, jerking aside, changing direction, bouncing against other protruding obstacles.

Then the realization dawned.

"The foreigner," she gasped. "He fell into the falls!"

Frowning, Anowara shouted to his friend who began paddling more vigorously again.

"We'll get as close as we can, and see."

However, the spitting torrents revealed nothing but more of their usual white foam and some split branches, carried into their pool now.

"Oh, Mighty Spirits," whispered Kahontsi, her chest squeezing with fright. "Don't let this man die. Please keep him safe, I beg you."

She should have offered a gift to the spirits, she knew. Or maybe a truly decent prayer, accompanied with tobacco offering on the night before, or when the dawn just broke. Hastily muttered words when it was already too late were of no help. They would only serve to offend the Spirits.

"Look there!" Tsitsho's scream tore her from her reverie, making her gaze leap.

"Where? What?" Anowara was asking.

"There, by that rock, behind the second waterfall."

She shielded her eyes against the splashing sprays, leaping to her feet, making their canoe nearly tip. Both youths glared at her direfully, but she didn't care, her eyes searching the sleek rocks and the swirling water around them. The second waterfall? By the large rock?

"Get the boat as near as you can. We'll take a look," shouted Anowara, assuming control. "Kahontsi, for all forest spirits' sake, sit down already!"

But she ignored what he said, as her eyes caught the movement – a head coming up, struggling against the current, to be pulled back again.

"There, there, I saw him," she screamed, then realized that they were paddling in that direction already, with Anowara leaning forward, scanning the water, ready to dive.

The head came up again, and this time the man was more successful, his hand grabbing a protruding rock, clinging to it with an obvious desperation, beating the water with his other arm.

"Let go," screamed Anowara. "We'll catch you down here. Let go!" He cursed loudly. "He doesn't hear me. Or maybe he is too stunned."

"What do we do?" whispered Kahontsi, her heart beating so loudly she was afraid they would not hear what she said.

"We keep screaming," tossed Anowara angrily. "I'm prepared to swim and catch him when he reaches our pool, but I'm not trying to go up there. Tekeni can risk his life for his foreigner. I won't do it."

She watched the man moving, more visible now as he pulled himself up, coming back to his senses, maybe.

"Let go of that rock," she yelled, cupping her palms around

her mouth, to make herself heard. "We'll catch you down here. Let go."

The head turned carefully, blinking against the sprays.

"Here," she waved her hands, making their canoe waver. It was difficult to keep her balance, but the chance of catching his attention was too great to miss. "Swim here. We'll catch you."

Now she was sure he saw her, as his shoulders turned too, and it seemed that his eyes narrowed. Waving more vigorously, she began imitating swimming movements.

"Swim here!"

And now, as the youths joined her screaming, she knew he understood, for he let the rock go, diving back into the current, just as Anowara's hand pulled her backwards.

"Don't join him in his swimming. If you go overboard, you will be swept straight away into the next rapids."

"Oh, please," she muttered, glaring at the youth. "I can swim better than you!"

But Anowara's eyes were back upon the struggling man, following his progress, ready to jump into the water should the slide prove to be difficult. Missing their boat would do the man no good, bringing him straight into the next rapids, to drown for sure this time.

Holding her breath, she watched him struggling with the current, disappearing from the view every now and then, but coming back up each time, navigating around the larger rocks.

"Please," she whispered, clenching her teeth until her jaw hurt. "Oh revered Right-Handed Twin, if you were the one to send him here, please let him make it."

His head was again out of her view, swallowed by the angry white foam, eager to claim its victim, the insolent foreigner who dared to challenge the mighty falls.

"Please!"

She shut her eyes for a heartbeat, trying to reach the benevolent sky deity with her spirit, to make it help. He had to help. If Tekeni was right and this man was, indeed, the messenger of the Great Spirits, then the Right-Handed Twin would not leave him struggle alone.

A tug on the other side of their vessel made her lose her balance and stumble to her side, while Tsitsho cursed, leaping past her in order to stabilize their canoe, she realized. Struggling to get back to her feet, she saw a hand clutching the wooden curb, gripping it desperately, its knuckles white and bleeding. Anowara was cursing loudly too, while it seemed that only Tsitsho's weight kept their boat from overturning.

"Get here!"

A hand pulled her strongly, making her lose her balance once again, crashing against the other side, scratching her limbs. The canoe jerked wildly, on the brink of overturning, as she watched Anowara grabbing the hand, pulling the man up, moving with his whole body as it seemed.

Now even Tsitsho was hissing through his clenched teeth, struggling with his paddle, but Anowara joined the rowing already, with both youths breathing heavily, desperate to keep their boat from being caught in the current and swept over the border and into the raging water of the next rapid.

Her instincts guiding her, she crouched at the bottom of the canoe, minimizing its unsteadiness as much as she could; the deed that had put her next to the crumbled form of the foreigner, now just a heap of limbs. He was breathing heavily, coughing and spitting, his forehead trickling blood, the rest of his body bruised and cut.

Trying to be of use, she supported his head as he retched more water, obviously having not eaten any food on this particular morning. Which was a good thing, she decided. Handsome and important as he was, she didn't want to be trapped at the bottom of a boat next to a puddle of someone's vomit.

"You are safe now," she whispered, trying to reassure him, as he fell back, bumping his head against the hard wood, exhausted.

Worriedly, she peered at him. He might have been safe from drowning, but he didn't look as though he had made it just yet, not with his face so drawn and pale, smeared with blood and bluish with bruises, with his eyes lifeless and sunken, and his lips just a colorless line.

"We'll get you to the shore and take care of you."

His eyes focused and he blinked, narrowing them painfully, trying to see better.

"You are alive, and you did the test of the falls," she went on, leaning closer, smiling with relief. He looked better now, with a little color creeping into his face.

His eyes widened, grew in proportion, staring at her in pure wonder. "You," he whispered. "You saved me. You are beautiful."

She felt the blood rushing up to her face, making her cheeks burn. "No," she muttered. "Tekeni and Anowara did this, and Tsitsho too. I was just…"

A sharp bump made her waver again, but she kept her arms under his head, making sure he wasn't hurt as she fought to keep her balance. Tsitsho was cursing, as the screeching went on, making their boat reel.

"What's happening?" she asked, looking up, still sheltering the wounded.

"Almost there." Anowara beamed at her from above, difficult to see against the glow of the high noon sun that had finally broken through the clouds. "Is he alive?"

"I think so, yes. But he is wounded, and, well, I think his mind is wandering."

But maybe not, she thought to herself. She was among those who saved him, oh yes; and she was held to be beautiful. She knew all about it.

"So what do we do now?" asked Tsitsho as the boat bumped again, more softly this time, cutting the rocky shore, its screeching more peaceful.

"I go and find Tekeni." Businesslike and full of purpose, Anowara leapt out of the boat. "You two take care of his foreigner. The wild twin will take it from there, I predict, but I would better hurry, before he jumps into the falls himself, to find out what happened."

The Crooked Tongues man pulled himself up, clutching to the side of the canoe, evidently feeling a little better with the boat steady and near the firm land.

"I'm grateful, so very grateful," he said quietly, wiping the blood off his face. "I will never forget."

They all stared at him as though the canoe itself had spoken.

"Well, it was nothing. Not much of an effort," muttered Tsitsho, suddenly at a loss.

"No, it is not. It is much, much of an effort." His accent actually pleased the ear when he tried to speak their tongue, much more so than his native crooked way of talking. "And I will remember, always."

They watched him getting up with an effort, clutching onto the side of the boat for support.

"Do you think you need to see a healer?" asked Anowara, the uncertainty in his voice sounding strange.

"No, no." The foreigner shook his head vigorously, but his face contorted, losing the little color it had gained. "I'm good. Just need some rest. They won't, won't expect... not until sunrise. The head of the council said..."

Not fully aware of what she was doing, Kahontsi rushed to his side, catching his arm and putting it over her shoulder, supporting. The touch of his skin, although wet and bruised, was pleasant, disturbingly so. He reeked of river and blood, but somehow, she enjoyed his smell, and it embarrassed her.

"We should find a good place to warm up." Taking some of his weight, she looked straight ahead, watching their step, guiding him out of the boat.

"I'll bring Tekeni here. You just get up there and maybe make some fire." Frowning, Anowara eyed them thoughtfully for another heartbeat, his gaze lingering upon her, disapproving somewhat. Then he was gone.

"I'll see if there is any firewood around," contributed Tsitsho hastily, anxious to be gone for some reason as well. He didn't feel comfortable around the strange foreigner, that much was obvious. He agreed to help, but only because his friends had asked him to do so.

Which left her alone with the man, struggling up the slippery path in the cold wind and the roaring of the rapids behind their backs.

"Tekeni will be here shortly," she said, uncomfortable in the silence that ensued.

"Yes."

Picking his step carefully, the foreigner made tremendous efforts not to lean on her, still enough of his weight was there to make her struggle.

"Do you think you broke something? Does it hurt when you walk?"

"No, I don't... don't think so..." With an evident relief, he slipped onto the ground the moment they reached the end of the path and a small clearing. "Just bruises. Hits. Too many rocks in your river." His smile flashed out suddenly, catching her unprepared, making her heart race. "I hope they don't ask me to jump, jump again. Hope one time enough... enough evidence."

"So you are not the messenger of the Right-Handed Twin," she said, irritated for no reason. "You are going to lie to them about that jump. You and Tekeni." She hesitated. "And us, too."

He frowned. "Yes and no." His gaze held hers, suddenly piercing, difficult to stand. "It is not that simple, Flint People girl. One can carry the message of the Great Spirits, even if one is not endowed with the powers of the sky dwellers. People tend to think simple, to ask for proof when everything is obvious, thrust into their faces." The grin upon his lips was thin and mirthless. "But these are people for you."

"And what makes you different?" It was difficult to understand him now that he had switched back to his native tongue. "Why are you not like other people?"

"It's not only me," he said, leaning against a tree with a sigh of relief. "There are people who are not a part of the crowd.

Tekeni is one good example. Your father is another." His gaze measured her again, in a way that made her feel naked. "You too, I think. There are many such people. They can see beyond the obvious, and most importantly, they are willing to do so."

"I'm not sure I want to see beyond the obvious," she said, desperate to conceal her embarrassment. Oh, if only he did not look so attractive, even though bruised and battered.

"Talk to your father. He is an exceptionally wise man." Grimacing, he straightened a little, inspecting his torso, running his palms along the bluish mess surrounding his ribs. "I hope they are not cracked," he muttered. "I have to be as good as new before dawn."

"Why dawn?" Coming closer, she tried to see the wound behind the plastered mess of his soaked hair, the obvious source of the bleeding.

"They said if I come back with sunrise, they will listen," he said, tilting his head obediently when she took hold of it.

"And you want to make them think you enjoyed your refreshing swim, don't you?"

"Yes, I do." His laughter made her feel strangely pleased. It was as though they had known each other for a long time already. Suppressing her smile, she tried to reach his wound without hurting him, doing her best at parting the wet, sticky tendrils, feeling him flinching, nevertheless.

"We need to wash it thoroughly." She looked around, acutely aware of his nearness and again, embarrassed by it. "I suppose Tsitsho will be here shortly. And Tekeni. Tekeni will surely know what to do."

"Oh, yes, he will." He sobered all of a sudden, his eyes losing the trace of mischievous amusement that filled his gaze since reaching the clearing. "This young man lives up to all expectations and more. An outstanding man. The Right-Handed Twin could not have given me a better partner."

"It was prophesied that he would do great things."

She remembered Tekeni as a boy, strong, restless, mischievous, always more vital and better looking than the other twin, always noticeable, for better and for worse; in trouble more times than not, but managing to wriggle out of it most of the times, having a winning smile and too much of a good-natured, natural confidence. And of course, the smarter, more cunning twin-brother that was always ready to back him up. A lucky child, the boy of the prophecy, now a tremendously impressive young man, a zealous follower of the strange foreigner, bent on bringing her people and their neighbors together, to live in peace. What a thought!

"They all expected him to do great things," she said, running her fingers along the rest of his head, looking for more sources of bleeding. "But no one expected him to take the path he is walking now." She could feel him tensing under her touch and it pleased her, made her feel powerful, somehow. He might have been the Messenger of the Great Spirits, too busy with his mission to fall in love with a woman if Tekeni were to be believed, yet her touch did not leave him indifferent, that much was obvious. "His father thought he would bring great victories to his people."

"He will." The foreigner's voice rang strongly, echoing between the trees. "But in a better way than a few more successful raids. He will make his people prominent and strong, like even the former War Chief could not have dreamed them to be."

"I would like to see it, and I would like to be a part of it."

He looked up sharply, his eyes glowing, boring at her. "Would you?"

Yes, I would, but with you, she thought, her excitement welling, his gaze making her feel powerful and lightheaded. It held the flicker of the same wonder, like back in the boat, when he had opened his eyes for the first time. He *did* think her beautiful!

"I want to be a part of the change. Yes, I want to help, like Tekeni does."

She watched him nodding, his smile flashing again, an open, unguarded smile. It made her heart race. Whatever his plans were, she cared little for the details. He may wish to unite her people and their neighbors, bending his energies and everything he had to that end.

Maybe he would succeed, or maybe he would not. She didn't care. But if she was to help, there would be enough opportunities to draw closer, to make a good impression. She was held to be smart and not only beautiful, and when he learned that, he would not be able to keep from falling in love with her.

Satisfied, she returned his smile, striving to appear innocent, as though caring for his mission and nothing else, until Tsitsho came up the path, carrying an armload of relatively dry branches.

"If not for the night storm," the youth breathed heavily, dropping his cargo and scanning the place for a good spot to make a fire. "I would have come back faster."

"Yes." Embarrassed, Kahontsi moved away from the wounded, feeling as though being caught doing something wrong. "I suppose when Tekeni and Anowara are here, we'll manage to have a nice fire and a nice meal going. I hope they'll have enough sense to bring food and maybe a blanket or two."

CHAPTER 20

Atiron squinted against the glow of the afternoon sun, the aroma of broiled meat tickling his nostrils, making his stomach growl.

"Aren't you going to get your plate filled?" asked Ohonte, brushing past him, beaming. "Come and enjoy the feast. They will not talk any more important matters, not for a while. Our guest needs to eat too."

Yes, indeed, thought Atiron, turning to follow, reluctant to leave. The foreigner, divine messenger or not, needed to eat, and maybe to rest as well, judging by the haggardness of his face and the way he made an obvious effort to stay upright, to listen to everyone and talk when required.

Eager, his gaze sought the formidable man in the crowd again, surrounded by people, the center of their attention, his food untouched upon his plate, but not from lack of appetite, of that Atiron was sure. Their guest was obviously hungry and exhausted, but trying to be polite, to address everyone's questions and concerns.

He eyed the pale, bruised face, and the way the man stood somewhat awkwardly, as though it took him an effort to maintain the natural pose of calm dignity and pride. A long-sleeved shirt covered the upper part of his body, concealing whatever damage his fall into the waterfalls might have caused. No, the messenger of the Right-Handed Twin or not, this man did not enjoy his swim in the Little Falls' rapids, that much was obvious.

He remembered the night and their conversation, glad that he had had an opportunity to have the fascinating foreigner all for himself before the rest of the town was convinced, before the test of the falls. Shaking his head, he sighed, not amused but confused more than ever. *Was he or was he not?*

The man, indeed, climbed the tree that was cut, disappearing into the worst of the rapids. He had seen it all, along with every dweller of the town. Everyone who could walk came. Everyone! No person in his or her right mind was ready to miss the spectacular challenge. They would have stayed for a whole day, if necessary, had it taken that long to cut the tree. But luckily, the tree was old and wobbly, so it was over soon enough, with the foreigner disappearing into the roaring horror, swallowed by the swirling mist. The end of the story.

It left the people to talk and argue, gesturing, peering into the chasm below, trying to see through the angry drizzle, eventually going back to the town, disappointed somehow. Had they expected the Messenger to come back right away, flying through the mist or just reappearing among them? Maybe, was Atiron's private conclusion. People liked miracles. They wanted to see the definite proof.

Oh, but there was more to it, much more. He grinned to himself, remembering the way Tekeni had sneaked away, quiet and unnoticed, while his country folk crowded the cliff, craning their necks in an attempt to see better. His gut feeling prompting him to watch, Atiron followed the young man with his gaze, watching him backing away, slipping out of the crowd, his lips pursed, face sealed, eyes worried but concentrated, determined. A man on a mission. The twin was not anxious to get back to the town, so much was obvious. He was up to something.

The suspicion that bore fruit when the youth stayed away for the whole afternoon, while the town buzzed and talked, speculating on the chances of the foreigner to be back with sunrise as directed by the Town Council. It seemed impossible, and yet the people were expectant. They wanted the strange man to come back, realized Atiron, pleased. They were ready to listen.

He himself was as anxious, but Tekeni's behavior gave him hope. The resourceful youth was up to something, with his old friends from Little Falls missing as well, Anowara and a few others. Had they hatched a plan? Was the foreigner alive, sound and safe somewhere, hiding until the morning? But how? He had seen him going down into thundering cascades. He had seen it happening with his own eyes.

"Father!" Kahontsi's voice tore him out of his reverie. "You are not eating. Why?" The girl beamed at him, more beautiful than ever, having a new glint to her large, doe-like eyes, her face glowing with excitement. "I'll bring you food."

"No, no, there is no need. I can get a plate of corn balls all by myself." He eyed her thoughtfully. "What are you up to, little one? You look excited."

"Oh, nothing!" The girl's eyebrows climbed high, a picture of an innocent surprise, but her lips twisted into an unmistakably smug female grin. "I'm just happy with what is going on. All the changes. It's so exciting." She glanced at the group Atiron was eyeing before. "This foreigner is fascinating. He talks interesting things. When one is able to understand him, that is." Her giggle was as melodious as a trickling of the water in a brook. "I hope he learns our tongue fast."

Atiron frowned. "Have you talked to him? When?"

"Oh, yes, I have. For quite a long time, too." Her smile was innocent, with not a trace of shame in it. "He tells interesting things. There will be quite a lot of changes."

"Yes, there might be changes. Maybe. But," he eyed his daughter closely, alarmed for no reason, even angered. "None of it will involve a young girl like you."

"Of course it will. He wants me to help. He told me so." She returned his gaze, her smile gone. "Everyone will be involved, and nothing will be the same anymore."

"You are talking nonsense, Daughter. Girls like you will go on with their lives, enjoying the changes, yes, if we are successful. But not as a part of the process." Her defiant gaze made his anger worse. "When you are old and one of the Clan

Mothers, you will do the changes. But not a heartbeat before."

She scowled in reply. "The twin is involved, and he is of my age."

"The twin is merely helping. He is translating for this man to be understood better."

"He does more than that, Father!"

He glanced at the group once again, finding it easy to pick Tekeni out in the surrounding people, impressively tall and broad shouldered, prominent in the crowd. Anything but a youth of no importance.

"The twin is an exception. He went through much, and it served to shape him into a man before his time."

"I'm not a girl of no importance, either," muttered Kahontsi, but her lovely face closed, turned wary.

He knew the signs. "Kahontsi, put any sort of these thoughts out of your head. You will stay away from this man. Do you hear me? You will not be involved in any of it. If I see you trying to approach him, I will be very angered. Do you hear me? Do you understand?"

She took a step back, staring at him, aghast. The reproaches of her mother were a routine, but a stern reprimand from him was a novelty.

"I… I didn't do anything wrong," she muttered, but by the way she dropped her gaze, he knew she'd done things she was not ready to confess.

"Did the twin get you involved in his schemes to get the foreigner out of danger yesterday?"

She mumbled something inaudible, her eyes boring at her prettily embroidered moccasins, threatening to make a hole in them.

"In what way?" It came out too sharply, but he didn't care. "Tell me!"

However, it was neither the time nor the place, with the townsfolk crowding all around, chatting loudly, their curious glances already shooting in their direction. He took a deep breath, summoning all his patience.

"We will talk about it this very evening, Daughter. Now go and think about your behavior."

Her cheeks burning, eyes glittering with tears, the girl stalked away, disappearing into the crowds, not returning his gaze. He watched the print her moccasins left in the dust. Did he take it too far? After all, he was the one to send her to talk to the twin on the evening of the youth's return, to make him feel at home. With all the commotion aroused by their dramatic appearance, Tekeni was not made truly welcomed, truly at home. They were all too busy with his foreigner to greet the returning son of the late War Chief properly.

However, the girl should have known better. There was a difference between greeting an old friend and a cousin home, and getting into some dubious enterprises. The twin might have been desperate to use any help he could get, having no time to renew his old contacts and friendships, but Kahontsi was held to be a smart girl. She should have known better.

"Come, sit with us," people called, waving at him invitingly.

He nodded and smiled, refusing to join, wishing to be alone, to think the things over. So the foreigner survived and, as promised, he had been listened to now, free to talk about his plans and ideas.

He remembered the night before the last and the fascinating conversation. It was difficult to understand the man without the twin's translation, still what he caught was more than enough to make him appreciate this strange visitor to their lands greatly. Those were no mere ideas but well-thought-out plans, elaborate and detailed, extensive, encompassing plans, that, given a chance, might, actually, bear a fruit. A peace with their neighbors maintained and nurtured through the Great Council of the Nations? Inconceivable and yet...

Could they truly live in peace? To sit together, smoking the sacred pipe, offering the Great Spirits and praying to them, and then just conversing, resolving the conflicts by talking and arguing, respecting each other? And who would be sitting in this council? Representatives of how many peoples? Two, three?

Maybe all five nations, the dwellers of this side of the Great Sparkling Water?

Involuntarily, he drifted closer to the group surrounding the foreigner and the twin, all the respectable people of the settlement, the members of the Town Council and other elders, sprinkled by the Clans Mothers aplenty. Oh yes, this man was listened to now.

He watched the outlandish, prominent face, seeing the strength behind the sunken, fatigued eyes, the courage, the conviction. Oh yes, this man knew what he was talking about, and he was listened to now by the people of Little Falls, such a large, influential town. If it decided to back the foreigner up, the People of the Flint may be considered as convinced already. With the coming of the Awakening Season they would be united, ready to approach their neighbors, and from the stance of strength and superiority at that.

Coming closer, he heard the foreigner's strange words, and the twin's rapid translation. First of all, the council of the Flint People would have to be formed, he thought, not listening. To talk the things over. Would they have to reach their decisions unanimously too, like the foreigner's projected Great Council of the Nations?

He watched the man's eyes light up as some obviously interesting question was translated to him. Exhausted and bruised as he was, the man enjoyed being listened to, oh how much he enjoyed it!

Then his eyes caught the sight of his daughter, standing among the crowd, surrounded by other youths, boys and girls, but oblivious of her friends, devouring the foreigner with her large, glowing eyes, instead. His sense of well being began to evaporate. Kahontsi was a stubborn little thing, and when she decided to do something…

He pursed his lips. Exciting changes or not, he would have to watch the girl closely because the foreigner, even if interested, was no man for her.

AUTHOR'S AFTERWORD

According to the various versions of the story, after crossing the Lake Ontario, the Great Peacemaker was, indeed, first greeted by a casual hunter upon the high banks of the Great Lake.

> *"... It happened at the time a party of hunters had a camp on the south side of the lake now known as Ontario, and one of the party went toward the lake and stood on the bank, and beheld the object coming toward him at a distance, and the man could not understand what it was that was approaching him; shortly afterward he understood that it was a canoe, and saw a man in it...*
>
> *Then Dekanahwideh asked the man what had caused them to be where they were, and the man answered and said: "We are here for a double object. We are here hunting game for our living and also because there is a great strife in our settlement."*
>
> *Then Dekanahwideh said: "You will now return to the place from whence you came. The reason that this occurred is because the Good Tidings of Peace and Friendship have come to the people... and if asked, you will say that the Messenger of the Good Tidings of Peace and Power will come in a few days."*
>
> *Then the man asked: "And who are you now speaking to me?"*
>
> *Dekanahwideh answered: "It is I who came from the west and am going eastward and am called Dekanahwideh in this world."*
>
> *Then the man wondered and beheld his canoe and saw that his canoe was made out of white stone..."*

A.C. Parker, "The Constitution of the Five Nations or
The Iroquois Book of the Great Law"

Next he approached the old woman Jikonsahseh, who was

living alone, feeding the warriors who happened to pass her dwelling.

> *"…Then after saying these words, Dekanahwideh went on his way and arrived at the house of Ji-kon-sah-seh and said to her that he had come on this path which passed her home and which led from the east to the west, and on which traveled the men of a blood-thirsty and destructive nature.*
>
> *Then he said to her. "It is your custom to feed these men when they are traveling on this path on their war expeditions" Then he told her that she must desist from practicing this custom. Then he told her that the reason she was to stop this custom was that the Good Tidings of Peace and Power had come… Then also, "I now charge you that you shall be the custodian of the Good Tidings of Peace and Power so that the human race will live in peace in the future. Then Dekanahwideh also said, "You shall, therefore, now go east where I shall meet you at the place of danger (Onondaga), where all matters shall be finally settled, and you must not fail to be there on the third day. I shall now pass on in my journey…"*

A.C. Parker, "The Constitution of the Five Nations or
The Iroquois Book of the Great Law"

Then he sought out legendary Hiawatha, who, according to some versions of the story, was *"… a man who instilled great fear in the people who knew him because after his wife became a victim of tribal warfare and his daughters perished (some stories claim it was due to sorcery), he became a hermit (self-exile) and estranged from the Onondaga's community and a man of hate who practiced a form of cannibalism on victims of his wrath. The Peacemaker was able to counsel Hiawatha and change his heart and help him to overcome his resentment and sorrow…"*

This deed being accomplished, the Great Peacemaker then went to the lands of the Mohawks (People of the Flint) where he was required to prove the divine nature of his mission by climbing a tree which was being cut down, falling into the worst of the falls.

"... *Then one of the chief warriors asked: "What shall we do with the powerful tribes... who are always hostile to us?"*

Then Dekanahwideh answered and said that the hostile nations referred to had already accepted the Good News of Peace and Power.

Then the chief warrior answered and said: "I am still in doubt, and I would propose (as a test of power) that this man (Dekanahwideh) climb up a big tree by the edge of a high cliff and that we then cut the tree down and let it fall with him over the cliff, and then, if he does not die, I shall truly believe the message which he has brought to us."

Then the deputy chief warrior said: "I also am of the same opinion, and I approve of the suggestion of the chief warrior."

Then Dekanahwideh said: "I am ready and most willingly accede to your request, because the good Tidings of Peace and Power has come unto us, I now confidently place myself in your hands."

Then the chief warrior said to Dekanahwideh: "I made this proposal, and therefore, you will now climb this tree so that it will be a sign of proof, and the people may see your power. If you live to see tomorrow's sunrise then I will accept your message."

Then Dekanahwideh said: "This shall truly be done and carried out." And then he climbed the tree, and when he had reached the top of the tree, he sat down on a branch, after which the tree was cut down, and it fell over the cliff with him.

Then the people kept vigilant watch so that they might see him, but they failed to see any signs of him... Now when the new day dawned, one of the warriors arose before sunrise and at once went to the place where the tree had been cut, and when he arrived there he saw at a short distance a field of corn, and nearby the smoke from a fire...and after seeing a man, he at once returned and said that he had seen the man, and that it was he who was on the tree which was cut the evening before..."

A.C. Parker, "The Constitution of the Five Nations or
The Iroquois Book of the Great Law"

And so the Great Peacemaker had gained the trust and the backing of the powerful nation, the People of the Flint (Mohawk), and the tentative proposals of the People of the Hills (Onondaga), but still there was much work ahead of him. He was yet to convince the remaining nations, and then to confront powerful Tadodaho and make him listen.

The continuation of his story is presented in third book of The Peacemaker Series, "**The Great Law of Peace**."